IN THE REGENCY BALLROOM COLLECTION

Louise Allen has been immersing herself in history, real and fictional, for as long as she can remember. She finds landscapes and places evoke powerful images of the past—Venice, Burgundy and the Greek islands are favourite atmospheric destinations. Louise lives on the North Norfolk coast, where she shares the cottage they have renovated with her husband. She spends her spare time gardening, researching family history or travelling in the UK and abroad in search of inspiration. Please visit Louise's website, www.louiseallenregency.co.uk, for the latest news, or find her on Twitter, @LouiseRegency, and on Facebook.

NO PLACE FOR A LADY

Louise Allen

First published in Great Britain 2013
by Mills & Boon, an imprint of Harlequin (UK) Limited,
Large Print edition 2014
Eton House, 18-24 Paradise Road,
Richmond, Surrey, TW9 1SR

ISBN: 978 0 263 24552 3

Harlequin (UK) Limited's policy is to use papers that are natural, renewable and recyclable products and made from wood grown in sustainable forests. The logging and manufacturing processes conform to the legal environmental regulations of the country of origin.

Printed and bound in Great Britain
by CPI Antony Rowe, Chippenham, Wiltshire

Chapter One

Almost 1:00 a.m. on the Bath Road outside Hounslow—September 1814

We are going to crash. The thought went through Max's brain with almost fatalistic calm. There was not enough room, even if the stage pulled over, even if it were broad daylight—even if he were driving and not his young cousin.

'Rein in, damn it, it's too narrow here!' He had to shout over the wind whipping past them and the thunder of hooves. The stage held the crown of the road, as well it might. At this time of night it was the safest place to be—unless you had a private drag bearing down upon you, driven at full gallop by an over-excited eighteen-year-old racing for a wager.

The coach was lit with side lanterns, as they were, and the moon was high and full, bathing the road and the surrounding heath in silver light, but Max did not need it to judge the road—he knew it like the back of his hand.

'I can make it!' Nevill looped the off-lead rein and the team, obedient to the lightest touch, moved out to the right ready to overtake, and they were committed.

Snatching the reins would not help; they were going too fast—the big Hanoverian bays, full of oats and more than a match for any stagecoach team, especially night-run horses, were too powerful to stop in this distance. And somewhere behind them, moving just as fast, was Brice Latymer, out for blood, and behind him, Viscount Lansdowne.

Max raised the yard-long horn to his lips and blew, more in hope than expectation. If they were lucky, if the driver of the stage was alert, strong and experienced, they might get away with a sideways collision and at least the horses would not plough straight into the back of the stage. Unlucky, and there would be a four-coach pile-up and carnage.

And the miracle happened. The stage, scarcely checking its speed, drew tight to the left, the whipping branches of the hedgerow trees lashing the side, forcing the rooftop passengers to throw themselves to the right. It was lurching, its nearside wheels riding the rim of the ditch, but if Nevill could keep his head they might just make it through.

'Go, damn it!' he thundered. Nevill dropped his hands and the bays went through the gap like a cavalry charge. The drag tilted to the right, bounced, branches scored down the length of the black lacquer sides and then they were neck and neck with the stage.

Now he had created the space the other driver was slowing, fighting his team to keep the vehicle steady and out of the ditch it was teetering on. Max looked across, wanting to send a silent message of apology, and found himself looking into an oval face, white in the moonlight, the eyes huge, dark and furious, the mouth lush. *A woman's face?*

Then they were past. Max shook himself—he was mistaken, or in the confusion of the moment he had seen the face of one of the rooftop passengers, not the driver.

He glanced to the side. Nevill was visibly shaken now the crisis had passed, his hand lax on the reins. 'Here, take them. I'm going to be sick.' He thrust the reins towards Max, making the bays jib at the confusing signals.

'No, you are not—drive! This is your bet, your responsibility, and I just hope to hell the others were far enough back to miss that.'

The Bell was perhaps three minutes ahead. The end of the race. If the stage didn't come through in five minutes it would be in the ditch and he would have to go back and see what he could do to help.

Who is she? The glimpse of that exquisite face seemed burned into his mind. *Just a hallucination*

*caused by fear, excitement, the relief of finding we
were through after all? Or a flesh-and-blood woman?*
His blood stirred. He realised, with shock, that he was
aroused. *I want her.*

'We're here,' Nevill said with a gasp. 'The Bell.'

Two and a half hours earlier

'Have you heard a word I said?'

'Probably not.' Max Dysart looked up from his contemplation of the firelight reflected in the toes of his
highly polished boots and grinned unrepentantly at
his young cousin.

Despite the fact that the clocks on the high mantel
had just struck half past ten, and the darkness outside
was pierced by countless points of flickering light, he
and all the men in the noisy, convivial company were
dressed in buckskin breeches, riding boots and care-
lessly open coats. Only the elegance with which they
wore their casual dress and the pristine, uncreased
whiteness of their Waterfall cravats hinted that these
were members of the Nonesuch Club and not deni-
zens of some sporting tavern.

'What were you thinking about?' Nevill demanded,
folding himself down on to the buttoned-leather top of
the high fender and holding out one hand to the fire.

'Women,' Max drawled, knowing it would bring a
blush to Nevill's cheeks. The boy was on the cusp of
ceasing to find women terrifying and unnecessary

and discovering that they were still terrifying, but mystifyingly desirable, as well. He was too easy to tease, although women had certainly been the subject of Max's brooding thoughts.

Max gave up trying to solve the conundrum of how he was going to find a suitable bride he could tolerate, marry and produce an heir with when he was, when he came right down to it, not certain he was in a position to make anyone an offer. He gave his cousin his attention, focusing on the youth's eager face. He could just give up on the problem and accept Nevill as his heir, he supposed. Or was that the coward's way out?

Nevill Harlow was just eighteen and appeared still to be growing into his hands and feet. He was also by far the youngest member of the Nonesuch Whips, gathered for their monthly meeting in their usual room at the Nonesuch Club on the corner of Ryder Street and St James's. Young he might be, but even the highest stickler amongst the members accepted him for his growing skill with the ribbons and his relationship to Max Dysart, Earl of Penrith, acknowledged nonpareil amongst drivers.

Acknowledged by everyone except, inevitably, Brice Latymer. Latymer was sitting beside the betting book, tapping his teeth with the tip of a quill pen and regarding the cousins sardonically.

Max let the cool regard slide over him without giving any sign he had noticed it. Sometimes he thought

Latymer lived to antagonise him. The man's scarcely veiled pleasure whenever he bested Max, whether in a race, at cards or by cutting him out for a dance, mystified him.

'What should I have been listening to?'

'I've had a bet with Latymer.' Nevill was grinning with excitement. 'But you'll need to lend me your bays.'

'My *what*?' Max swung his feet down off the fender.

'Your bays. And the new drag. I've bet I can beat him and Lansdowne to the Bell at Hounslow.'

'In my new drag, driving my bays? My four expensive, perfectly matched, *Hanoverian* bays?' Max enquired ominously.

'Yes.' Nevill was not known for the strength of his intellect, more for his abounding good nature, but it was obviously beginning to dawn on him that his magnificent cousin was not delighted by the challenge he had accepted. 'They're more than able to beat Latymer and his greys.'

'*They* are. Are you? Are you aware what I will do to you if you sprain so much as a fetlock?'

'Er…no.' Out of the corner of his eye Max could see the rest of the Nonesuch Whips watching them, most with good-natured grins on their faces. They all knew Max's feelings about his precious bays, and they all liked young Nevill, but the rare opportunity to view Max Dysart, Earl of Penrith, losing his fabled self-control was eagerly anticipated.

'I will tear your head off your shoulders,' Max promised softly, dropping his arm over Nevill's shoulders and smiling a crocodile's smile. The younger man flinched, his nervous grin wavering. 'I will knot your arms behind your neck and I will use your guts for garters.'

'Right.' It was a strangled squeak.

'And do you know what I will do if you lose to our friend Mr Latymer?'

'No.' That was a gulp.

'Never let you drive one of my horses again, as long as you live.' Max imbued his smile with all the menace he could muster and felt the bony shoulders under his arm quiver. 'Are you allowed passengers?'

'No. Just a guard to carry the yard of tin.'

'Right. I'll do that.' He felt the relief run through the young man. 'When is it for?'

'Midnight, tonight. Leaving from here. I wanted to send round to your mews and get them harnessed up....' Nevill's voice began to trail away.

'Just ask next time before you lay the bet,' Max said mildly, creating major disappointment amongst the audience as they realised the anticipated explosion was not going to happen.

But, damn it, he had taught the boy to drive, starting with a pony cart, graduating through curricle and phaeton until he could manage a drag, the heavy private coach drawn by four horses, and a match in size, weight and speed for the Mail or the stagecoaches. If he could not trust Nevill with his team now, it was to mistrust his own teaching.

'Send to the mews. And, Nevill,' he added as his cousin made for the door, enduring amiable joshing as he went. 'Bespeak dinner—I'm damned if I'm waiting until we get to the Bell!'

'Have you had any dinner yet?'

Bree Mallory pushed back her chair and saw Piers standing in the doorway, a pint tankard in his hand. 'No. What time is it?'

Her brother shrugged. 'Nearly eleven. I had the ordinary in the snug an hour past.'

Bree got to her feet, stretched and glanced out of the window overlooking the main yard of the Mermaid Inn. The scene outside in the glare of torches and lanterns would have struck most people as chaos. To Bree's experienced eye it was running like clockwork and the whole complex business of the headquarters of a busy coaching company was just as it should be.

Pot boys were pushing through the crowd with tankards and coffee pots; at least three women appeared to have lost either children or husbands, and in one case, a goose, and through the whole turmoil the grooms leading horses to coaches or to stables wove the intricate pattern that sent out a dozen coaches in the course of the night, and received as many in.

A coach, the *Portsmouth Challenge*, was standing ready, the porters tossing up the last of the luggage and a reluctant woman being urged on to a roof seat by her husband. Over her head Bree could hear the grinding of the clock gears as it made ready to strike the three-quarter, and she glanced towards the door of the tap room in anticipation. A massive figure in a many-caped greatcoat strode out, whip in hand, jamming his low-crowned hat down as he went. It was Jim Taylor, the oldest and most cantankerous of all the Challenge Coaching Company's drivers.

As the clock struck Jim swung up ponderously on to the box, arranged the fistful of reins in his left hand without glancing at them and shouted, 'Let them go!'

'You could set your watch by him,' Piers commented, strolling across to join his sister at the window.

'You can by all of them,' she riposted, 'or we wouldn't employ them.'

'You're a hard woman, Bree Mallory.' He gave her a one-armed hug round the shoulders in passing, grinning to show he was only teasing.

Bree smiled back. 'I have to be. This is a hard business. And why haven't you gone home to bed?' He might look like a man, her tall, handsome, baby brother, but he was only seventeen and, if he hadn't been recovering from a nasty bout of pneumonia, he would have been at school at Harrow. 'And my excuse, before you ask, is that the corn chandler's bill is completely at odds with the fodder records *again* and either he is cheating us, or someone is stealing the feed.'

'I was finishing my Latin text.' He grimaced. 'It's enough to put me into a decline, the amount of work the beaks have sent me home with.'

'If you hadn't spent most of the day hanging round the yard, you'd have been done hours ago,' Bree chided mildly. Piers was itching to finish at school and come to start working at the company. It was his, after all. Or at least, he owned half of it, with George Mallory, their father's elder brother, retaining his original share.

Bree had a burning desire to protect the company for Piers. Uncle George, with no children of his own, would leave his half to his nephew eventually and then there would be no stopping her brother.

He already knew as much as Bree about the business, and rather more about the technical aspects of coach design and the latest trends in springing than she ever wanted to know. 'Where are my journals?' he wheedled now. 'I have finished my Latin, honestly.'

'They look even more boring than the grammar texts,' Bree commented, lifting the pile of journals dealing with topics such as steam locomotion, pedestrian curricles and canal building off the chair by her desk. 'Here you are.'

'I am giving up on the mystery of the vanishing oats for the night.' Bree blotted the ledger and put away her pens. 'Come on, let's go and find some dinner— I expect you can manage to put away another platter of something.'

They rented a small, decent house in Gower Street, but the sprawling yard of the Mermaid seemed more like home for both of them and they maintained private rooms up in the attic storey for when they chose to stay overnight.

Bree stopped and looked back over the yard, seized with a sudden uneasiness, as though things were never going to be the same again. She shook herself. *Such foolishness.* 'You weren't born when Papa bought this—I can only just recall it.' She smiled proudly. 'Twenty years and it's turned from a decaying, failed business into one of the best coaching inns in the capital.'

'*The* best,' Piers said stoutly, cheerfully ignoring the claims of William Chaplin at the sign of the Swan with Two Necks, or Edward Sherman's powerful company with its two hundred horses, operating out of the Bull and Mouth.

From small beginnings, with his own horses and a modest stage-wagon service, William Mallory had built it into what it was today, and Bree had grown up tagging along behind him, absorbing the business at his coat tails.

It had worried her father, a decent yeoman farmer, that his daughter did not want to join the world of her mother's relatives, but Edwina Mallory had laughed. 'I was married to the son of a viscount, my eldest son *is* a viscount and I am delighted to let him get on with it! Bree can choose when she is older if she wants a come-out and all the fashionable frivols.'

And perhaps, if Mama had lived longer, Bree might have done. But Edwina Mallory, daughter of a baron, once married to the Honourable Henry Kendal, had died when Bree was nine, and her relatives seemed only too glad to forget about the daughter of her embarrassing second marriage.

'What does Kendal want?' Piers asked, hostility making his voice spiky. He had picked up the letter lying on her desk, recognising the seal imprinted on the shiny blue wax.

'I don't know,' Bree said, taking it and dropping it back again. 'I haven't opened it yet. Our dear brother is no doubt issuing another remonstrance from the lofty heights of Farleigh Hall, but I am in no mood to be lectured tonight.'

'Don't blame you,' Piers grunted, handing her the shawl that hung on the back of the door. 'Pompous prig.'

She ought to remonstrate, Bree knew, but Piers was

all too correct. Their half-brother, James Kendal, Viscount Farleigh, was, at the age of thirty, as stuffy and boring as any crusted old duke spluttering about the scandals of modern life in his club.

As soon as Bree was old enough to realise that her mother's connections looked down on her father, and regarded her mother's remarrying for love as a disgrace, she resolved to have as little as possible to do with them. Now, at the age of twenty-five, she met her half-brother perhaps four times a year, and he seemed more than content for that state of affairs to continue.

'I don't expect he can help it,' she said mildly, following Piers out into the yard. 'Being brought up by his grandfather when Mama remarried was almost certain to make a prig out of him. You won't remember the old Viscount, but I do!'

Bree broke off as they negotiated the press of people beginning to assemble for the Bath stage in less than hour.

'Hey, sweetheart, what's a pretty miss like you doing all alone here in this rough place? Come and have a drink with me, darling.'

Bree looked to her left and saw the speaker, a rakish-looking man with a bold eye and a leer on his lips, pushing towards her.

'Can you possibly be addressing me, sir?' she enquired, her voice a passable imitation of Mama at her frostiest.

'Don't be like that, darlin'—what's a pretty little trollop like you doing in a place like this if she isn't after a bit of company?'

As Bree was wearing a plain round gown with a modest neckline, had her—admittedly eye-catching— blonde hair braided up tightly and was doing nothing to attract attention, she was justifiably irritated. But it was the rest of the impertinent question that really got her temper up.

'A place like this? Why, you ignorant clod, this is as fine an inn as any in all London—as fine as the Swan with Two Necks. I'll have you know—'

'Is this lout bothering you?' At the sight of Piers, six foot already, even if he had some growing to do to fill out his long frame, the rake began to back away. 'Get out of here before I have you whipped out!'

'Honestly, Bree, you shouldn't be here without a maid,' Piers fussed as they pushed their way into the dining rooms and found their private table in a corner. 'You're too pretty by half to be wandering about a busy inn.'

'I don't *wander*,' she corrected him firmly. 'I run the place. And as for being too pretty, what nonsense. I'm tolerable only and I'm bossy and I'm too tall, and if it wasn't for this wretched hair I wouldn't have any trouble with men at all.'

The waiter put a steaming platter of roast beef in

front of them and Bree helped herself with an appetite, satisfied that she had won the argument.

Half an hour later she sat back, replete, and regarded her brother with fascinated awe as he dug into a large slice of apple pie.

'This is your second dinner tonight. I think you must have hollow legs, else where can you be putting it?'

'I'm a growing boy,' Piers mumbled indistinctly through a mouthful of pastry. 'Look, here comes Railton. I think he's looking for us.'

'What is it, Railton?' The Yard Master was looking grim as he stopped by their table.

'We'll have to cancel the Bath coach, Miss Bree.'

'What? The quarter to midnight? But it's fully booked.' Bree pushed back her empty plate and got to her feet. 'Why?'

'No driver. Todd was taking it out, but he's slipped just now coming down the ladder out of the hayloft and I reckon his leg's broke bad. Willis is taking the Northampton coach later, and all the rest of the men are spoken for too. There's no one spare, not with you giving Hobbs the night off to be with his wife and new baby.' His sniff made it abundantly clear what he thought of this indulgence.

'Are you sure it is broken?' Bree demanded, striding across the yard, Piers at her heels. 'Have you sent for Dr Chapman?'

'I have, not that I need him to tell me it's a break when the bone's sticking through the skin. You've no cause to go in there, Miss Bree. It's not a nice sight and Bill's seeing to him.'

Even so, one did not leave one's employees in agony, however much of a fix they had left one in through their carelessness. Bree marched through the hay-store door and was profoundly grateful to see there was no sign of blood and Johnnie Todd was neither fainting nor shrieking in agony.

'He'll do.' Bill Potter, one of the ostlers and the nearest they had to a farrier on the premises, got to his feet and walked her back firmly out of the door. 'Doctor will fix him up, never you fret, Miss Bree.'

That was good, but it didn't solve the problem of the Bath coach. 'I'll drive it.' Piers bounded up. 'Please?'

'Certainly not! It's one hundred and eight miles.' Bree knew the mileages to their destinations, and all the stops along the way, without even having to think about it. 'The most you've ever driven is twenty.'

'Yes, but I don't have to drive all the way, do I?' Piers protested as they walked back to the office.

'What?' Bree broke off from wondering if she could possibly send round to one of the rival yards and borrow a driver. But that put one in debt...

'Johnnie would only have driven fifty miles,

wouldn't he? Whoever the second half-driver is, he'll be ready and waiting in Newbury.' Piers banged through the door and started rummaging in the cupboard for his greatcoat.

'Fifty miles is too far. I've driven thirty, and that was hard enough, and I wasn't recovering from pneumonia.' *Thirty miles. Thirty miles with Papa up beside me, in broad daylight and with an empty coach coming back from the coach makers. Even so, can it be that much harder to do it with passengers up and at night? There's a full moon.*

'I'll drive,' she said briskly, trampling down the wave of apprehension that hit her the minute she said it. 'The Challenge Coach Company does not cancel coaches and we don't go begging our rivals for help either. Shoo! I'm going to get changed.'

Chapter Two

Bree thrust the whip into the groom's hands and used both hers on the reins. Behind her the passengers were screaming, the inner wheels were bucking along the rough rim of the ditch and branches were lashing both coach and horses.

Thank God she had never followed the practice of so many companies and used broken-down animals for the night runs, she thought fleetingly, as the leaders got their hocks under them and powered the heavy vehicle back on to the highway. The lurking menace of a milestone, glinting white in the moonlight, flashed past an inch from the wheels.

The coach rocked violently, throwing her off balance. Her right wrist struck the metal rail at the side of the box with a sickening thud. Bree bit down the gasp of pain and gathered the reins back into her left hand again, stuffing the throbbing right into the space between her greatcoat buttons.

Hell, hell and damnation. Ten miles gone, another

forty to go. Her arms already felt as though she had been stretched on the rack, her back ached and now she had a badly bruised wrist. *I must have been mad to start, but I'm going to do this if it kills me. It probably will.*

The team steadied, then settled into a hard, steady rhythm. 'Slow down, Miss Bree,' Jem the groom gasped as she took the crown of the road again. 'You can't spring them here!'

'I can and I will. I'm going to horsewhip that maniac the length of Hounslow High Street, and we've lost time as it is,' she shouted, as the sound of another horn in the distance behind them had the groom staring back anxiously. 'If they can catch us up before the inn, they can wait,' Bree added grimly. And if they didn't like it, they had one very angry coaching proprietor to deal with.

'You won. Congratulations.' Max fetched Nevill a hard buffet on his back as the young man climbed stiffly down from the box.

'I...Max, I'm sorry. I nearly crashed it.' He stumbled and Max caught him up, pushing him back against the coach wheel. The others would be here in a moment; he wasn't having Nevill showing them anything but a confident face. 'If you hadn't told me when to go, shouted at me... I was going too fast on a blind bend. I'll understand if you never let me drive your horses again.'

'Are you ever going to do anything that stupid again?' Max demanded, ignoring the bustle of ostlers running to unharness his team. 'No?' His cousin shook his head. 'Well, then, lesson learned. I once had the York mail off the road, although I don't choose to talk about it. I was about your age, and probably as green. Now, get the team put up and looked over and then get us a chamber. I'm going to save your bacon by doing my best with the coachman.'

'But I should—'

'Just do as I ask, Nevill, and pray I don't look at the damage to my paintwork before I've had at least one glass of brandy.'

The average stagecoachman would have the boy's guts for garters—their temper and their arrogance were legendary. Max heard the sound of the horn and the stage swept into the yard: at least he wasn't going to have to organise its rescue from the ditch. He scanned the roof passengers as they clambered down, protesting loudly about their terrible experience. No young woman—he must have been dreaming. His heart sank and he grimaced wryly; he was acting like a heartsick youth after a glimpse of some beauty at a window.

The groom swung down beside the grumbling passengers. 'Brandy on the company,' he said, urging them towards the door of the Bell and the waiting landlord.

He swung round as Max strode up. 'You driving that rig just now, guv'nor?' he demanded belligerently.

'No, my young cousin was, but I am responsible. Allow me to make our apologies to the driver, and to you, of course.' He slipped a coin into the man's hand and stepped to one side to confront the other who was slowly climbing down, his back to the yard. The groom shifted as though to protect his driver's back. Max dodged—and found himself face to face with the smallest, strangest, and certainly most belligerent stagecoach driver he had ever met.

'You oaf!' It was his young woman. In the better light of the inn yard she was even more striking than he recalled from that startling glimpse, her looks heightened by shimmering fury. No classical beauty, although a low-crowned beaver jammed down almost to her eyebrows so that not a lock of hair showed, did not help. And goodness knows what her figure was like under the bulk of the caped greatcoat. But her face was a pure oval, her skin clear, her eyes deep blue and her mouth flooded his mind with explicit, arousing images

'What are you staring at, sir?' she demanded, giving him the opportunity to admire the way those lovely lips looked in motion, glimpsing a flash of white teeth. 'Haven't you ever seen a woman driving before?' She grounded the butt of her whip with one hand and glowered at him. *Tall, she's tall for a woman*, he thought irrelevantly as she tipped her head, just a little, to look at him.

'Not one driving a stagecoach,' he admitted. Somewhere behind him the increase in noise heralded the arrival of the two rival drags. Max moved instinctively to shield her from sight. 'Madam, I must apologise for that incident. Naturally I will meet any damages to the coach, and you must allow me to pay for whatever drinks the passengers are taking in there.'

'Certainly. Your card for the bill?' That was businesslike with a vengeance. Max dug into the breast pocket of his coat and produced his card case. 'Send me a round sum, I am not concerned with detail—it was our fault.'

'It most certainly was, and *I* am concerned with detail. You will get a full accounting. Now, if you please, I must see to having my next team put to.'

'Wait. You surely do not want to be seen by the other drivers.' She did not appear in the least discommoded by being found, dressed as a man, in the midst of a group of boisterous gentlemen.

'Really, Mr...' She glanced at the card, tilting it to catch the lantern light and her eyebrows rose. '*Lord* Penrith, I am in a hurry.' If it had been a young man with that accent and that attitude he would have assumed it was some young sprig of fashion out for a thrill. But women did not drive stages, and ladies most certainly did not drive *anything* on public highways outside the centre of town.

'Damn it, Dysart, if it wasn't for that damnable stagecoach I'd have had you in that last straight.' Latymer.

Max swung round, the flaring skirts of his great-coat effectively screening the willowy figure of the woman. 'Go and argue the toss with Nevill,' he suggested. 'But I say you lost it on the pull past Syon House. How far behind was Lansdowne?'

'One minute, but I still maintain—'

'I'll be with you inside in a moment. I've just got to argue this blockhead down from claiming half the cost of his damn coach,' he added, low-voiced, taking Latymer by the arm and turning him away. 'I told Nevill to get the brandy in.'

As he suspected, that was enough to turn the grumbling man back to the warmth of the inn parlour. As usual, whenever Latymer lost something, he would insist on a prolonged post mortem, the aim of which would be to prove he had failed for reasons entirely outside his control.

When he turned back, the young woman, far from taking advantage of his efforts to shield her, was engaged in spirited discussions with the head ostler about the team he was proposing to put to. 'And not that black one either. It's half-blind,' she called after him as he stomped back to the stables to fetch another horse.

'I will not run with those broken-down wrecks they try and fob one off with at night,' she pronounced as he came up to her.

'Madam—'

'Miss Mallory. Bree Mallory.'

'Miss Mallory, you cannot be intending to continue driving?'

'As far as Newbury.' She turned an impatient shoulder on him, watching the team being put to. It would take only a few minutes, now the horses had been agreed. 'Jem, get the passengers.'

'But wait, you've had a nasty shock.' Max put out his hand and caught her by the right wrist, then dropped it as she went white and gasped in pain.

For a sickening moment the yard spun and Bree found herself caught up hard against Lord Penrith's chest.

'Let me go!' The effect of being held by a strange man—no, by *this* strange man—was making her as dizzy as the pain. Reluctantly, it seemed, he opened his arms.

'You are hurt. Let me see.' *What a nice voice he has*, she thought irrelevantly. *Deep, and gentle and compelling.* She had no intention of doing as he asked, and yet, somehow, her hand was in his again and he was peeling back the cuff of the gauntlet to examine her wrist. 'Has that just happened?' She nodded. 'Can you move your fingers?'

'Yes. It isn't broken,' she added impatiently. His concern was weakening her; she had to tell herself it was nothing, that she could drive despite it.

'Well, you aren't driving a stage with that. You had best go inside and get it bound up.'

'Yes, I am driving! I cannot abandon a coach full of passengers here, let alone the parcels we're carrying. The Challenge Coach Company does not cancel coaches.'

'There are entirely too many *c*s in that sentence,' Lord Penrith remarked, 'but it does at least prove that you haven't been drinking if you can declaim it. The coach won't be cancelled. I'll drive it. Wait here.'

'You...I...you'll do no such thing!' She found herself talking to his retreating back. He was already striding off towards the inn door to where the youth who had been driving the drag was waiting. There was a short conversation—more an issuing of orders, she decided, going by her short experience of his lordship's manner, then he was coming back.

'Right. Is there room for you inside, Miss Mallory?'

'Certainly not. I am staying on the box.' Bother the man, now he had tricked her into accepting that he was going to drive! 'Are you any good, my lord?'

She knew who he was, of course—one glance at his card, and the cut of his own drag and team, told her

that. But she was not going to give Max Dysart, Earl
of Penrith, the satisfaction of acknowledging that he
was one of the finest whips in the land. Piers would
be mad with jealousy when he found out with whom
she had virtually collided.

He turned, pausing in the act of climbing on to the
box, one hand still resting on the wheel. 'Any good?
At driving?' One eyebrow arched.

'Yes, at driving,' she snapped. *If only he didn't keep
looking at me like that. As though he knew me, as
though he owned me...*

'Certainly. Much better than my young cousin, I
assure you, Miss Mallory. Then...I am quite good at
most things.'

Furious at what she suspected was an innuendo that
she didn't understand, Bree marched round and got
Jem to help her up on the other side of the box. She
could have made it on her own, she told herself resent-
fully, but she wasn't such an idiot as to strain her hurt
wrist just to prove a point. Without thinking about it
she flicked the tails of her coat into a makeshift cushion under her, and settled back. Jem swung up behind.

Lord Penrith already had the reins in hand. He certainly looked the part. 'Have you ever driven a stage
before?' she demanded. It would not be surprising if
he had—it was a craze amongst young bucks to bribe
a coachman to let them take the ribbons. More often
than not, the entire rig ended up in a ditch.

'Let them go!' He turned his head and grinned at her as the wheelers took the strain and began to move. 'Now I am wounded. You think I'm the sort of fellow who gets drunk and overturns stages for kicks? No, I drive a drag and my own horses when I want a four in hand. This lot aren't too bad.'

'Stick to ten miles an hour,' Bree cautioned. 'No springing them.'

'Yes, ma'am,' he said meekly as they got back on to the road and the leaders settled into their collars. 'There's a clean handkerchief in my left-hand pocket if you want to tie up your wrist.'

Gingerly Bree fished in the pocket and pulled out the square of white linen. She wrapped the makeshift bandage round her wrist, then tucked her hand back into the front of her coat. Just the knowledge that she did not have to drive another forty miles was bliss. Surreptitiously she rolled her aching shoulders.

'Thank you, my lord.'

'Max,' he said absently, his eyes on the road ahead. 'What sort of name is Bree?'

'My sort. It was my father's mother's name.'

There was a flash of white as he grinned. 'Tell me, Miss Mallory, how does a lady, who speaks with an accent that would not be out of place administering set-downs in Almack's, come to be driving a stagecoach?'

'I had an excellent education.' *Bother.* She had been

so shaken she had let her guard down. Both she and Piers were perfectly capable of switching their accents to suit their company, whether it was disputing the price of oats with the corn chandler or holding a stilted conversation with their half-brother. If she had been thinking, she would have let a strong overtone of London City creep into her vowels.

It was entirely possible that this man knew James, and if *he* discovered she was driving on the open road, and in men's clothes, then the fat really would be in the fire. One more of James's ponderous and endless lectures on propriety and she would probably say something entirely regrettable and cause a permanent family rift.

She shot an anxious glance over her shoulder, but the roof passengers were huddled up, scarves and mufflers round their ears, hunched in the misery of open-air, night-time travel. She could confess to robbing the Bank of England and they would not hear.

'My parents were perfectly well to do. Just because we're in trade does not mean elocution was neglected,' she added starchily.

'So how is it that you are driving?' he persisted.

'Because the driver broke his leg and there was no one else to send out, and the Challenge—'

'Coach Company does not cancel coaches,' he parroted. 'Yes, I know. Do you drive often?'

'I haven't driven a stage for three years,' Bree admitted. 'And I've never driven one in service or at night. But Piers—my younger brother—is recovering from pneumonia. I couldn't let him drive. It's his company, his and my uncle's. And I drive four in hand all the time.' She didn't add that she liked to drive the hay wagon up from the family farm near Aylesbury, or that she'd driven the dung cart before now when the need arose. Let him think she bowled round Hyde Park in a phaeton.

'Your driving is superb. I don't know how you held the stage out of the ditch when we overtook,' he said.

Neither do I! Terror and desperation, probably. The compliment from such a master warmed her. 'Why, thank you, my lord.'

'Max.'

'Max. It was sheer necessity. I doubt I could do it again. I was using both hands by that point, and I had abandoned my whip,' Bree confessed. 'The old coachmen in our yard would be shocked to the core.'

There was a chuckle from her companion, then he fell silent, intent on navigating the moonlit road.

It was curiously companionable, riding through the chilly darkness on the jolting, hard box beside this stranger. The team were trotting out strongly, then gathering themselves to canter when Max gave them the office on the better stretches. Her wrist throbbed painfully and her shoulders ached, but

Bree realised she was enjoying herself. The man was a superlative whip.

'You had better blow for the gate,' Max remarked, jerking her out of her reverie. 'The next toll bar's coming up.'

'I can't. I've tried and tried to master the horn, but I can't do it.'

'Fine guard you are,' Max grumbled. 'Here, take the reins.'

He held his left hand towards her and she slid her own into it, fingers slipping down his wrist and over his palm until the ribbons lay between the correct fingers and he could pull his own free. The team pecked a little at the strange position, then settled.

Max lifted the horn and blew, the long notes echoing through the clear night. 'Just in time,' Bree said as the toll gate keeper stumbled out in his nightgown to drag open the wide gate.

'We're going to have to do this for every gate, you realise,' Max commented, his big hand sliding into hers as he took back the reins. It brought them close together again and the fleeting memory of his arms around her in the inn yard made Bree catch her breath.

'We could stop a moment and pass the horn back to Jem,' Bree suggested reluctantly. It was the sensible thing to do, of course, but that had been rather fun.

'And lose more time?' Max flicked the whip close to the ear of the offside wheeler that seemed to have decided it didn't want to share the work. 'I'm sure the Challenge Coach Company is always punctual. Hmm, not enough *c*s. I shall have to think of a slogan.' Bree chuckled. 'Besides,' he added, echoing her own thoughts, 'it was rather fun.'

'In what way, exactly?' she enquired repressively. It might be very stimulating to be sitting here enjoying a master class in four-in-hand driving, but one had to recall that she was also alone, unchaperoned, with a man she was certain James would stigmatise as a rake. On the other hand, if James would disapprove, it made it all much more pleasurable.

'It's a form of trick driving in its way. And, of course, there's the opportunity to hold hands with a pretty girl. Now, what have I said to make you snort?'

'I do *not* snort. And if you find any female dressed as I am pretty, my lord, there is something wrong with you.'

'I have exceptionally good eyesight.'

'And a vivid imagination,' she muttered. He probably *was* a rake, and flirting with anything female under the age of ninety was doubtless a prerequisite.

Max smiled, but all he said was, 'We shall see.'

By the time they reached the last toll gate before Newbury Bree thought she had never been so stiff, nor so exhilarated, in her life. She seemed to have passed through some barrier of exhaustion and now, at almost four in the morning, she felt wide awake.

Probably because my bottom-bones are bruised black and blue, she concluded ruefully. The old coachman's trick of making a cushion with her coat tails was not as effective as she had been led to believe, or perhaps she simply had less natural padding than they did.

It was time to sound the horn again. They had the rhythm of it now. Bree felt the warmth of Max's large hand slide over hers, then she had the reins and he was blowing for the gate. But when they were through and he reached for her in his turn he did not slip his fingers across her palm; instead, he closed his hand around hers and held it lightly.

'We'll drive the last bit together,' he said simply, and she wondered at the warm rush of pleasure the words and the action brought her.

I'm getting light-headed, Bree thought, flexing her fingers within Max's grip and fighting the urge to lean into his body. It was deliciously like being drunk.

The sensation lasted as long as it took William Huggins, otherwise known as Bonebreaker Bill, to come striding out into the yard of the Plume of Feathers and see who was driving his coach through the arch.

'Miss Bree! What do you think you are doing?' He glowered up at the box of the coach, meaty fists on his bulky hips, booted feet apart.

'We didn't have a driver to send out, Bill,' she said placatingly. Bill had known her since she was six and had proved a far stricter guardian than either of her parents ever had.

'Who's this flash cove, then?' he demanded, swivelling his bloodshot eyes to Max. 'Some break-o'day boy who's cozened you into letting him take the ribbons for a thrill?'

'This is Lord Penrith, Bill. My lord, allow me to introduce William Huggins, the finest coachman on this, or any other, road.'

Bill brushed aside the compliment, taking it as his due, but his eyes narrowed. 'Penrith? From the Nonesuch Whips?'

'For my sins.' Sensibly, Max was staying on the box where he had the advantage of height. But the coachman had lost all his hostility.

'Well, I'll be damned! If half they say about you is true, my lord, then it's a privilege to have you drive my coach, that it is! Why, you can take it all the way to Bath if you be so wishful.'

'Thank you, but no, Mr Huggins.' Max began to climb down. 'This was a long enough stage for me—I had no idea those box seats were so hard.'

'Hah! You should fold your coat tails under you, my lord. That's the way to save your bum bones.'

'It doesn't work, Bill,' Bree said, causing him to go

scarlet. 'I tried. Now, come and lift me down, please. I'm as stiff as a board.'

The ostlers, spurred on by the presence of their severest critic, completed the change in under two minutes and Bill took the coach out on to the highway with a roar of farewell and a flourish of his hat. Poor Jem, expected like all guards to work the whole distance, was back up on the box beside him.

'There you are,' Max said, fishing his pocket watch out. 'Dead on time. The Challenge Coach Company never compromises with the clock,' he added with satisfaction. 'You may have it engraved on your stationery with my compliments.'

'Thank you so much.' Bree turned to him, tipping her head back to smile up into his face. It was one part of him, she realised, that she hadn't been able to study during the last four hours. She knew the feel of his hands on hers, the range of his voice, and the height and breadth of his body had bulwarked hers like a rock all night.

It was difficult to make out colours in the lamplight, but his eyes were dark under dark brows, his cheekbones pronounced, his chin rather too decided for her taste, and his mouth—which was within a fraction of a smile as he watched her—was generous. It was a good face, she decided. A tough face, but in a good way. He made her feel safe.

'Thank you,' she said again. 'Goodbye, my lord.'

'And just where do you think you are going now, Miss Mallory?'

'To bespeak a room, of course.'

'With no maid, no luggage and at four in the morning?'

'They will know who I am when I introduce myself.'

'It is not the inn staff I am concerned about. Really, Miss Mallory, you cannot stay here—goodness knows who you might encounter. Think of your reputation.'

'I do not have one!' Really, he was as bad as James. 'Not that sort of reputation. I am not in society, I am not in the marriage mart. I am in *trade*, my lord. Besides, what alternative do I have, other than to wait for the next stage back and be jolted for another five sleepless hours? I have, I regret to say, no convenient maiden aunt in Newbury.'

His mouth twitched. She could not tell, in this light, whether he was annoyed that she was arguing with him, or amused by the maiden aunt. 'I was going to take a private parlour for you to rest in for a while and I will hire a chaise to take us back to London.'

'A chaise? A closed carriage? For the two of us? All the way back to London? And just what will that do for my reputation, pray?'

'Ruin it, I imagine,' Max said amiably.

Chapter Three

Max watched the expressions chase across what little he could see of Bree's face. *Oh, to get that damned hat off her head.* 'At least, it would ruin you if you were the young society lady you speak of, with vouchers for Almack's and a position in the marriage mart to defend. Then, if it should be known that you had spent five hours in a closed carriage with a man, it would be a disaster.

'But you aren't, are you? You are much safer being whisked home in comfort by me than you are sitting in a public house where you will be recognised by anyone who does business with your company, and at the mercy of any passing rakes and bucks who chose to prey on unprotected women.'

'And you aren't, I suppose? A rake, I mean.' That lush mouth looked gorgeous even when it was thinned to a suspicious line.

'No, I am not, if by that you imagine I will take the opportunity to ravish you. But I cannot prove it—you will have to make your own judgment on my character.' He studied Bree's face, expecting anything from anger to the vapours, and was taken aback when she laughed.

'My lord, if you feel moved to ravish any woman looking as I do now, *and* after driving through the night, then I both pity your need and admire your stamina. I would appreciate the comfort of a chaise very much. Thank you.'

Enchanting. Oh, enchanting, he thought, returning the smile. 'Let us find you a room for half an hour, for I am sure you would want to wash your hands, have a cup of tea and have your wrist better dressed. I will hire a chaise. Even stopping for breakfast along the way, we will be home for luncheon.'

When he tapped on her door she emerged promptly, discreetly wearing the voluminous greatcoat and with the low-crowned beaver down over her eyebrows. But as soon as the chaise turned out on to the highway she tossed the hat into the corner and shrugged off the weighty coat with a sigh of relief.

'Max? What are you staring at?' she asked, watching him with narrowed eyes in the light of the two spermaceti oil lamps that lit the interior.

'I...I...your hair. I was not expecting it to be so long.' *God, I'm babbling like some green boy. Even Nevill would be showing more address.*

Bree flipped the thick braid back over her shoulder. 'I should have it cut, but it is easier to manage plaited.'

'Don't cut it,' he said abruptly. It was a lovely, unusual, wheaten gold without any hint of red in it. Not brassy or silvery or any of the usual shades of blonde. Where it escaped from the severity of the braid tiny wisps curled at her temples and across her forehead, which was smooth and touched with just a hint of the sun. So unfashionable to have blonde hair. So unladylike to allow oneself to be caught by the sun. His gaze wandered down to arched brows, three shades darker than her hair, to deep blue eyes watching him back somewhat warily from the shelter of long lashes.

'Do I have a smudge on my nose?' Bree enquired, seemingly ignoring his comment about her hair.

'No. I am just getting used to you without that hat.' *And without that greatcoat, and in breeches and boots, Heaven help me!* Her legs were long and shapely, her figure, flattened by a waistcoat and shrouded by her coat, was more difficult to judge, but even the best efforts of men's tailoring could not completely submerge womanly curves that had Max's heart beating hard.

He wanted her, but not because she was beautiful, because she wasn't exactly that, and he should know, he had kept some diamonds of the first water in his time. *What is it about her?* He struggled with it, trying to identify the elusive something that had shot an arrow straight under his skin in that first fleeting exchange of glances.

More for something to occupy himself than for comfort, Max took off his own greatcoat, stuffed his gloves in his pocket, and ran his hands through his hair, which had suffered from having his hat jammed down hard to keep it on against the wind.

'Is that a Brutus, that hairstyle?' Bree was watching him, head on one side a little. She had the faint air of a woman sizing up a purchase. Max had the uncomfortable feeling that if he were a chicken she would have inspected his feet for signs of age, or if he were a horse she would be checking his teeth. He was not at all sure he was passing muster.

'My own variation on it, yes.'

'I only ask because Piers says that is how he has had his hair cut. I can see the resemblance, but yours is far more successful.'

'Thank you,' Max said gravely. Contact with Miss Mallory handing out lukewarm compliments was chastening to one's self-esteem. 'How old is your brother?'

'Just seventeen. We have a half-brother, James, who is thirty. Mama married twice.'

When she talked about Piers her voice was warm, loving; when she spoke of her other brother, it was cool. 'Is James concerned with the business?'

'Goodness, no.' That was apparently funny enough

to make her laugh. Max was filled with an ambition to make her laugh again, to hear the rich, amused chuckle, but his usually ready wit appeared to have deserted him. 'James has nothing to do with it. Piers inherited my father's half and Uncle George holds the other. He founded the company with Papa and he still runs both family farms and breeds most of our horses. I run the office.'

'So you own nothing, but do all the work. That seems a little unjust.'

'It is merely the lot of most women,' Bree observed drily. 'Piers will take over as soon as he is of age, although I suspect I will still manage things day to day. Piers is far more interested in the technical side of the business—improved springing, horse breeding for stamina, that sort of thing. And he believes that we will need to keep an eye on all the new forms of transport that will come in the next few years.'

'Such as? Nothing will replace the horse, however improved the carriages may become.'

'Canals, steam locomotion...'

'Never catch on,' Max said confidently. 'Canals are fine for heavy transport, I'll give you that, and steam is good for industry and mining. But these steam locomotives are nothing but dangerous gimmicks.'

That luscious chuckle again. 'Should you ever meet Piers, I advise you not to air such opinions. I usually have to rescue the unenlightened after an hour's lecture.' She yawned suddenly, hugely, clapping both hands over her mouth like a guilty child. 'Oh, I beg your pardon!'

'Go to sleep,' Max suggested. 'Here.' He stripped off his coat, folded it so the soft silk lining was outermost and offered it to her. 'Use that as a pillow. And take your own coat off. You'll be more comfortable. You can put one of the greatcoats over you, if you feel chilly.'

Bree regarded him, the laughter gone from her face, her eyes a little wide. Max realised that taking off his coat had probably been unwise, and expecting her to abandon herself to sleep under the circumstances was asking too much.

'Thank you,' she said, surprising him. She shrugged off her own coat, giving him a glimpse of the label. Not such a good tailor as his, but not contemptible either. She saw the direction of his gaze. 'Yes, I was so brassy as to have these clothes made by a tailor, but he came to the house—I draw the line at marching into a gentleman's establishment to order breeches, whatever James might think.'

Max sat back, his arms folded, and gazed out of the window on to darkness while Bree made herself comfortable. She placed her own greatcoat on the seat at one end, patted his coat carefully into a pillow at the other, then swung her feet up and curled on to her side.

'Are you warm enough?' He shook out his caped greatcoat and offered it.

'If I take it, then you might be cold.' She looked up at him, suddenly so vulnerable on the makeshift bed that something inside him twisted.

'I'm warm,' Max assured her. 'Very warm indeed.' *Too damned hot, in fact.*

'Thank you.' She simply closed her eyes and snuggled down as he draped the heavy cloth over her, careful not to touch her body. As if it were something she did every night, Bree fished out the golden plait and let it lie on the covering. 'Goodnight.' Her lips curved into a smile.

'Goodnight.' Max flattened his shoulders against the squabs, crossed his arms, crossed his legs and gazed fixedly at the webbing of the small luggage holder above Bree's seat. How was that made? Netting, presumably. How was netting made? Try to work it out. Or count the number of diamonds it made. Or think about how much damage tonight's little adventure had done to the immaculate lacquer of his drag's sides. Or anything other than the fact that the woman opposite trusted him enough to fall asleep like this, and that he wanted to abuse that trust, very, very badly.

Why? It all seemed to go back to his musings in the club, so many hours ago: he should get married and start his nursery. He had a title, an estate, a family name to consider.

There was no one to nag him to do it except his grandmother, who on their last meeting had informed him with some asperity that if he wanted to go racketing around like a twenty-year-old instead of a man who had just had his thirtieth birthday, then she washed her hands of him. 'Either sort out that business over Drusilla once and for all and find a suitable young woman to marry, or decide to accept Nevill as your heir. He's a nice enough young cub,' the Dowager had pronounced flatly. 'I expect I can lick him into shape if I start now.'

Nevill was, indeed, nice. The word just about defined the boy. But Max didn't want him as his heir, he wanted his own son, he realised. That decision at least seemed to have hardened since he was thinking about it last night.

A son meant a wife. He had done his best to reform his life, he assured himself. He had danced attendance at every function the Season could throw up. He had spent the summer at a number of house parties—he had even spent two weeks in Brighton.

I have been giggled at, simpered at, flirted with. I've chatted endlessly to tongue-tied girls, I've done my duty by well-bred wallflowers, I've risked my skin by talking to forward young madams with bold manners and overprotective brothers and I've done the pretty by every matchmaking mama in town. And not one of them has stirred me as much as that first sight of this woman.

The honourable thing—the rules—were quite simple. Well-bred virgins were for courting, respectfully. Young matrons who had not yet produced their husband's heir and spare were for avoiding. Decent middle-class women of any description and servants were out of bounds. Professionals, flighty widows and married women with a quiver full of offspring and a yen to stray—they were all for pleasure.

What he had before him was a decent, if unusual, middle-class woman. Which meant she was out of bounds for any purpose whatsoever. *Except friendship.* That was a startling thought. Men did not have women friends. Women were to be married to, or related to or for making love to or for employing. But this one, this Bree Mallory, made him want to talk to her, as well as reduce her to quivering ecstasy in his arms.

He thought he could talk to her about the problems with the Home Farm, his efforts to make Nevill less awkward around ladies, his search for a decent cook, his doubts about government policy and whom he should support in the House.

Talk about big things or utter trivia, both comfortably, with a friend.

For a moment, thinking about that fantasy, he had forgotten the reality. To marry, a man must be single, unattached, free. And he had no idea whether he was or not, whatever his lawyer assured him. And reforming his life in order to find himself a wife was meaningless when he was still avoiding the same issue that he had been for ten years.

Bree sighed and stirred in her sleep, and the heavy plait slithered over the rough wool, hairs snagging in it. Then it fell. Max sat watching it swing with all the focus of a cat confronted by a mouse. He wanted to catch it, pat it, stroke it, play with it. He wanted to feel the texture of it in his hands. It would be like silk, he just knew. Most of all, he wanted to see it loose.

He must not touch her. He knew that as he knew the sun came up in the morning. But the thin ribbon that tied the end of the plait, that was another matter. The bow had come undone, so only one crossing of the tie held the knot. Max bent, caught one end in his fingers and tugged gently. It was brown velvet, prickling against the pads of his fingers. The tug loosened it. He tweaked the other end, the weight and springiness of the hair working with him. The ribbon caught for a moment, then fell to the floor.

He sat upright, away from Bree, his eyes on her hair as the plait, freed, began to part and come undone, his breathing as tightly controlled as though he were about to fight a duel.

The lack of movement woke Bree, then the noise from outside. Confused, she lay with her eyes closed.

It sounded like the yard of the Mermaid during a change, but she hadn't fallen asleep at her desk…the bed she was lying on lurched slightly and her eyes flew open.

'Oh! Oh, I'm sorry, I had forgotten where I was.' Lord Penrith, no, *Max,* was sitting opposite her, the lines of his face harsh in the morning light filtering through the drawn blinds. His cheeks were darkened with stubble. 'What time is it?'

'Almost seven. You've slept through two changes and we are at an inn on the far side of Reading. I thought it might be better to stop here for breakfast.'

'Why? Oh, you mean more discreet?' Bree sat up, rubbing her eyes. 'For goodness' sake, look at my hair.' It had managed to free itself almost entirely from its plait and the ribbon lay twisted on the floor. She pushed back the greatcoat and sat up, gathering the mass in both hands and dragging it back off her face. Max stood up abruptly and reached for his coat.

'I'll go and bespeak a private parlour and breakfast.' He almost snatched up his hat and the door was banging shut behind him before she could respond. 'Wait here.'

What is it about men and mornings? Papa was just the same, and Uncle George still is, and I cannot get a coherent or intelligent word out of Piers before at least nine. Shrugging, Bree raked her fingers through her hair and began to plait as best she could with no mirror. She pulled on her coat, then the greatcoat, jammed on her hat and got out of the chaise into a familiar scene.

The poles of the chaise were grounded, the postilions leaning against them chatting with an ostler, knowing that they had at least half an hour before their passengers finished breakfast. A pair of stable boys in breeches and waistcoats scurried across the yard carrying buckets, and a stout man with a gig was engaged in earnest conversation with a groom over a problem with the harness.

It was a small inn, not one she knew, which meant it would not accommodate a stage changing. But the horses looking over the stable doors were healthy stock, from what she could see, and the place was well kept. It was a wise choice for a discreet stop, she realised, wondering if Max knew all the inns along the Bath road where a man might halt with a woman and expect privacy and a good meal.

No one took any notice of her as she walked across the yard and in through the inn door. A maid was bustling through with a loaded tray. Bree stopped her with a query and received a startled glance when the girl realised she was a woman.

'The privy's through there, sir...I mean, ma'am.'

'And the gentleman who just bespoke a private parlour for breakfast?'

The maid's face cleared. Obviously this was an illicit liaison, which was an easy explanation for the strangely dressed woman in front of her. 'Second on the left, ma'am, Miss…er.'

Max was brooding over a day-old news sheet when Bree came into the parlour and tossed her hat on to a chair. He got to his feet, a frown between his level brows. 'There you are. I couldn't find you.'

'Privy,' Bree explained briskly. No point in being coy about it. 'The maid thinks we are eloping,' she commented, peeling off her greatcoat and sitting down in the chair he was holding for her.

'How the devil do you deduce that?'

'Well, when a woman in man's clothes asks which parlour a gentleman is in, there are very few alternatives that are likely to occur to her.'

'Do you mind?'

'Not at all. I certainly won't be stopping at this inn again, so where's the harm?'

'I am beginning to have grave doubts about how I am going to explain this to your male relatives.'

'I cannot imagine Uncle George coming up from Buck- inghamshire armed with his horsewhip, and Piers will be too busy worshipping at your feet to notice, even if I staggered through the door shrieking that you had ruined me.' Bree found she enjoyed watching Max's face, even when he was scowling.

He definitely was not handsome. She had long ago decided that her taste ran to slender gentlemen with dark hair and green eyes, the refined, artistic type. The earl was big, tough, and did not look as though he had an artistic bone in his body. His eyes were brown, his hair the deep colour of dark honey. The decided chin she had already remarked upon. And his mouth—now that was very expressive.

His lips quirked as she studied him. 'And why should your brother do anything so outlandish?'

'Because, although he has altogether too much interest in steam engines and canal boats, his absolute passion is driving. And he knows all about the exploits of the Nonesuch Whips—meals are frequently rendered hideous by his mistaken belief that I must be just as interested. You, my lord, feature frequently. Oh, thank you.' The maid came in with a large platter of ham and eggs, followed by a pot boy with a teapot in one hand and a tankard in the other and another girl with the bread, butter and preserves.

'So you knew who I was from the moment you saw my card?'

'Of course.' Bree began to cut bread.

'So you knew I was a perfectly competent driver?'

'A nonpareil, according to Piers.' She passed him the bread and helped herself from the platter. 'I am *starving.*'

'Yet you asked me if I was any good?' That obviously rankled.

Bree smiled sweetly. 'I could not resist. I was some-what annoyed with you, if you recall.'

'You, Miss Mallory, are a minx and I hope your young man has the measure of you,' Max said warmly, taking out his feelings on a slice of ham.

'My what?'

'Young man, follower, betrothed.'

'I don't have one.' She regarded him, surprised, her forkful of food half-raised.

'Why ever not?'

'Most of the men I meet are employees. And I don't mix socially with the other coaching company pro-prietors, because…I don't know really, I just don't. When we are at the farm there are our neighbours, but I've never met anyone I felt I wanted to be closer to, somehow.' Her voice trailed away.

How could she explain that the farmers and the coaching proprietors all regarded her warily because of her titled relatives, and her half-brother and that side of the family thought of her and Piers as an embar-rassment hardly to be acknowledged. She fell neatly between two stools, but she had no intention of re-vealing her family circumstances to the earl. He too would despise what she knew James regarded as her mongrel breeding.

The vertical line between Max's dark brows was deeper now. 'That's a waste.'

'I am too bossy anyway,' she said with a laugh, de-

termined that he would not pity her. 'What about you?
Is Lady Penrith wondering what has become of you?'

'I am not—' He broke off. 'There is no Lady Penrith at home waiting for me.'

'So is there a young lady expecting to become a
countess shortly?'

'No.' He frowned again and there was a bleakness
at the back of those warm brown eyes that spoke of
banked emotion. 'If I were looking for a wife, I would
first have to find one who isn't a ninny.'

'They can't help it, you know.' Bree cut some more
bread. 'They are brought up to believe that the slightest show of independence, the merest hint of taking
an intelligent interest in anything besides fashions and
dancing, housekeeping and babies, will brand them
as either bluestockings or fast.'

'How do you know?' Max was enjoying watching
her eating. Her table manners would have graced a
banquet, but her appetite was extremely healthy. It occurred to him that Bree Mallory was one of the fre-
est women he knew: she said what she thought, she
made up her own mind about things and she did not
appear to feel she had to hide things just for the sake
of convention.

'I...' It seemed he was wrong. What had he said?
She had coloured up and was looking thoroughly self-
conscious. 'I read fashionable journals, if you must
know. And I observe people.'

'Of course,' Max agreed. There was a mystery about Miss Mallory, and one he was only too well aware he was not going to be able to investigate. Whatever he felt about her—no, *because* of what he felt about her—the only honourable thing to do would be to drop her at her own front door and never see her again.

Chapter Four

'That was a good stretch,' Bree remarked, looking out on the countryside rushing past as the postilions took advantage of the famously fast road between Staines and Hounslow.

'Yes.' Max nodded agreement. 'I would reckon we made thirteen miles an hour there. We'll be at the bridge over the River Crane in a moment.'

'Then the Heath, then Hounslow and we'll be back where we started,' she said brightly, trying to keep the conversation going. That sentence was the longest Max had uttered since they left the inn, replete with ham, eggs and cherry preserve.

'Yes.'

Bree watched him from under her lowered lashes as the chaise slowed and clattered over the bridge. He wasn't sulking; he did not appear to be sleepy. Perhaps he was simply irritated to have lost so much time over her concerns. She hoped it was not that; she had been enjoying the adventure—even her wrist had stopped aching so much. And, if truth be told, she was enjoying Max's company.

The chaise lurched on the well-worn road and the Heath unfolded on either side with its rough grazing, spiny cushions of gorse and occasional copses of trees.

'The gorse is still in flower.' Max was resting his forearm on the window ledge.

'Love is out of fashion when the gorse is out of bloom.' Bree quoted the old adage with a smile. 'I love the scent of it in the summer when the sun's on it. It smells of—'

There was a shot, very close, and the chaise juddered to a halt to the sound of shouting outside.

'Hell.' Max shifted to stare forwards out of the off-side window, pushed Bree firmly into a corner and rummaged urgently in the pockets of his greatcoat as it lay on the seat. 'Highwaymen. Two of them.' He dragged a pistol from the pocket. 'Stay there.' He opened the door and climbed out slowly, the hand holding the pistol slightly behind his back.

The moment he was out of the door Bree slid along the seat and squinted round the corner of the window frame. There were two of them, each with an ugly-looking horse pistol, one covering the postilions who were out of her sight, the other now training his weapon on Max.

'Not good odds,' Bree muttered. Her heart was banging somewhere in the region of her throat, but she tried to think calmly. The fact that they probably did not have much of value about them, beyond a few coins in her pocket and Max's watch, signet and what money he had left after hiring the chaise, was not particularly encouraging. She had heard of highwaymen shooting travellers out of sheer frustration at a disappointing haul.

She dug into the pocket of her own greatcoat and produced her pistol. Not as large, and by no means as elegant, as the firearm Max was carrying, it was still perfectly capable of doing the job. Not that she had ever used it in anger. Bree checked it carefully, brought the hammer to half-cock and slid out of the opposite door, opening it as little as possible.

'Hand it over, guv'nor.'

'I am not carrying more than a few sovereigns.' Max sounded bored.

'We'll have them. And yer watch and yer rings.'

'I'll be damned if you do.'

Bree peered round the back of the chaise. The position hadn't changed, although the man covering the postilions had turned slightly, his pistol wavering between the riders and Max.

'Well, if you wants to go to hell, guv'nor, I'm sure we can manage that. Just hand the dibs over first.' The closer man seemed to be the leader—he was certainly doing all the talking. She tried to commit his appearance to memory for later reporting to the magistrates, but between a kerchief covering him from the nose down, and a battered tricorne jammed on his head, there was little to identify him.

She couldn't see properly to get a clear shot at the other, not without coming right out into the open, and she didn't want to do that until Max made his move. Her bruised wrist was already aching abominably with the weight of the pistol; she just wished he'd do something.

When he did, it took her by surprise as much as it did the highwaymen. His head snapped round as though he had just seen someone approaching and both men responded. In the second it took them to realise nothing was there, he had the pistol trained on the nearer rider.

Bree saw the man's hands tighten on the reins and his horse began to sidle. 'Just need to point out, guv'nor—there's two of us. You loose off that pop, you're going to get shot.'

'And you will be dead. I am an excellent shot,' Max rejoined calmly. 'Might I suggest we call it quits and you leave before you get hurt?'

'Nah. You cover him, Toby. He won't do nothing. The odds aren't right.'

'They are now.' Bree slid out from behind the carriage and ducked under Max's arm before any of the men could react. 'I've got your friend Toby right in my sights.' *For just as long as I can hold this thing steady, which isn't going to be for much longer....*

'That's a woman!' the nearer rider said indignantly. He fired at Max just as Max pulled the trigger. Bree took aim at the centre of Toby's chest and squeezed. The air seemed to be full of the sound of gunfire; something whistled past Bree's ear and struck the coach. Toby was clutching his right hand, swearing, his horse rearing. The other man was slumped over the pommel of his saddle, one hand groping for the reins.

Bree turned to Max, expecting him to go forwards to grab the horse while the man was incapable, and found he was on his knees, one hand pressed to his shoulder, blood showing between his fingers.

'Max!' The sound of hooves made her turn to see both men, lurching in their saddles, cantering away. 'Max!'

He shook his head as if to clear it. 'I think it's just a graze, across the top of my shoulder.'

'Come here, help his lordship up!' The postilions hurried over, and between them got Max to his feet.

'It's all right. I can manage.' He shook them off and climbed into the carriage, muttering words under his breath that Bree was fortunately unable to hear clearly. 'Drive back to London before anyone else decides to have a go at us.'

'We should stop in Hounslow, find a doctor. Max, you're bleeding.'

'Not much. Don't fuss.' His teeth were gritted and he was pale across the cheekbones, but the bleeding did not seem to be getting any worse. 'That was one hell of a shot—you took the pistol right out of his hand.'

So that was what had happened. Bree realised she'd shut her eyes the moment she'd pulled the trigger. The temptation to take the credit for such a feat was acute. 'I was aiming at his chest,' she admitted. 'I've never shot anyone before.' And would not again, if she could help it. Her ears were still ringing, her wrist felt as though it had been hit by a hammer and she didn't like to contemplate how she would be feeling if she had killed the man.

Max gave a shout of laughter that turned into a gasp as the chaise lurched forwards again. Was there anything this woman wouldn't attempt? And then to have the honesty to admit she had missed by a foot. He was going to get her back home before anything else happened, and he certainly did not intend her spending any time in Hounslow in broad daylight, dressed like that, while they found a surgeon.

He dragged off his neckcloth, wadded it up and pushed it under his coat.

'What *do* you think you're doing?' Bree was watching him, hands fisted on her hips.

'Stopping it bleeding.' *Ouch.*

'We need to look at it, bandage it properly. It could

be bleeding worse than you think and with that dark coat I can't tell.'

'I'll take off the coat,' Max conceded. *Anything to stop her fussing*, he told himself, trying to ignore the very real anxiety in her blue eyes.

Shrugging out of it, in a moving carriage, was not easy. He could feel the sweat beading his forehead, and he almost bit his tongue with the effort not to swear out loud.

Bree came and sat next to him. 'Now take off your shirt.'

'No.' He could feel the colour rising in his face and tried to fight it.

'Why ever not? How can I bandage this if you don't?'

'It doesn't need bandaging.'

'I will be the judge of that. You can't sit in a jolting chaise for another hour with it oozing like that.' He heard her swallow hard. Obviously dealing with oozing gunshot wounds was not something Miss Mallory dealt with daily. He was almost surprised.

'I will hold my neckcloth over it.'

'You will not. Take off that shirt.'

'No.' Max groped for a convincing explanation. 'It would not be proper.'

'Oh, for goodness' sake! I've seen men's bare chests before. I have a brother, don't forget. And the men are always sluicing off under the yard pump. I'm sure a lord has nothing they don't have.'

He could feel it now, the blush was positively burning. 'I am not going to take off my shirt.'

'Don't be such a baby.' She had her hands on the collar. It was quite obvious the wretched woman had a younger brother.

'I am not being—'

Bree simply gripped the shirt either side of the tear made by the bullet and yanked. Max clutched the tatters of the garment to his chest and glared at her. 'Satisfied?' he demanded, glancing down and flattening his palms firmly to his pectorals.

'Better, but you are making this very difficult.' She peered at the wound. 'It is just a groove, but it is really deep. It must hurt.' She lifted the neckcloth and dabbed gently at the edges. 'I'll make a pad with some of the shirt fabric and then tie it up with the neckcloth. Will you *please* let go of it!'

Max clung on grimly while Bree wrenched at the shoulder seams until the whole back of the shirt came away. She made a neat pad and pressed it to the wound, then stared at him. 'It isn't the pain, is it? You're embarrassed—in fact, you are blushing. For goodness' sake, you're a man of the world, a rake probably—what is there to be embarrassed about?'

'I am not a rake,' he ground out between clenched teeth.

'Well, you certainly aren't a monk! Women must have seen your chest before now. Lots of them. Oh, have it your own way—just sit still.'

He should have realised, if he had been thinking clearly, that the only way to secure a pad on his shoulder was to place the middle of the long neckcloth on top, cross it under his armpit and then bring one end across his chest and the other around his back, to tie under the opposite armpit.

But it did not occur to him until her right hand was diving under the front of his shirt, pushing his own hand out of the way.

'What on earth?'

Oh, Lord. If she laughed, he'd strangle her. Reluctantly Max unbuttoned the wreck of his shirt and pulled it off. 'Before you ask, I was very drunk, very young and it was a bet.'

'But…' She was staring, obviously fascinated. The effect of her wide-eyed, innocent regard was damnably arousing. He concentrated grimly on the embarrassment. 'It's pierced, only not like earrings. It's a sort of stud.' She reached one exploratory finger towards his right nipple, realised what she was doing, flushed as red as he knew he was, and snatched her hand back. He thought he might simply faint from lust, there and then. 'What is it?'

'I was nineteen,' Max said, determined to get this

said and finished with. 'We went to a house of…a place…'

'A brothel?'

'Yes, a brothel. And there was a tableau…'

'Really?' Bree's eyebrows shot up. 'What of?'

'Never you mind. Anyway, the man had his nipple pierced, and there was an argument about how much it hurt to have it done, and like an idiot I said it couldn't be that bad, women had their ears pierced all the time—I did mention that I was very drunk, didn't I?—and one thing led to another, and there was a bet. And there I was.'

'Did it hurt?' Her eyes were enormous.

'I cannot begin to describe it.' He winced even now at the memory. 'This shoulder is nothing in comparison.'

'Can't you have it removed?' She was staring, openly fascinated despite her blushes.

'No. It's shaped like a tiny dumbbell with ends that seem to self-lock. I went to my doctor. When he'd finished falling about hooting with laughter he said I risked losing significant bits of flesh if he tried to cut it off, so I'm stuck.'

Bree was still staring, transfixed, and the blush was ebbing away to leave her looking positively intrigued. 'Does it still hurt?'

'No.'

'Why do people do it, though?'

'It's considered erotic.' *And I hope to Heaven she doesn't ask me what I mean.* 'And don't you dare laugh.'

'I wouldn't dream of it,' Bree assured him, biting the inside of her cheeks in an effort to keep a straight face. The poor man was mortified—who wouldn't be? But it was very endearing to see such a very male creature reduced to blushing confusion. She busied herself with catching the ends of the makeshift bandage and tying it, which was not at all easy without brushing against the unmentionable stud.

But erotic? Why would such a thing be erotic? she wondered as Max rearranged the shredded shirt as best he could and then eased the coat back on.

She knew what the word meant. She understood in principle what went on between men and women—you didn't grow up on a farm and run a public hostelry without working *that* out—but what on earth had nipples to do with it?

The problem was, just thinking about it made her own begin to tingle in a most extraordinary way. In fact, they were positively aching and she was finding it very difficult to meet Max's eyes and her breath felt as though it was tight in her throat and something of the dizziness she had felt when he had caught her in his arms in the inn yard returned.

So, this was sexual attraction. *Oh, my goodness! Well, thankfully I haven't felt this way until this stage in the journey and Max is doubtless too embarrassed, and in too much discomfort, to notice anything odd about my manner. Am I blushing? He's stopped blushing. That's all right then.*

Max crossed his legs abruptly, making Bree certain he was in more pain than he was admitting. He was fiddling with the tails of his coat, flipping them across his lap and turning in the seat away from her.

'I should have asked you,' he said suddenly. 'Are you all right? The shock of the highwaymen must have been considerable.'

'No, I'm absolutely fine,' Bree said brightly, well aware that she was overdoing the cheerfulness by several degrees. She glanced out of the window and saw the glint of water to the right. 'The Thames—we're nearly at Kew.'

'I told the postilions to take me home first, to Berkeley Square. Then they can take you on to your home. I thought that would be more discreet.'

'Yes, of course. How thoughtful.' She was sounding like one of the ninnies he said he disliked. But what did it matter? Bree realised with a sinking heart what should have been obvious from the start of this adventure: she was never going to see Max Dysart, Earl of Penrith, again.

This attraction was too new, too strange to handle. If she said anything, she'd be sure to betray herself, she was certain. Better to be safe than sorry. With an artistically contrived yawn Bree turned her head into the corner squabs and pretended to settle down and sleep.

The rumble of carriage wheels over cobbles signalled their return to town and gave Bree an excuse to wake up. It was a relief—sitting with one's eyes closed, and nothing to think about but a disturbing gentleman only inches away, was not a comfortable way to pass the time. Especially when the man in question was about to become nothing but a daydream.

The imposing houses around the square were a far cry from the modest respectability of Gower Street, but Bree had a fair idea of what they looked like inside. James's own town house was just a stone's throw away in Mount Street.

Max looked very much more himself, she noted. Doubtless relief at seeing the back of this inconvenient adventure acted as a powerful tonic. 'Miss Mallory.' He was being very formal all of a sudden. 'It has been a pleasure.'

'I am quite sure it hasn't,' Bree retorted, smiling. 'Your handsome drag is no doubt scratched all over, you've lost a night's sleep and been shot in the shoulder—you must have a very strange idea of pleasure if the past twelve hours have been entertaining.'

'It all depends on the company,' he said, surprising her by catching up her hand and touching his lips to her fingers where they emerged from their makeshift bandage.

'That, my lord, is very gallant.' *Ye gods! What must he be like if he sets out to flirt in earnest? The women must fall at his feet in droves.* Those dark brown eyes were melting something inside her in a way that was, strangely, both painful and enjoyable.

'Gallantry does not come into it. What direction shall I give the men?'

'Oh, um—' She almost said Gower Street, then thought rapidly. 'The Mermaid Inn, High Holborn.'

'Home of the Challenge Coach Company? Of course. Good day, Miss Mallory.'

Not *goodbye.* 'Good day, my lord. And thank you.' Impulsively Bree leaned forward and kissed his cheek, and sat back, flustered, as he stared at her, a smile just curving the corner of his mouth. Then he had stepped back, the door was closing and the chaise moved off.

Piers came bounding out of the office as she climbed down from the chaise and thanked the postilions. 'What on earth are you doing in that? It's not like you to spend that sort of money. Still, I don't blame you. You must be exhausted. How did it go? Tell me all about it, Bree. I wish you'd let me go too.'

'Do hush a minute!' She threw up a hand to silence him and hastened into the office. 'The sooner I get out of these clothes the better. Help me with this great-coat, will you?'

'What have you done to your wrist? Let me see.' Piers pushed her firmly down into her desk chair and began to untie it. 'Ouch! That looks painful.' The fine square of white linen, soiled now where it had been on the outside, flapped open as he shook it out, revealing a fine white-work monogram in one corner. 'D? Where did this come from?'

'It stands for Dysart, and it belongs to Max Dysart, Earl of Penrith. And yes, he is *that* Max Dysart, your hero from the Nonesuch Whips.'

'You've met Lord Penrith? Tell me—'

'I will tell you all about it when I've got out of these clothes, had a bath and we're eating our luncheon. Is everything well here?'

'Oh, yes, fine, except I can't work out what's going wrong with the oats bill either. But what happened— Bree, you cannot leave me in suspense...'

'Oh, yes, I can,' she said, making for the door and the blissful prospect of a deep, hot bath. 'Just watch me.'

'If you're going to be mean, then I'll spoil your bath by telling you that James sent a message round to ask why you haven't answered his letter. So I thought I'd better read it in case it was something serious.'

'And is it?' Bree stopped in the doorway.

'He's getting married.'

'At long last! To whom? And why is that such a matter of urgency for us to know about?'

'He's engaged to Lady Sophia Lansdowne, the younger daughter of the Duke of Matchingham.'

Bree whistled soundlessly. 'That's a very good match. Brilliant, in fact. She's supposed to be very beautiful and extremely well dowered.'

'Yes, and she's got a fierce grandmother who has heard that James has some disreputable relations and she's not willing to give her blessing until she's inspected us for herself. Apparently she's heard we run a broken-down ale house and are in the horse-coping business or some such.'

'Well, why doesn't James put her right?' Bree demanded. 'Snobbish old harridan.'

'*Rich,* snobbish old harridan, if you please. Apparently she's likely to leave the bulk of her fortune to Lady Sophia—*if* she approves of her marriage.'

'So we have to be taken to be inspected, I collect? I'm half-inclined to dress like a Covent Garden fancy piece and have you borrow an outfit from one of the grooms.'

'We'd look very out of place.' Piers grinned. 'We're to attend the ball to celebrate the betrothal and, what's more, we're invited to the dinner beforehand.'

'To make certain we don't eat peas off our knives and spit in the finger bowls, I suppose. Honestly! We visited with James at the town house only six months ago—he must know we have presentable society manners.' She sighed. 'We had better go. James is a tactless idiot, but he *is* our brother. What will it be, trollop and ostler or lady and gentleman?'

'Lady and gentleman, I think,' Piers said reluctantly. 'Less fun, but we'd only give him heart failure otherwise. And look on the bright side, Bree—you'll need a new gown.'

Chapter Five

'**A**re you writing a poem, Dysart?'

'A what?' Max put down the glass of brandy he was nursing and focused on the amused face of his friend Avery, Viscount Lansdowne. 'Of course not. Are you foxed?'

'I've been holding what I thought was a perfectly sensible conversation with you for the past ten minutes and you've just said "The underside of bluebell flowers" in answer to a question about what you were doing next Thursday night.'

'Was I being coherent up to that point?' Max hoped so. And he was damned if he was going to explain that his mind had drifted off in an effort to find just the right colour to describe Bree Mallory's eyes.

'Probably. You have been saying, "yes", "no" and "I see what you mean" in approximately the right places. On the other hand, so does my father when my mother's talking to him, and I know he doesn't hear a word she says.'

'I am not your father, thank God. Start again.'

'All right. But you haven't seemed to be yourself ever since we had that race to Hounslow.'

'It was a long night of it, and then I got shot in the shoulder coming back, if you recall.'

'You're getting old,' his friend retorted with a singular lack of sympathy. 'Don't tell me that driving a stage is so much more tiring than driving a drag.'

'Well, it is. You've a team that is any old quality, and just when you get used to it, they change it. You've a strict schedule to keep to and a coachload of complaining passengers to look after. And it's heavier than a drag. You're only nagging me because you lost to both Nevill and Latymer and you want to try a stage.'

'I expected to lose to young Nevill, with you up on the box alongside him,' Lansdowne retorted. 'That was no great shock. But I don't say I wouldn't have minded putting Latymer's nose out of joint for him. And as for driving a stage—now you've got the "in," can't you arrange for the rest of us to have a go?'

'No.'

'Selfish devil. Well, then, forget whatever you're brooding about and tell me—are you going to come?'

'To what?'

'There! I knew you didn't hear a word I've been saying to you.' Avery crossed his long legs and made himself more comfortable. 'To my sister Sophia's betrothal party. Grandmama Matchingham has insisted on the full works—dinner first, ball after, all relatives from both sides mustered.'

'Who did you say she's marrying?' Max ignored Avery's exaggerated eye-rolling.

'Kendal. You know, Viscount Farleigh. You must have met him, gets to everywhere that is respectable. Prosy type, if you ask me, but Sophia seems to like him, so there you are, another sister off my hands.'

'Prosy he might be, but at least with him you can be sure he's not setting up a chorus dancer on the side, or running up gaming debts for you to settle.' Max thought about what he knew of Farleigh: all of it was boringly ordinary.

'There's that to be said for the match. I'd be as worried as hell if she fancied one of the Nonesuch crew.' Avery grinned. 'Anyway, I need some leavening at this party—what with Grandmama Matchingham insisting he bring along his entire family for inspection, and Sophia inviting every insipid miss she calls a friend, it'll be a nightmare. I'm asking all the Whips in sheer self-defence—at least we can get up a few card tables.'

'You make it sound so tempting, how could I resist such a flattering desire for my company?' Max murmured. 'Why does the old dragon want to inspect all the Kendals—no black sheep in that lot, are there?'

'Apparently there are some rattling skeletons she's heard about. Anyway, Kendal pokered up and said he had no concerns about producing the entire family down to third cousins once removed, if required, so I expect it's all a hum.

'Say you'll come, there's a good fellow. I'll put you next to a nice girl at dinner.'

'I thought you said they were all insipid,' Max grumbled mildly. Of course they'd be insipid; there was only one woman who wouldn't be. 'All right, I'll come. Anything for a friend.' *Anything to take my mind off going to the Mermaid in High Holborn and committing a monumental indiscretion with Bree Mallory.*

'Miss Mallory, I implore you, allow me to cut your hair! How are we to contrive a style even approaching the mode with this much to deal with?' Mr Lavenham, the excruciatingly expensive *coiffeur* Bree had decided to employ, lifted the wheaten mass in both hands and looked round with theatrical despair. His assistant rushed to assist with the weight of it, clucking in agreement.

She dithered. It was heavy, it took an age to dry when she washed it, the fashion was for curls and crops. *Don't cut it.* The deep voice rang in her head. Bree swung between practicality and the orders of a man she was never going to see again. *What is the matter with me? There is no decision to be made—I no longer take orders from anyone.*

'Leave it,' she said decisively. 'I am paying you a great deal of money, Mr Lavenham—I expect you to work miracles.'

'Your Grace, may I introduce my sister, Miss Mallory, and my brother, Mr Mallory, to your notice?'

How very condescending, as though we are actually well below *her Grace's notice*, Bree thought, the fixed smile on her lips unwavering. *At least he hasn't slipped in the* half *sister and brother, just to distance himself as much as possible.*

Bree swept her best curtsy, watching out of the corner of her eye as Piers managed a very creditable bow. In front of them the Dowager Duchess of Matchingham narrowed her eyes between puffy lids and assessed them.

How old is she? Bree wondered. *Old enough not to care about anyone or anything beyond her own interests and those of the family, and she is one of the generation for whom very plain speaking was the norm.* The washed-out blue eyes focused on her.

'I hear you run some sort of inn.'

'My brother is half-owner of the Challenge Coaching Company, your Grace. It operates from the Mermaid Inn in High Holborn.'

'Hmm. What's this I hear about horse dealing?' *Definitely a throwback to an age where good manners were considered a weakness.*

'My Uncle George breeds the horses for the company, your Grace. He also manages the two farms the family owns. They are very extensive and situated near Aylesbury.'

'Your family owns land?'

Time to bite back. Bree raised one eyebrow in elegant surprise. 'But of course, your Grace. Our father was one of the Buckinghamshire Mallorys—Sir Augustus is a cousin.' The baronet was a fourth cousin once removed and she'd never met him, but he was suitable for these purposes.

'Indeed.' Her Grace's nose was slightly out of joint, Bree could see. The prejudice she had formed could not be sustained, which was always uncomfortable. Time to move on—it would not be politic to rub it in. The Dowager turned her attention to the next person in the receiving line. 'Lady Bracknell, it must be an age since we met...'

Bree swept another curtsy, thankful, for once, for her mama's insistence on deportment lessons. Piers was close at her side. 'Phew, what an old dragon!'

'And we slew her nicely,' Bree murmured. 'Now, time to do the pretty to everyone else.'

Lady Sophia was pale, beautiful in a way that had Piers gazing with dropped jaw until Bree dug him in the ribs and painfully correct. 'Miss Mallory, Mr Mallory. I am so pleased to meet you.'

'And we are delighted to meet you,' Bree rejoined

warmly, meaning it. Surely this lovely creature would make James more human? 'I wish you every happiness.'

Freed from the principals, they were still faced with a formidable line. The Duke, the Duchess, Viscount Lansdowne, all waited to be greeted. Bree liked Sophia's brother on sight. He was languid, elegantly handsome and had a twinkle in his green eyes that had her dimpling back. It occurred to her, with startling suddenness, that he was exactly the sort of man she had believed was her model of excellence. Until she had met one large domineering gentleman with brown eyes, a stubborn jaw and strong, gentle hands.

'Run the gauntlet, Miss Mallory?' the viscount enquired softly.

'I am afraid the family skeletons were not up to scratch, my lord,' she rejoined demurely, wondering what possessed her to be so bold. 'We scarcely rattled at all.'

'Good. Grandmama deserves the occasional setdown. Will you save me a dance, Miss Mallory?'

'I would be delighted, my lord.'

'You *are* going it!' Piers observed as they emerged, with some relief, from the end of the receiving line. 'Dancing with a viscount, indeed.'

'Why not?' Bree demanded. 'I have been having driving demonstrations from an earl, after all.' She glanced around the big reception room. 'You should go and find yourself a pretty heiress to flirt with.'

Piers, predictably, went pink to his hairline, but strolled off, heading for a group of young men around the fireplace at one end of the long room.

For an unchaperoned single woman, things were more awkward. She assumed a confident smile and drifted towards a group of gossiping young matrons.

Her silken skirts swished reassuringly as she moved, reminding her that, in this department at least, she had nothing to fear. Sea-foam green silk trimmed with tiny gilt acorns and fine gilt ribbon clung in elegant simplicity. Her hair, braided and curled by a master, was dressed into a style where the intricacies of plait and twist were all the ornament it needed, and, to complete her air of confidence, Mama's thin gold chains and aquamarine ear bobs provided a refined hint of luxury.

Bree rarely had the opportunity, or wish, to dress up, but when she did, she found a totally feminine delight in it. In fact, after the events of a few days ago, shedding every trace of the booted, overcoat-clad stagecoach driver was a pleasure to be revelled in.

As she came up to the group, a young woman stepped back, squarely on Bree's foot. 'I am so sorry! How wretchedly careless of me. Are you all right?'

She was black haired, lovely and vivacious and her wide, apologetic smile had Bree smiling back, despite her sore toes. Then she realised who this lady must be: the likeness was unmistakeable. 'Excuse me, but are you related to Lady Sophia?'

'But, yes, she is my baby sister, and Avery is my big brother.' Her new friend linked a hand confidingly through Bree's elbow. 'I am Georgy—Lady Georgiana Lucas, if you want to be stuffy. So now you'll have met all of us except Augustus and Maria, and they are still in the schoolroom.'

Slightly dazed by the flow of information, Bree allowed herself to be steered to a sofa. 'I couldn't bear another minute of Henrietta Ford's account of her last confinement,' Lady Lucas continued. 'It's bad enough having babies oneself, without someone going through all the details endlessly, don't you think?'

Georgy stopped, her head on one side, waiting for a response. 'I'm not married,' Bree explained. 'So people don't talk about that sort of thing in front of me.'

'Aren't you? Good heavens! You look married.' Bree must have appeared puzzled, for Lady Georgiana went off in a peel of laughter. 'You know—confident, poised. Not at all like someone just out.'

'Well, I'm an old maid, so that accounts for it.'

That provoked more mirth. 'I don't believe you—and I'll wager next month's allowance that Avery has already asked you for a dance. He always asks the prettiest girls. I just wish he'd marry one. Would *you* like to marry him? He's very nice and badly in need of a wife to make him settle down.'

'He seems charming, but I am quite ineligible for such a match.' Despite the shocking frankness of Lady Georgiana's conversation, Bree couldn't help liking her. Whatever did she make of dear James?

'Why?' Georgy demanded.

'My father was a farmer. My brother and uncle own a stagecoach company,' Bree confessed.

'Oh!' Georgy laughed delightedly. 'I know who you are—you are the black sheep!'

'I believe so. I am Bree Mallory, and that's my brother over there, the tall blond youth on the right of the fireplace. I think, to be accurate, we are the skeletons in James's cupboard. Our mother married the second time for love, you see.'

'Then you will be my sister-in-law. We will be the greatest friends. What fun I will have matchmaking,' Georgy announced. 'Admittedly, a country squire and a stagecoach company is just a teensiest bit of a handicap if you want an eldest son at the very top end of the aristocracy, but I'm sure I can find you a nice baron, or the second son of a viscount. In fact, I've got just the man in mind. Are you poor? I hope you don't mind my asking, only that does make a difference.'

'No, I'm not,' Bree said frankly, half-fascinated, half-appalled by this frankness. 'I'm very comfortably off, I'm happy to say.' And she was. She had money in her own right from her parents, Piers and Uncle George insisted she take a fair share of the company profits and she managed her money with care. A top-flight *coiffeur* and a fashionable evening *ensemble* had not caused her a moment's financial worry. 'But I am not—truly—in search of a husband. I'm not at all sure I could give up my independence now.'

'It will have to be a love match then. I do not despair.' Georgy got to her feet in a flurry of amber silk. 'Come along and meet people.'

Bree worried that Georgy would make the most embarrassing introductions, but she flitted amongst the growing crowd, talking to everyone, introducing Bree with a cry of, 'You must meet my new sister-in-law to be! Isn't she lovely?' Everyone seemed friendly, no one drew aside their skirts in horror at meeting Farleigh's embarrassing relative and she began to enjoy herself.

'And this is Mr Brice Latymer.' Georgy halted in front of a saturnine gentleman of average height and exquisite tailoring.

Latymer, the man from the inn yard, the man who was racing Max's cousin that night. Did he see me? Bree could feel the blood leaving her cheeks and forced a smile to match his.

'Miss Mallory, I am delighted. And I understand I have the pleasure of taking you in to dinner.' He was very suave, his eyes on her appreciative, without being in any way offensive. Bree felt herself relax. Of course he did not recognise her. He made her an immaculate bow. 'I shall seek you out again when dinner is announced, Miss Mallory. I look forward to it.'

'Phew, he is *so* smooth,' Georgy remarked once they were out of earshot. 'Really good company, and he makes an excellent escort, but I wouldn't waste time with him, Bree, dear. Not *quite* enough money.' She steered them firmly towards the fireplace. 'Now, introduce me to your handsome brother.'

'Miss Mallory?' It was Mr Latymer again, this time offering his arm to escort her in. She let him lead her, enjoying the sensation, just for once, of being comprehensively looked after. It would pall after a time, she knew, but it was quite fun, once in a while, to be treated like a fragile being.

The Duke took the head of the table and the party began to settle themselves. Just as the footman tucked the chair under Bree's knees there was a slight flurry as another couple arrived opposite. Beside her she felt Mr Latymer stiffen and glanced across to see what had caught his attention.

There, staring right back at her, was Max Dysart, arrested in the act of sitting. The earl looked blankly at her, and she realised, with an inward tremor of mischief, that he couldn't decide whether she really was the woman he had rescued in the inn yard.

It was unthinkable to speak across the table. Wickedly, Bree gave not the slightest hint of recognition. Doubt flickered in his eyes and there was a frown line between his dark brows. Bree fussed a little with her napkin, and turned her head sideways, allowing Lord Penrith—should he still be looking—the picture of upswept hair, elegant jewellery and the line of a white throat.

Then it occurred to her that, amusing as it might be to tease his lordship, he was now almost certain to approach her after dinner in an attempt to decide whether his eyes were deceiving him or not. And, if he said the wrong thing in this crowded assembly, she could find herself in a very difficult position indeed.

'Penrith's taking an inordinate amount of interest in this side of the table,' Mr Latymer observed, directing a hard look back. 'Are you acquainted with him?'

'Lord Penrith?' Bree laughed, hoping it was not as shrill as it sounded inside her head. 'Good heavens, no!' Now she had done it. *Damn, damn... I should have thought, said I had some slight acquaintance. Now if he seems at all familiar Mr Latymer may assume the worst.*

Bree Mallory. It has to be her. But how can it be? 'Miss Robinson, allow me.' Max handed his dinner partner the napkin that had slipped from her grasp.

The slender brunette at his side batted sweeping lashes and gazed at him admiringly as she prattled on.

Max smiled and nodded and murmured agreement with her inanities. *And Avery promised me a* nice girl *as a partner! Like the one opposite. Just what has Brice Latymer done to deserve her? It has to be Bree*….

Surely there was no mistaking that glorious wheaten-gold hair, the weight of it caught up into a masterpiece of the *coiffeur*'s art? And surely there was no mistaking that generous, lush mouth or those eyes, the colour of bluebells in a beech wood? A blue you could drown in.

But the elegant society lady across the table looked back at him without a glimmer of recognition. And besides, what would practical businesswoman Miss Mallory in her breeches and boots have to do with this gorgeous creature?

He realised he was staring as he caught Latymer's sharp green eyes glancing in his direction. Time enough to solve the mystery, Max decided, turning to show an interest in Miss Robinson's intensely tedious recital of her feelings upon being invited to this event. There was a sense of anticipation flowing through his veins, like the feeling before hounds draw first cover on a crisp autumn morning—it would more than support him for the duration of this meal.

As the covers were removed after the first course

Max took the opportunity to scan the couple opposite. The blond woman reached out her right hand to pick up her wine glass. She misjudged the distance and the back of her wrist knocked against the heavy cut-glass flagon of drinking water. Max saw, more than heard, her sharp intake of breath. Small white teeth caught on the fullness of her lower lip and she closed her eyes briefly before lifting the wine glass.

That clinched it—hair, eyes, mouth might all be some amazing chance likeness, but all that *and* a painfully injured right wrist, that was beyond coincidence.

He caught her eye and mouthed *Bree?* For a moment he thought she might continue to cut him, then a twinkle of mischief lit her eyes and she nodded slightly before raising one gloved finger to her lips in a fleeting warning.

How the Devil did she get in here? Max jerked his attention back to the young lady on his left who, unfortunately, showed no sign of wanting to prattle mindlessly, unlike Miss Robinson. He was going to have to exert himself to entertain this one, when all he wanted to do was speculate wildly about Bree's presence under the Dowager Duchess of Matchingham's roof. Admittedly, it was the current Duke's roof, but no one, let alone that nobleman, believed he had any chance of ruling it while the Dowager lived.

He offered peas to the young lady, agreed that the latest gossip about the Prince Regent was too intriguing for words and asked her opinion of the latest exhibition at the Royal Academy.

That at least gave him a chance to think about Bree. How had she obtained the entrée into such a gathering? And where, for goodness' sake, had she obtained a gown that was the work of a top-flight *modiste*?

The meal dragged on interminably, the passage of time doing nothing but build the tension in his nerves and the disconcerting feeling of arousal in his loins. How could he have guessed that the enchantingly different girl in her man's clothing was the possessor of an elegant neck, of white, sloping shoulders and the most deliciously rounded bosom? The gown she was wearing was apparently designed to make the very best of all these features and, unlike the very young ladies in their first Season, she had dispensed with the froth of tulle or lace that disguised them. If he had wanted her before, now the need was painful.

The ladies, called together by the Duchess rising, began to file out amidst a scraping of chairs. At the door Bree glanced back over her shoulder. Their eyes met. Was he imagining things or had she motioned with her head towards the terrace?

Chapter Six

Max waited a moment. Several guests rose and made their way out. He joined them, making his way out through the long windows on to the terrace that ran the full width of the gardens. At intervals steps went down to the lawns and at the far end there was a charming summerhouse.

Max strolled along. *Where is she?* Had he misunderstood? Then he glimpsed a flutter of pale draperies behind one of the pillars of the summerhouse. 'Bree?'

'In here, my lord. Thank you for coming. I could only hope you would understand my meaning. How is your shoulder?' Some light reached them from the house where every room blazed with illumination, but it was not intense and he moved close to study her face. Her voice was a touch breathless, but otherwise she was remarkably composed for a young lady in such a compromising position.

'A little sore, but healing well, thank you. I did not

expect to find you at such a party. I was having trouble believing my eyes.'

'I was shocked to see you too, although why I cannot imagine—I am sure you must go to endless smart parties. I was being mischievous, I am afraid, teasing you by pretending I was not myself. Then Mr Latymer asked me if I knew you. I should have said *yes*, in an indifferent way, and he would have thought nothing of it. Then I realised I risked all sorts of embarrassments if you greeted me later. I will warn Piers not to react if he meets you.'

Max took her by the elbow and steered her to the front of the summerhouse where its arcade overlooked the silent gardens. Bree perched on the balustrade and leant her back on a pillar.

'Your brother is here too?' How had both the Mallorys inveigled their way in?

'Of course—you do not know who we are. Viscount Farleigh is our half-brother. Our mama married twice. She was the daughter of Lord Grendon, so we have dozens of Grendon cousins—most of them are here tonight. Then, when James's father died unexpectedly, she married again, for love. It was very romantic—her horse bolted and Papa jumped a five-bar gate on his hunter and galloped after her and snatched her from the saddle. Mama used to say he snatched her heart and never gave it back.

'As you can guess, there was the most frightful row.

Mama was only just out of mourning and, although Papa was perfectly respectable and owned land, some of the family had drifted downstream socially. The cousin who was a highwayman was almost an insuperable obstacle, but fortunately—in the opinion of the old viscount—he was hanged just before the wedding, poor man. His grandfather insisted on bringing James up, so we are not at all close.'

'So you must be the skeletons in the cupboard Avery was telling me about.'

Bree gave a gurgle of laughter. 'That's us.' He could see from the glint of light on white teeth that she was smiling. 'James insisted we come along and demonstrate that we do not swig gin out of the bottle or try to sell doctored nags to the unwary or whatever it is the Dowager believes we do, the old gorgon. I think we surprised her.'

'*You* surprise me,' Max admitted. 'You must agree, breeches and beaver hat do not show you to your best.'

She chuckled. 'They are very practical, but I do prefer being a girl. I enjoyed dressing up for this evening. I took your advice, you know.'

'You did?' Max shifted his position so he could sit facing her. 'What about?'

'I almost had my hair cropped. My *coiffeur* wanted me to, I wanted to, or I thought I did. But at the last minute I remembered what you said, and didn't.'

'It looks…very well.' *And I want to take out every*

single pin and comb, very, very slowly, until it all tumbles down.

'Thank you! I must go back.' She jumped down off the balustrade, shaking out her skirts. Max smiled, his amusement at her lack of concern unseen in the gloom.

'Bree?'

'Yes?' She stood poised on the top step, ready to flit back along the terrace.

'Will you dance with me this evening?'

'Me?' Even in that light he could make out the incredulity on her face. 'My lord, *earls* are far too top-lofty for the likes of me.'

'Earls dance with the sisters of viscounts and the granddaughters of barons, and I'll wager Lansdowne has already asked you for a dance.' *And she is not an innocent little bourgeoise, she understands this world, my world, even if she is not actually a part of it. This is becoming something very different, and I can't fool myself it is not.* He stood looking at her, thoughts rushing through his mind. *Now I have to do something about Drusilla.*

'Yes, well…' She was in a delightful dither, his stare only adding to her confusion. Max found it strangely encouraging that he seemed to have this effect on her. 'Lord Lansdowne is about to become my brother-in-law.'

'Well…' Max pursued, moving closer '…I am so

top-lofty, as you put it, that I will dance with whom I choose, especially if they happen to be the most beautiful girl in the room.'

'*Me?*' Bree felt her insides execute a swoop of delight. It was not true, of course, although she flattered herself she was looking more than passable this evening. It was very strange being out here alone with a man like this. It was even stranger being here with the man she had been dreaming about for days and who, she had very sensibly decided, was completely beyond her touch.

Now she *was* here, such sensible considerations did not seem particularly relevant.

'Yes. You.' He was very close suddenly. The man seemed to move like a cat, for all his height and breadth. 'Do you think I deserve a reward for saving your hair?'

'I...you...' *He is going to kiss me.* 'Yes,' she whispered, although whether to his spoken question or his unspoken one she had no idea.

Bree had never been kissed before. Not by a non-related male. Not kissed full on the mouth by a man who appeared to have made a study of just how to reduce an independent, mature, sensible female to a state where all she was capable of was clutching as much of his torso as her hands could encompass and clinging on in the faint hope that her legs would continue to support her.

She hadn't known what to expect. Certainly rather more activity than was occurring. It was incredible that he could achieve the effect he was, simply by holding her very firmly against his chest with one arm and cupping the back of her head with the other hand whilst applying light pressure to her lips.

Only—it was not just pressure, she realised hazily. He was exploring her lips with his, moving from corner to centre, catching the fullness of her lower lip between both of his, releasing it to slide to the other corner and then back to the centre. This time he used his teeth in a light, teasing nip that shot sensation, shockingly, right to the core of her.

His tongue, sliding out to run along the join of her lips, made her gasp against his mouth. She felt his smile. 'Shh,' he whispered without lifting his mouth and the sound hummed against the sensitised tissue. Back came his tongue, sliding, pressing now. *What does he want? Oh!*

The invasion breached her feeble defences, leaving her shaken. If someone had told her a man would put his tongue in her mouth and she would like it, she would have been disgusted and incredulous. But it was… Bree gave up trying to think straight and tentatively touched her own tongue tip to Max's.

It was moist and velvety and hot, this intimate exchange of touch. This caress. And it was making her feel as though she were in someone else's body altogether. Her breasts, pressing heavy against cool linen and the fine friction of superfine cloth, felt decidedly swollen. They tingled most disconcertingly and it seemed that the only relief might be to press closer. And in the pit of her stomach—no, lower, in an area where no modest young woman should be giving any thought to, there seemed to be a strange, hot, liquid feeling.

As she shifted her grip to hold more securely to Max's shoulders, she became aware of a pressure against the curve of her belly. She might be inexperienced, but she wasn't ignorant. One knew the mechanics of the thing—in theory. But she hadn't exactly comprehended that a kiss could have quite such a startling effect on a man. Max lifted his head.

'Bree. I had not intended doing that.' He sounded rueful, and to her delight, shaken.

'Why not?' she asked, the poor light defeating her efforts to read his face.

'One does not kiss young ladies, on the terrace, in the dark. Surely your chaperon warns you about these things?'

'I do not have one.' She realised that Max was not the only one who was feeling shaken—her knees were trembling.

'You're going to need one if you are intending to attend any more social events. It will be noticed if you do not. The lady who resides with you will probably do.'

Why was he talking about chaperons when the presence of one would have stopped him kissing her as he just had? Bree blinked in the gloom; perhaps Max really was regretting that kiss. Perhaps he thought she would take it as some sort of declaration and chase after him.

'I do not have a female companion,' she explained, trying to keep any hint of chagrin out of her voice.

'Does Farleigh realise that?'

'No.' Bree bit her lip. Now that she and Piers had been introduced to the Lansdowne clan it seemed unlikely that they would be able to slide back quite so easily into social obscurity. 'I suppose I had better acquire one.'

'It's as well. Men really are not to be trusted, you know.' Max gave her a gentle push in the direction of the terrace.

Bree resisted the pressure. 'All men? You included?'

'Oh, me in particular, Miss Mallory.' The amusement in his voice had a hard edge. 'Definitely, you should be beware of me.'

'Nonsense,' she said stoutly. 'I asked you to come out here—and I could have left at any moment when you kissed me. And besides, if you are such a dangerous seducer, you could easily have had your wicked way with me the other night and you were the perfect gentleman.'

'I was, wasn't I? I wonder what came over me. Did it not perhaps occur to you, Miss Mallory, that I was behaving with such restraint with the intention of lulling you into a false sense of security in order to entice you into my power later?'

'Have you been reading sensation novels, my lord?' Bree enquired tartly. 'I realise that many men find a dangerous image to be an attractive one to cultivate, but I do credit you with more sense than that.'

He laughed, a genuine snort of amusement. 'You never answered my question about a dance.'

'Certainly, my lord—I have an entire card full of country dances to fill!' Without waiting for his response, she picked up her skirts and ran down the steps to the terrace. The allegory about riding tigers floated into her mind from nowhere. She was riding a tiger now, and very exhilarating it was. But how did one get off?

Bree studied her face in the mirror in the ladies' retiring room while a maid valiantly brushed at the lichen clinging to her skirts. The effect on her face of being thoroughly kissed was startling. Her cheeks looked as though she had rouged them, and her mouth was bee-stung and rosy pink. Her eyes were wide, and something sparkled in them, try as she might to lecture herself for wanton behaviour.

'Bree! There you are.' It was Georgy, sweeping in. 'Look at my hem! Oh, thank you.' She smiled sweetly at a maid who came forward with a sewing basket.

'I…I feel a little flushed,' Bree admitted. 'I came in here to cool down a trifle.'

'You look fine to me. The colour suits you,' Georgy assured her. 'You mustn't be shy—go on, they'll be starting the dancing in a minute, and you'll want to get your card filled up with all the most eligible men.'

That seemed unlikely to occur, but Bree was pleasantly surprised. The attentions of Viscount Lansdowne and the approval of his sister apparently gave her a certain *cachet* and, although her card was not full, it was gratifyingly almost three-quarters complete when she showed it to Piers.

'Am I too late, ma'am?' The deep voice made her jump, even though she had been tensed for Max's appearance ever since she had come into the ballroom. 'I apologise for addressing you before being introduced, but I am not acquainted with your chaperon.' Bree narrowed her eyes at him and he smiled back with an air of perfect innocence. 'Max Dysart, Ea—'

'But, Bree, you must know Lord Penrith, he rescued yo—' Piers's clear, excited voice cut through the hum of conversation. Interested faces turned.

'Lord Penrith? Why, of course, you came to the

aid of young Hinkins, our driver, at Hounslow a few evenings back, did you not? Piers told me all about it—thank you so much.' She directed a look of such quelling intensity at her brother that he shut his mouth with a snap and melted back into the crowd.

But the group of men he was with had heard more than enough to pique their interest and he found himself the centre of attention. 'I say, Mallory, do you have anything to do with the stagecoach Penrith was driving?' one gentleman demanded.

'I own the company,' Piers admitted. 'Half of it, that is.'

'I see your brother has fallen amongst the Nonesuch Whips,' Max commented softly. 'Tell me which dance I may have, and then I'll go and distract them if I can. Otherwise you'll have a yard full of bucks all wanting to drive a stage.'

'The second cotillion?' Bree asked distractedly. 'And thank you, I would be grateful.'

Max bowed gracefully and strolled off to join the crowd around Piers. To her relief the focus of their attention switched immediately to him. *For such a big man, he really looks surprisingly good in evening dress*, Bree mused. *I would have expected him to look his best in buckskins and boots, but he appears positively elegant. Good tailoring, of course, but—*

'What an extraordinary coincidence that Penrith

should be sitting opposite you at dinner.' Mr Latymer's voice in her ear jerked her abruptly back from her contemplation of broad shoulders under well-fitting superfine.

'Er…yes, it was, was it not? Naturally I am glad of the opportunity to thank him.'

'Yet you did not mention the acquaintance earlier.' Mr Latymer raised an eyebrow. 'In fact, you denied it.'

'Of course. I had not been introduced.' Bree pulled herself together. 'And, however grateful I was to his lordship—given that I understand it was his drag that caused the accident in the first place—the fact that he was able to assist one of Piers's drivers is stretching an excuse to claim acquaintance to its limit.'

'Hmm. Our dance, I believe.'

Almost half an hour spent executing intricate figures with a number of other couples was not the best situation in which to carry out a conversation, and Bree was grateful for it. But Mr Latymer obviously had something on his mind, and she was not surprised when, after the dance, while she was sitting fanning herself, he returned to her side with a glass of lemonade.

'I would be fascinated to see around the headquarters of your coaching company, Miss Mallory. Might I call?'

'Why, of course, but it is not my company—Piers

can make arrangements for you to see behind the scenes.'

'Then you have nothing to do with it?'

'I occasionally assist with a little paperwork,' Bree said airily. It would be just her luck to be there when Brice Latymer turned up.

'What a good sister you are.' There was warmth in his tone. Bree shot him a glance from under her lashes and was surprised to see warmth in his eyes also—the sort of warmth she had discerned in the gaze of another gentleman altogether. *Goodness*, she thought, flustered. *Piers is right, I am going it!*

'I am very fond of Piers, and he intends to take over the running of the company full time when his education is finished. My uncle is the other owner, but he lives in the country, so I do what little I can to help,' she added, hoping it sounded as though she occasionally glanced at the bill for candles.

'But you could spare some time to drive with me?'

'Drive?' Bree, feeling herself going hot and cold all over, plied her fan energetically.

'Yes. I have a new phaeton you might enjoy.'

'Oh. Your phaeton. Of course.' *Of course, not a stagecoach... Of course, he doesn't know...* 'Thank you.'

Bree shot a distracted glance in Piers's direction, hoping he was being discreet. To her horror he was deep in conversation with the lanky young man she recognised as Max's cousin. There was nothing for it, she would have to go and extract him before he did any more damage.

'Miss Mallory, our dance, I believe?' It was Lord Lansdowne.

'Yes, of course.' Bree flipped open her card. It was a country dance and immediately afterwards she had the cotillion with Max—all she could hope was that he had discouraged the Nonesuch Whips from a mass descent on the Mermaid.

She curtsied and took her place. At her side Lord Lansdowne waited while the first couple set off down the double line. 'Would you care to drive with me some time this week?' he enquired.

Another one! Really, this would be quite amusing if it were not so awkward. She could hardly abandon the business to its own devices until the Whips lost interest in the possibility of a whole stagecoach company to play with. Yet, on the other hand, if she was discovered to be the actual manager of the business, James would be mortified and the Dowager deeply disapproving. One look at the Lansdownes had left Bree very clear about who called the tune in that household. The old besom might well take it into her head to forbid the match.

'Of course, my lord, I would be delighted.' What else could one possibly say? The dance took them off down the line, into an intricate measure at the far end and left them separated by several couples. The necessity of keeping a smile plastered on her face for the length of the dance did nothing for Bree's nerves, nor for her temper.

Lord Lansdowne, obviously impervious to her simmering state, swept her an extravagant bow and deposited her neatly in front of Lord Penrith.

'Thank you so much, my lord.' Bree curtsied, smile intact.

'It was a pleasure. I will call at the earliest opportunity.' Lansdowne made a mocking bow towards Max. 'I yield to you, Dysart.'

'Miss Mallory. Our cotillion.'

'Oh, no, you don't.' Bree tucked one hand firmly into Max's elbow and headed for the doors on to the terrace. 'I want to talk to you.'

'Really, ma'am, you have me all of a flutter. Alone with you on the terrace *twice* in one evening—people will begin to talk.'

'They'll have to see us first,' Bree retorted, marching down the steps into the maze of clipped yew that framed the formal pool.

'Your friends the Whips! You said you'd distract them, but two of them have asked me to drive with them and your dratted cousin is exchanging cards with Piers, and the rest are hanging around him like wasps round a honeypot and how am I to run the business not knowing which gentleman is about to appear in the yard and start poking about? I can hardly wear breeches and a false beard until they lose interest, can I? And stop laughing at me!'

Max had folded up on to an ornate bench and was clutching his sides in abandoned amusement. 'Oh, please, try the false beard....'

'Wretch!' Bree took a swipe at his elegant crop with her fan. 'It is *not* funny.'

'I can quite see that from your point of view it is not,' Max agreed, getting his laughter under control with an effort. 'But, Bree, this may be a blessing in disguise. At least now you are forewarned of the danger—after all, once your brother became betrothed to Lady Sophia your days of managing the yard were doomed. Sooner or later someone is going to find out, and then think of the kick-up there'd be.'

He looked up at her standing in front of him, and smiled. Bree took her hands off her hips and tried not to glower. 'A chaperon, a business manager—what are you going to tell me I need next? James is costing us a great deal of money.

'What is it with you men and stagecoaches? You've got drags, you've got much better bloodstock than we can afford—why do you want to play with my stage-coaches?'

'It is not *your* company, when all is said and done. Don't you want to get married, have a family of your own?'

'I suppose so, but I am resigned to it. By the time

Piers is old enough to take control, I will be too old to find a husband.'

'So find a business manager, then find a husband,' Max said. 'And don't frown at me, it creases your very nice forehead.' He got up and smoothed the furrow between her brows with his thumb. 'I fail to see why you cannot find a good man to manage your business.'

'Piers would resent it.' It was tempting and yet, what on earth would she do with herself all day without the company to run? Shopping and calls and parties until she found a husband? Then more of the same, plus children? The children were intriguing, the unknown husband and the daily social whirl were not. 'I would die of boredom.'

'Find a man with an estate you can become involved with, start a charity, play the 'Change, take a lover...'

'Max!' He was altogether too close. She could smell the light, citrusy cologne he wore, the trace of soap, the exciting tang of masculinity overlaid with all the refinements of clean, well-groomed sophistication. He was showing an altogether commendable, if very disappointing, restraint about trying to kiss her again.

Perhaps he didn't like it last time. I am very inexperienced after all. Completely *inexperienced. Perhaps he doesn't want to do it again. I shouldn't want him to—this can't possibly lead to anything.*

'You are a delicious innocent, Miss Mallory, and I should not be out here with you.'

'That's true. But you were in the carriage with me before, so I know I can trust you. But then I looked dreadful.'

'You looked edible,' Max said, reminiscently. He reached out and let one finger trail lazily up and down the column of her neck. It felt strong, hard, slightly rough against her soft skin.

'You, my lord, must have a very strange taste in women, if you thought I looked better then than I do now,' Bree observed as repressively as she could manage, given that her insides appeared to be hollow and her breathing was not working properly.

'I did not say that.' The finger was exploring the whorls of her ear now, rubbing the lobe, then drifting up behind it into the soft hair. 'Now, I think you look utterly seductive.'

'Are you trying to seduce me?' Bree asked, swallowing hard.

Chapter Seven

'Seduce you? No.' Max's mood of gentle sensuality seemed to have quite vanished. 'I am getting you in a fluster and I am ensuring that I spend an acutely uncomfortable evening.'

'Why?' Bree demanded.

'Why am I getting you in a fluster?'

'No. I know the answer to that—you're a man. Men flirt, and I was silly enough to come out here with you—I expect it is quite automatic on your part. No, why will you be uncomfortable?'

'Um…my conscience will be troubling me,' he said. Bree narrowed her eyes. That was not the truth, but he would refuse to tell her if she pressed. 'May I call and take you driving?'

'You are number three,' Bee informed him, torn between smugness and exasperation. 'Am I to go driving with all of the Nonesuch Whips while you take it in turns to try to persuade me to let you drive a stage? It is a deeply unflattering motive.'

'But you may acquit me, for I have already driven your stage, have I not?'

Time to take the bull by the horns, my girl, Bree told herself. 'Then what *is* your motive, my lord? You do not want to drive a stagecoach, you do not want to seduce me...'

'I said I was not trying to, not that I did not want to.'

'Now you are teasing me. I know perfectly well that you are too much the gentleman.' He grimaced. In the flare of the torchlight his face looked stony. Bree blinked; it must be a trick of the light.

'Perhaps I am amusing myself by bringing you into fashion, perhaps I enjoy flirting with you or perhaps I enjoy your company and would like to be your friend. What do you think, Bree?'

'Perhaps all three?'

'Clever girl.'

She slapped at him lightly with her fan. 'Do not patronise me, my lord, or we will not be friends for long.'

Max stood and held out his hand to help her to her feet. 'That would be a pity, Bree Mallory, because I think you will be very good for me.'

Max watched Bree take the hand of her next dance partner and walk gracefully on to the dance floor. Another of the Whips, he noted. He really should do something about that, but it was too tempting to let them lay siege to the Challenge Coach Company—

nothing was more certain to drive Bree out of the office and into the life that was proper for her. Into his company.

'Don't you go hurting my about-to-be-sister-in-law,' a voice at his elbow chided him, like the echo of his conscience.

He looked down and met the sparkling green eyes of Georgy Lucas. 'What do you mean, Lady Georgiana?'

'You know perfectly well what, and you know who, as well—don't go getting all starchy with me, Max,' she said, slipping her hand companionably under his elbow as they stood there. 'I know what they say about you.'

'And what is that, pray?' Georgy's challenging gaze was not at all shaken by his coolness.

'That you gave your heart very unwisely when you were young, had it broken and now have no heart at all.'

Damn the woman! Max bit down a sharp retort. *What does she know, really? Not the whole truth—very few people know that.*

'Oh, I have a heart, Georgy, just not one I care to hazard any more.'

'You will have to marry one day, Dysart—think of the title.'

The title. And my heart—if anyone wants it.

'And if you really choose to be unconventional, why, you have the standing to carry it off. Miss Mallory is not so very unsuitable after all—think of all the members of the House of Lords who have married actresses, for goodness' sake. She is perfectly respectable, with some excellent, if distant, connections.'

'I assume you are trying to matchmake as usual, Georgy. I hope you know what you are talking about, for I have no idea,' Max lied. She was a disconcerting little minx, but talking to her had given him an idea.

He began to steer her down the edge of the floor. 'Where is your husband? I feel the need to advise him to lock you up on his most remote estate until you learn better conduct.'

Georgy, whom he had known since she was in leading strings, pouted. 'Darling Charles is in the card room, and he dotes upon me, so it is no use grumbling to him, Max.'

Darling Charles was Lord Lucas, not only an influential magistrate, but one with close ties both to Bow Street and in government.

'I think I will have a little chat with your Charles,' Max said meditatively, disentangling Georgy's hand from his arm. 'Go and flirt with your numerous admirers.'

She dimpled at him and strolled off in a swish of expensive French satin, leaving Max wondering how to broach his request to her husband. At the card room his luck was in; his quarry was just settling up after a game of piquet and was more than happy to join Max for a hand.

Max selected the table in the farthest corner, passing several empty ones on the way. Lord Lucas's slightly raised eyebrow at this odd behaviour did not escape him, but the magistrate settled back in his chair without comment while Max summoned a waiter to fetch them claret.

Max looked into the shrewd grey eyes and wondered if the rumours about the baron being the government's leading spymaster could possibly be true. If they were, it seemed an odd occupation for a man whose taste in wives ran to Georgy and all her frivolity.

'This is an excuse,' he said baldly, cutting the fresh pack and offering it to Lucas. 'I wanted to ask your advice on a matter of some discretion. It is a problem upon which I have only just reached a decision.'

'Indeed.' Lucas shuffled the cards and dealt, his face blandly amiable. 'I will be glad to help if I can, Dysart.'

'It is a personal matter.' Max picked up his cards, one part of his brain assessing the hand, even as he spoke. 'It concerns an affair that very few people know of, and one I would wish to keep from being any more widely known.' He laid down a club.

The baron merely nodded, played in his turn, then remarked, 'I spend my life hearing things that must never be spoken of. I have the habit of secrecy. Why not tell me your problem? I will see what I can do to help.'

Max folded the cards in his hand and snapped them down on to the table. 'It concerns my wife.' He picked up the hand again, irritated to find himself so lacking in control. 'I need to be certain that she is dead.'

Bree sat down next to Piers and fanned herself. 'Phew! That was very energetic. You are a good dancer, my dear.'

'I am, am I not?' he observed smugly.

'At least when you are dancing with me you are not being indiscreet with your new friends from the Nonesuch Club. Honestly, Piers—you almost blurted out that I was driving the stage that night! Can you imagine the scandal that would cause if it were known?'

'I'm sorry. I will try to be very careful—but what can I do about them calling? They wanted to know our direction so they can visit—I could hardly refuse to say, could I?'

Bree nodded. 'We cannot keep fobbing them off. I'll have to think of something harmless for them to do that does not involve fare-paying passengers.

'But as for calling, I'm afraid I am going to have to find myself a companion-cum-chaperon, and I do not think I can spend so much time working at the inn either. We need a business manager. Lord Penrith pointed out to me that now we are known widely as James's relatives we are going to have to keep up this level of respectability. Or, at least, I am. I have to admit, I did not think this through at first, but he is quite correct. Our brother is marrying the daughter of a duke, for goodness' sake! That is not going to be something that goes away after tonight, or even after the wedding.'

Her brother grimaced. 'Isn't it going to be expensive to hire these people? And won't you miss it? Working at the Mermaid, I mean?'

'Yes, I will, and I will miss my freedom as well, but it cannot be helped. Leaving James's opinions to one side, I do not really want to figure as a hoyden, nor do I want to cut myself off from society altogether. Tomorrow I will try the agencies, see what I can find out about what rates of pay would be expected. We can afford it, Piers. The business is doing well, and I can still keep overall control from a safe distance.'

'I could leave school,' he suggested, with a sideways glance from under ridiculously long lashes.

'And act as my chaperon, do you mean?' Bree laughed at him. 'I don't think so!'

'As our business manager, of course.' Piers laughed back. 'And I think you are quite right, it isn't proper, and it is not fair that you have to do all that work.' He bit his lip thoughtfully. 'Won't it be difficult at home, though, if you are going to employ a starched-up chaperon to live with us?'

'Lord, yes! It would be ghastly,' Bree agreed, taken aback by the thought. Really, the pitfalls of all this respectability stretched way beyond the cost of it. There would be a loss of privacy, the need to run a more regulated and formal household—and the fact that a chaperon would expect to…well, to *chaperon* her. 'What I need,' she said reflectively, 'is the appearance of rigid respectability combined with the freedom to do whatever I like.'

'Mmm.' Piers raised an eyebrow, a skill Bree wished she could perfect. 'I would love to be a fly on the wall when you explain that at the employment exchange.'

Lord Lucas's hand froze in the moment of making a discard, then he recovered himself smoothly and laid down the card. His face did not betray any emotion beyond an interest in the fall of the cards. 'Indeed? I assume that you do not mean to imply that you wish this lady found and then—how can I put it?—removed?'

'No. Never that.' Max fanned out his cards with steady fingers. The Queen of Spades, the Knave of Hearts, the King of Diamonds. It summed the whole wretched business up somehow.

'Forgive me, Dysart, but I was not aware that you had a wife.' The man opposite did not raise his eyes from his study of his hand.

'Very few people are. A vicar somewhere in Dorset

who may be dead, a certain adventurer who may also be dead—and will be if I ever find him—my grandmother, my man of business, my groom and some old, very loyal servants.

'It is seven years since money was last drawn on the funds I set up for her. If she is still alive, I will divorce her. If she has died, then I need take no further action.' *How would it feel to see her again? Or to stand by her graveside? Will it still feel as though something is ripping into my heart, or will I still feel nothing, as I have taught myself to do these past years?*

'After seven years she may legally be presumed dead.' Lord Lucas played a card. 'My hand, I think.'

'So my legal advisor tells me, but I wish for certainty. A presumption is not enough, should I wish to marry again.'

'I see.' The magistrate—if that was all he was—glanced towards the ballroom, then back at Max. He kept his face shuttered, willing himself to show no emotion. 'Yes, I see. Despite what my dear wife believes, I do actually listen to what she says, and I begin to see your predicament. Young ladies do have a not unreasonable expectation that a man who courts them is free to do so.' He hesitated. 'You contemplate divorce if Lady Penrith should still be alive? You do understand what that would mean?'

'Legally, emotionally or in terms of my reputation and honour?' Max enquired, then answered his own question. 'Yes, to all of those. I understand exactly what it would cost.'

'Has it occurred to you that the other lady in the case may hesitate to commit herself in the face of such notoriety?'

Max picked up the pack and began to shuffle it. He moved the cards in his hand aimlessly, looking unseeing at the painted faces. 'If I were to have a lady in mind—and we are speaking hypothetically, you understand—I would need to be very certain of my own feelings, and of hers also. Even then, I must decide whether I can square my conscience with placing her in that position, if I do find myself seeking a divorce.'

'If there was someone,' the older man responded carefully, 'your sudden desire to discover the truth implies that it is a fairly recent acquaintance. Perhaps such a lady would not have the stomach for being at the centre of a scandal.'

'Do you know, if her heart was engaged in something, I do not think anything would give her pause.' Max smiled wryly. 'Speaking hypothetically, of course.' *But one wife left me within weeks—why am I such an optimist as to believe I might find another who will love me?* He realised, with a stab, almost of irritation, that he could no longer contemplate simply a *suitable* marriage. Now, all of a sudden, he was demanding a love match for himself. And that, surely, was an impossible dream.

'This anxiety may not be necessary,' Lord Lucas pointed out, cutting across his thoughts. 'You may indeed be a widower. After seven years and no word of her, that is the most likely assumption.'

'Yes, I may.' *Drusilla.* Sweet, playful, lovely, innocent Drusilla, who had dismissed her responsibilities as Countess of Penrith as a tiresome bore, and himself for a stuffy tyrant, within days of that impetuous secret marriage, and who had set her desires higher than his honour when she found herself a lover within the month. She had not spurned his wealth though, not while it could support both her and the man she fled with. Yet, how could he wish her dead? Even asking these questions seemed perilously close to it. 'How do I find out?'

'You need an investigator of experience and discretion. I know a man who fits that description. If you will permit me to consult him, without mentioning names, naturally, I will discover if he is available and what his fee would be. If you decide to proceed, we can then arrange a meeting.'

'Money is not an object,' Max said harshly. 'Speed and discretion are.' For nine years he had done nothing. Now even nine days of uncertainty were intolerable to contemplate.

After he parted from Georgy's husband Max made his way back to the edge of the dance floor. His nerves stretched raw by the conversation he had just had, and the memories it evoked, he stared out coldly at the noisy throng, the weaving lines of dancers, the nodding chaperons, the chattering girls, the dark elegance of their men folk. It was all a mask over—what? Did every face, serious or laughing, conceal some painful secret?

'Are you well, my lord?' A hand touched his arm and he looked down, startled. It was Bree, her long fingers in their elegant kid gloves startlingly white on his dark sleeve. 'You look so—' She wrestled for a word, frowning up into his eyes. 'So bleak.'

'I felt bleak,' he confessed, feeling the blight lift as he looked at her. She seemed so right, standing by his side, as though some benevolent deity had created her, just for him. How long had he known her? All his life, it seemed. 'What would you say if I told you that I had a secret that would scandalise society?'

'I know you have.' She dimpled a smile, lifting her hand to brush fleetingly over the right breast of his waistcoat. Desire hit him like a blow and he was conscious of his nipples hardening at her touch.

'Not that, you minx.' He found himself smiling at her and shook his head. 'No, this is something far more serious.'

'I see.' Bree bit her lip, her eyes thoughtful. 'I should say that I am very sorry it makes you so sad, and I would ask if there was anything I could do to help you.'

'Why? Why would you do that?'

'Because we are friends.' She flattened her palm against his left lapel. He was conscious of his heart beating beneath the pressure—surely she could feel it too? 'And because I am a little outside society and I am not easily scandalised.' She took her hand away and Max realised he had not been breathing. He dragged the air into his lungs as she smiled mischievously. 'And I am very intelligent, so perhaps I can think of something to help.'

'Your company and your friendship already help,' Max said seriously. 'I hope that perhaps my secret may prove not to be too terrible after all.'

'And if it is?' The calm oval of her face tilted up as she looked deep into his eyes. 'No, do not answer— you will still find me your friend, whatever the problem.' He found he was watching her mouth, certain that it was as expressive as her lovely eyes. Now it went from composed, serious lines into a soft, tentative smile. 'Would you wish to be left in peace?'

'What, now?' He met her eyes. 'No, not by you, Bree. Why?'

'We never had our dance,' she pointed out.

'Whose fault was that?' He found he was already leading her on to the floor where the next set was forming.

'Mine,' she admitted with a twinkle. She moved in close to his side as the other couples shuffled and sorted themselves out. 'Do you dance as well as you do other things?'

'Such as?' The bleak mood had lifted completely. Somewhere at the back of his mind was the shadow of it, the looming cloud of approaching scandal and old heartbreak, the wrenching decision whether to cease all contact with Bree now, before she could be embroiled in this, hurt by it. And under it the nagging uncertainty that any woman could truly love him, Max, just for himself. But that was like a storm gathering over distant mountains. Here it was as though he were in a sunlit valley.

'Such as…driving.' The tip of her tongue just touched the full pout of her lower lip. Max could have sworn it was a quite unconscious provocation, but her body was betraying her and he had a silent bet with himself that he knew what she was thinking about.

'Not as well as driving,' he admitted, low-voiced as the music started and he swept her a formal bow. 'And definitely not as well as kissing.'

His daring words had caught her at the bottom of her curtsy. Bree gasped, stumbled, and he caught her up in his arms before she could fall. 'Do take care, Miss Mallory,' he said, loudly enough for the surrounding couples to hear. 'The floor seems quite slippery here.' He steadied her on her feet again and swung her into the first measure.

'You are an unmitigated rake,' she whispered as she pivoted elegantly beneath his raised hand.

Max caught the gleam in her eyes. 'I fear you have led me astray, Miss Mallory.' He swung her neatly round at the end of the turn and they came to the end of the line and were able to catch their breath while the next couple worked their way down the ranks of dancers. 'May I call on you?'

'For what purpose, my lord?'

'To take you driving, as you promised. And possibly to practise my other skills.'

'But of course, my lord. I would be delighted to go driving.' Bree made her curtsy to the gentleman opposite them and prepared to step out to take his hand. 'I do not, however, consider that you require any further practice in the exercise of that other talent you mentioned.'

Max found he was grinning broadly and hastily got his face back under control before the young lady opposite decided she was about to be partnered by a lunatic. Why was it that being chastised by Miss Mallory was as gratifying as any amount of admiration from any other woman?

He watched her as she turned, following the lead of her partner, moving away from him down the floor. Away. His heart contracted painfully. He should move away from her in real life, dissociate himself from her entirely until he was certain no stain of scandal attached to him and that there was no need for the public shame of a divorce.

But if he did, now she was out in society, who would move to claim her while he waited, silent, uncertain and unfree, in the wings? He had only just found her—must he let her go?

Chapter Eight

'A lady's companion would be *how* much a year?' Bree demanded, even though she knew she had heard correctly the first time. It was not as though she could not afford the rates the Misses Thoroughgood's Exclusive Employment Exchange demanded, but they seemed extreme for something she did not want in the first place. However, common sense told her she should, so, the Monday morning after the ball, here she was.

Miss Emeline Thoroughgood looked down the length of her thin nose. 'If one desires a lady companion of breeding and refinement, and one who can undertake the delicate and sensitive duties of a chaperon with discretion yet firmness of purpose, I am afraid one must expect to pay premium rates, Miss Mallory.'

'I simply require the look of the thing, Miss Thoroughgood.' Even as she said it, she realised that the lady would leap to entirely the wrong conclusion. 'I live with my brother,' she said hastily. 'He is most rigorous in his care of me. However, a respectable female to accompany me when he cannot would be desirable.'

Miss Emeline's expression softened slightly at the reas- surance that she was not dealing with some kept woman who needed to cloak her activities in a veil of respectability. *Actually, she is not so far wrong*, Bree thought with hidden amusement. *Only my activities are not quite what she imagines.*

'I may be able to suggest a solution,' Miss Emeline said pensively. She rang the hand bell on her desk. 'Smithers, has the client with Miss Clara departed?'

'No, Miss Emeline.' The clerk consulted the clock on the mantel. 'I would expect her to come out at any moment.'

'Ask her to come in here when she is free, would you?' He bowed himself out. 'I make no claims for this suggestion, Miss Mallory, however, Miss Thorpe may answer your purposes at a most reasonable cost.'

A tap at the office door heralded the entrance of a woman in her late thirties. Her dress, from bonnet to half-boots, proclaimed the governess in its drab anonymity, and her hair, dark brown, threaded with grey, was drawn back tightly under her bonnet. But her eyes looked out steadily from under rather thick brows and met Bree's with an assessing intelligence that instantly appealed to her.

'Miss Mallory, this is Miss Thorpe. Miss Thorpe

is an experienced governess with admirable qualifications. However, we understand that she no longer wishes for that form of employment. It occurs to me that possibly she may suit your requirements.'

'Miss Thorpe.' Bree got to her feet and offered her hand. 'I am looking for a companion. Why do we not have tea together in Gunther's and see how we suit each other?'

This unconventional approach appeared to startle Miss Thoroughgood, but Miss Thorpe's eyebrows merely lifted slightly and she smiled. 'Thank you, Miss Mallory, I would be pleased to.'

'That's settled, then. Thank you, Miss Thoroughgood. I will let you know how we get on.' Bree shook hands briskly and ushered Miss Thorpe out in front of her. 'Now, we just need to find a hackney carriage.'

'There's one.' Miss Thorpe hailed the cab authoritatively, securing it under the nose of a soberly dressed City type clutching a bundle of papers tied in red tape. Bree was impressed.

'Well…' she settled back and regarded the other woman '…I will be frank, Miss Thorpe. I have never had a female companion before, nor a chaperon, and I suddenly find myself in a situation where that has become, if not essential, at least highly desirable. But— and here is where the frankness comes in—I have no intention of losing my freedoms and suddenly becoming a sheltered society miss. I run a stagecoach company.' That did provoke a reaction from the self-controlled Miss Thorpe. Her lips pursed in a soundless whistle, then she smiled.

'Unconventional indeed, Miss Mallory. Would I be required to assist with this enterprise?'

That had never occurred to Bree. 'Would you be interested to?'

'Why, yes, I believe I might. I am a competent bookkeeper and I used to run a school—quite a large one, in Bath—until the proprietor decided to sell up, and I did not have the resources to buy her out. Then I found myself having to work as a governess, but I do miss having the variety of managing the school. You will be wanting to take up references, Miss Mallory, and to have a trial period, I imagine.'

'I hire and fire staff for the company on a regular basis, Miss Thorpe. Few of them come with references, so I have come to trust my judgment on first impressions. I would be very happy if you would join us on the basis that you assist with the running of the office, accompany me in the evenings and act as my chaperon whenever I have company. We will give it a month and see how we feel at the end of it. What do you think? You may find us unacceptably unconventional.' There was something about the governess that appealed to Bree. It was not so much what she said, but the calm confidence with which she said it.

'It sounds fascinating, Miss Mallory.' Miss Thorpe

looked out of the window as the hackney drew up to the pavement. 'I have never been interviewed for a position at Gunther's. I think that bodes very well!'

'Excellent.' Bree led the way into the tea shop, glanced around and found a table in a quiet corner. 'This will do. Now, what shall we have? Hot chocolate? I suppose it is really rather cool for ices, and perhaps too early in the day,' she added reluctantly.

'I never think it is too *anything* for ices,' Miss Thorpe declared robustly.

Bree found herself laughing. 'I really think we will suit, Miss Thorpe! Now, let me tell you all about ourselves. The household consists of my brother Piers and myself…

'…and so you see, what with Lord Farleigh's engagement and the interest the members of the Nonesuch Whips are taking in the company, things cannot go on as they are.' That account had skimmed lightly over some of her feelings on the stage, and censored completely that kiss the other night. Bree stopped talking at last and peered into the depths of the chocolate jug. 'Shall we have some more?'

'Yes, please, Miss Mallory.'

'Bree, please. What is your name?'

'Rosamund. My father was a Shakespeare enthusiast.' Miss Thorpe smiled. 'I answer very well to Rosa.'

'Rosa it is, then.' Bree gestured to the waiter. 'Another jug of chocolate, and a plate of macaroons, please. So, what do you think? And when can you start?'

'I think that it sounds fascinating, and I could start immediately, if that is what you would like. But I am afraid my wardrobe is singularly unfitted for the role as your companion, especially if you intend to accept any evening engagements.'

'Goodness, we have not discussed salary, have we?' Bree thought rapidly. She had not yet investigated the wages a business manager might expect, but now she might well not have to. The Yard Master, Railton, and his men were more than capable of supervising the operation in the evenings and at night as they did now, provided there was someone taking the major decisions and doing the bookwork. She named the amount Miss Thoroughgood had asked for a top-flight lady's companion. 'How would that be? And a suitable wardrobe as well? And you can move in today.'

Rosa gasped. 'Are you sure?'

'Why, yes. It will be hard work filling two roles. Now that I have been forced into society, I suppose I had better enjoy it, so we will be out and about a good deal.' She poured the fresh chocolate. 'Have a macaroon.'

'I *will* need a new wardrobe if I am to eat many of these,' Rosa commented, biting into one of the confectioner's famous biscuits.

'Well, any excuse for shopping is welcome,' Bree said seriously, earning a chuckle from across the table. 'Let's make a list.'

Max reined in his team to a walk as they entered Gower Street. The road was relatively quiet and it did not require much concentration to negotiate it to the point halfway down where the Mallorys' home was.

Which left far too much mental capacity for indecision. The Earl of Penrith was not given to indecision. Max Dysart, the man, was discovering just how uncomfortable it could be. The choices before him were clear-cut enough, but none of them were easy.

One, Max tried rehearsing them again, *I can make no effort to see her again and treat her as a mere acquaintance whenever we meet. Two, I can attempt to act simply as a friend and an acquaintance and, thirdly, I can endeavour to attach her.*

He pulled up in front of Bree's house and sat there, the reins still in his hand. Gregg, the groom who was sitting up behind him, arms folded, jumped down from his perch behind and ran to the horses' heads.

They are all dangerous. Max stared ahead unseeingly between the ears of one of the dapple greys, causing an approaching gentleman to wonder anxiously if there was something amiss with the cut of his clothes, given that the swell in the fancy rig was frowning at him so ferociously. *Number one almost ensures that she will find herself courted by any number of other men before I am in a position to make my move.*

Two—he reflexively steadied the offside horse which was taking exception to a passing dog—*risks her thinking my interest in her is purely platonic and we are back to the numerous other suitors again. Three, I am risking everything on the chance I am no longer married. If I am wrong, then I am embroiling Bree in a scandal that will be plastered all over the papers in every ghastly detail. And all of this assumes I really do want to risk courting another woman and offering her marriage.*

'My lord?' Gregg was regarding him anxiously.

'Get back up,' Max ordered.

'I thought we were calling here, my lord. I could walk the greys if you are worried about leaving them standing in this wind.'

'I'll shake the fidgets out of them in the park,' Max declared as the groom walked back.

With the licence of long service, the man let his feelings show on his face: the pair were as calm as high-blooded driving horses could ever be, and his lordship had just driven past the park on his way here.

Max gave a mental shrug. If he was going to become indecisive, he might as well get on with it. *Once round the park, then I'll make up my mind,* he bargained with himself, lifting the hand that held the reins and sending the greys off down the street at a brisk trot.

'Oh.' Bree stood staring down Gower Street at the unmistakable back and shoulders of the driver of the retreating phaeton.

'Is something wrong?' Rosa climbed down from the hackney and joined her on the pavement.

'That was Lord Penrith, the gentleman I told you about. The one who drove the stage for me.'

'The one who advised you to employ a chaperon and a business manager.' Rosa nodded, obviously ticking off a mental list from her morning's briefing.

'He must have been calling,' Bree said, lamely stating the obvious. She gave herself a little shake and called up to the driver, 'Wait a moment, will you? Someone will be out to pay you and collect our baggage.'

The front door opened to reveal the Mallorys' one footman who doubled as Piers's valet. 'Peters, please pay the driver and fetch in the luggage. This is Miss Thorpe, who will be living here from now on. She will be having the blue bedroom.

'We employ Peters, a cook, Mrs Harris—a general maid—and an upstairs maid who will be looking after both of us now.' Bree urged Rosa in front of her into the hall and looked at the salver lying on the console table. It contained a number of calling cards and several envelopes. Bree flipped through the cards confidently. 'Mr Latymer, Lord Lansdowne, Mr Trenchard. Trenchard? Oh, yes, third country dance. Lady Lucas.' There was nothing with Max's crest.

'Peters?'

'Yes, Miss Mallory?'

'Did the gentleman who just called not leave a card?'

'No gentleman has called since eleven o'clock, Miss Mallory. There was a regular flurry of callers this morning, but no one yet this afternoon.'

'How very odd.' And how very… Bree searched for the right word to describe her emotions. How very flattening. Max had obviously intended to call and then thought better of it on the very doorstep. But why? She led Rosa upstairs, talking brightly about the household and pointing out the various rooms as they went, her mind almost entirely on Max and his motives.

Had he taken her in disgust when he reviewed the events of last night in the cold light of day? It would be hypocritical of him if he did, but then, that was the way of the world. Men expected to take their pleasures and keep their respectability. The women involved immediately lost theirs.

Did he think her pert and forward, or completely wanton? Her stomach churned uncomfortably and suddenly she felt quite ill with mortification. Last night it had seemed natural to respond to his advances, natural to return his kisses with what small instinctive skill she had. Max had not treated her with disrespect; she had seen no cynical gleam in his eyes.

Which made it worse, in a way. Thinking back, recalling with a blush just how she had responded to him, he must have taken a disgust of her behaviour. Or she was wrong about him and he was actually a rake, bent on her seduction after all—but why, then, would he not call? No, she could not be that wrong about him. *But what do I know about men?* It was a mystery, and a very unsettling one.

'Here is your room.' She threw open the door to the third bedroom. 'It looks out at the back, so it is very quiet.' Bree sat down on the edge of the bed and bounced a little. 'Yes, the bed seems to be all right. Now, what else can we do to make you more comfortable? There is an easy chair, and a dressing table and stool, and I think the wardrobe will be large enough.'

She got up and went to open the clothes press, trying to force her muddled brain to think of practical matters. 'Good, I think that will do. Would you like a small table and chair for a desk? There isn't much room in here, and, of course, we hope you will feel absolutely free to join us in the drawing room at any time, but you might like privacy for letter writing and so on.'

'It looks—' Rosa swallowed hard and blinked

'—it is lovely. It is such a luxury to have a pretty, well-furnished room again. I became used to it when I was running the school, but as a governess one soon learns one's place—which is in whatever spare room it is least inconvenient to put one.'

'That's horrid.' Bree smiled with a warmth that came hard, given that she was feeling so queasy. 'We both want you to feel at home here.'

'Your brother has not met me yet,' Rosa said cautiously.

'Piers will like you,' Bree said confidently. 'He is living in dread that I am going to bring home a starched-up widow who will make him take his feet off the furniture, mind his tongue at all times and button his waistcoat in the house.'

Peters arrived at the door and dumped the first of Rosa's bags on the floor. 'I'll fetch up the rest directly, Miss Mallory. What about the shopping?'

'Bring that up here too, and send Lucy to help Miss Thorpe unpack.' She turned to Rosa as the man clattered off down the stairs again. 'If you sort out the bits and pieces I brought for myself, Lucy will bring them along. You must treat her as your maid as well as mine. She will fetch you hot water, light your fire and so forth.'

She broke off at the sound of the knocker. 'I wonder who that is.' Leaning over the banisters, she could hear Peters below.

'I am sorry, my lord, I do not know if Miss Mallory is at home. Would you care to step into the drawing room whilst I ascertain if she is receiving?'

From her perch, hanging over the second-floor banisters, Bree had a bird's eye view of the hall and the tops of Peters's sandy head and the oval of a fashionable tall hat. The hat was doffed and handed to the footman along with gloves.

'Who is it?' Rosa came to her side.

The bared head below was unmistakably that of Max Dysart. Her complaining stomach performed another uncomfortable twist and Bree clutched the polished wood. 'Lord Penrith.' *So why has he come back?*

Peters was toiling up the stairs again, a silver salver in his hand. 'Lord Penrith, Miss Mallory.' He proffered the salver, the neat rectangle of pasteboard lying dead centre. 'Are you at home?'

'I don't know,' Bree said blankly. 'I really do not know.'

Peters, unused to such a response, gaped at her. 'Go down to the hall and wait a moment,' Rosa said firmly, taking control. The footman obediently began to descend again. 'What is wrong?' She took Bree's arm and guided her back into the bedroom. 'Do you not wish to see this man? I can go down and tell him you are resting or some such excuse.'

That was so tempting. Bree bit her lip, then decided that honesty was the only policy with her new companion. 'He kissed me last night, and then, later, I was out alone on the terrace with him. Now I am afraid he will think me very fast and will either be here under the mistaken assumption that I will permit liberties, or he considers me wanton and has decided he no longer wishes to have anything to do with me.'

'Why would he be here in that case?'

'Because he promised to help me with the Whips, and now perhaps he feels he does not care to.'

'Hmm.' Rosa pursed her lips. 'I think there is nothing to be gained by putting off the encounter. I will come down too. If he is a rake bent upon your seduction, my presence should serve to warn him off, and if he is hypocrite enough to despise you for a few innocent kisses, then he should be chastened by seeing you have taken his advice and have a companion.'

She whipped off her bonnet and stooped to check her reflection in the mirror. 'My goodness, I shall be pleased to get out of this hideous gown, but it certainly makes me look a dour chaperon.'

Bree managed a shaky smile. 'Come along, then. Let us put my reputation to the test.'

Chapter Nine

'Lord Penrith. Good afternoon.' Bree was proud of her calm tone. 'May I introduce Miss Thorpe, my lady companion? Miss Thorpe, Lord Penrith, who was so good as to assist when we found ourselves with a driverless coach.'

She studied him as he shook hands with Rosa. He seemed the same and yet, somehow, different. What was it? Bree puzzled and then stopped as she realised he was waiting while the ladies took their seats. 'Do sit down, my lord. Would you care to take tea?'

'Thank you, yes, I would.'

Rosa bobbed up and tugged the bell pull, then sat quietly while Bree spoke to Peters.

'You see, my lord, I took your advice and engaged a companion,' Bree said, attempting a rallying tone. It was impossible to read Max's feelings this afternoon; all the expressive light had gone from his eyes and he was sitting, perfectly composed, his face unreadable. There was an air of seriousness about him, that was what was different.

'I am flattered that you should take such heed of my advice.'

'Indeed. But how could I not, after you had demonstrated the need for one so clearly.'

'Demonstrated?' His eyebrows went up.

'By your lucid explanation—or should I say example?—of the dangers to a lady's reputation when in society.' She felt the need to provoke a reaction, any reaction. This was like talking to a polite feather pillow.

'It is a sad fact that a lady, incautiously without chaperonage, may find herself kissed, or worse,' Max remarked blandly.

'Outrageous,' Rosa contributed, her face studiously straight.

'Of course, the lady might allow such liberties,' Max added. 'A gentleman would do well to reflect that this may simply be the expression of innocence, inexperience or a certain naive generosity of spirit.'

'Or all three.' Bree could feel her colour rising. He was telling her—in a patronising manner—that he understood, excused and dismissed her behaviour last night. 'Doubtless the gentleman in question would also reflect that a further attempt would be doomed to failure.'

'I feel sure that would be the safest path for him.' His

smile was rueful and Bree thought she had glimpsed the first sign of genuine emotion since he had arrived. She decided that she was not being dismissed as wanton, nor was he bent on seducing her, which left the rather embarrassing situation of having kissed him and now not knowing how to behave with him.

'You may be interested to know that Miss Thorpe will also be taking over some of the office work at the Mermaid for me.'

'Have you any experience of such a business, Miss Thorpe?' Max turned his dark eyes on her.

'None at all,' Rosa smiled austerely. 'But I have run a large girls' school. I am sure my experience with accounting, keeping discipline and managing a complex timetable will come in useful.'

'I must congratulate you, Miss Mallory, on finding such a well-qualified candidate so quickly.' His eyes found hers and Bree racked her brain to decide exactly what colour they were. A very dark hazel, or brown? She pulled herself together and concentrated.

'I was lucky my lord. I hope you also mean to congratulate me upon taking your advice.'

'I do. And I wonder why.'

'Because it was sensible advice, of course.' Bree flushed at her own sharp tone and reached for the tea pot. 'Cream or lemon, my lord?'

'Cream. Thank you. Are you from London, Miss Thorpe?'

'Nottinghamshire originally, my lord.' He waited, his silence an invitation to prattle that Rosa ignored with a prim smile, much to Bree's admiration. She knew she would have plunged on with every detail of her life story, confronted by that coolly interrogative voice and the amount of sheer personality behind his bland expression. *What is he here for? I thought he was coming to ask me to drive with him.*

'Have you been able to solve my other problem and rein in your friends of the Nonesuch Whips?' she asked.

'No,' he said baldly, putting down his cup and crossing his legs. Bree forced herself not to stare at the length of tightly stretched pantaloons vanishing into glossy Hessians. 'I hinted, I suggested—and I found myself beginning to sound as though I had an ulterior motive. And that, I would suggest, is more dangerous than the original threat.'

'Oh…' Bree mentally passed in review a number of highly improper expressions she had learned in the inn yard. 'Drat,' she concluded regretfully. It really did not do justice to her feelings.

'Drat indeed,' Max agreed.

'Will they get bored and find something else if Piers gives them the run of the place for a couple of days?'

'I doubt it—not unless you let them drive. That's the big attraction, you see—driving a stage in cold blood, not as the result of a drunken spree. They are good drivers, all of them, they have a serious interest and an inn yard is a public space, when all's said and done.'

'Well, they are not getting anywhere near my passengers,' Bree declared robustly.

'You let me drive,' Max said softly.

'I knew of your reputation. In any case, I had no choice.'

'And were you satisfied?'

Bree swallowed. 'I was entirely satisfied with your driving.'

They sat silently looking at each other while the tick of the clock on the mantel seemed to fill the room and Bree felt her own heartbeat stuttering out of time with it.

'Ahem.' Rosa leaned forward. 'May I pass you a custard tartlet, my lord?'

'Thank you, but no.' The shutters were back. No, not even that—his expression was so unreadable that she had no idea whether there even were any shutters or whether there were simply no strong feelings for him to hide.

'I have had an idea,' she said suddenly. Goodness knows where it came from, other than from her desperate desire to distract the Whips and her equally urgent wish to be anywhere but here exchanging stilted conversation with Max Dysart. 'Do the Nonesuch

Whips have club days when they all drive to a specific destination, as the Four Horse Club does?'

'Yes, but we are not so hidebound as to insist on the same destination on every occasion, nor do we confine ourselves to trotting in single file the entire way as is the FHC rule. We seek out interesting inns and eating houses and make them the goal for the day. Why do you ask, Miss Mallory?'

'Because it occurs to me that on some days we do have a spare coach and that we might be prepared to allow that to be driven, without paying passengers, of course, on such an expedition. Would that slake your friends' thirst?'

'The very answer, Miss Mallory, I congratulate you. You and Miss Thorpe must be my guests in my drag.'

'I must insist on my own groom with the stage and Piers on the box as well,' she cautioned.

'That seems eminently reasonable to me,' Max agreed.

'And no racing.'

'I promise.'

'You can offer that on their behalf?' Bree realised she must have looked as dubious as she sounded when she saw the quirk of amusement at the corner of Max's mouth. *Thank goodness, some sign of humanity at last!*

'I will ensure that everyone who wishes to drive

must give me their word to that effect before we start. Does that satisfy you?'

'Yes. Yes, my lord, it does. Thank you.'

'The Club will, of course, pay whatever a return journey for the trip would be, assuming a full way-bill of passengers.'

Bree opened her mouth to agree that that would be very acceptable and closed it again. Now she had Rosa she did not have to fear curious strangers at the Mermaid any longer, not if they had an accept-able outlet for their desire to drive the stagecoaches. Piers had blossomed in the company of the Whips: he had enjoyed it and it was far better that he had his introduction into society with men who spent their time driving rather than frequenting gaming halls and brothels.

'No,' she said slowly, considering it. 'No, we will not charge, unless any damage is done. If it is suc-cessful, then we may repeat it. I see no harm, and perhaps it may give the Challenge Coach Company a certain *cachet*.'

And it also propelled her into the unsettling com-pany of the Earl of Penrith. *And that of a number of other pleasant and attractive gentlemen*, she added mentally. Max's words about finding a husband echoed with Georgy's teasing matchmaking. Not a gentleman of title, not with her pedigree. But there might be a nice younger son. She tried to feel enthusiastic about that possibility and found the thought strangely flat.

'That is very generous.' Max removed his pocket book and consulted it. 'The next meeting will be on Saturday the tenth.'

'I will check with the yard and see, then let you know. Where is the destination?'

'It depends on the weather, although there was discussion of taking a picnic to Greenwich Park, if it is fine.'

A whole day of frivolity. Bree tried to recall when she had last taken an entire day to devote simply to pleasure, and could not. And an entire day in Max's company. And that of Lord Lansdowne, Mr Latymer, Piers, Rosa and all the other Whips, of course.

'That sounds delightful,' Rosa observed sedately, jerking Bree back to the present.

'Delightful,' she echoed dutifully.

Lord Penrith put down his cup and saucer and got to his feet. 'I will wait to hear from you then. Thank you for the tea.' He bowed slightly. 'Ladies.'

Rosa jumped up and tugged the bell for Peters and then Max was gone, leaving Bree staring rather blankly after him.

'I thought he was going to invite me to drive in the park with him,' she said.

'Perhaps he forgot, thinking about your proposal

with the stage,' Rosa suggested, looking doubtful. 'Is he always like that?'

'No.' Bree wrinkled her forehead. 'But I've only met him twice before, of course. How did he strike you?'

'At first, just as he meant to—a conventional, rather cold-blooded English gentleman making a social call. But he isn't just that.' Rosa was frowning now too. 'There's humour there and warmth in his eyes when he looks at you and you are not looking at him. And something else. Something dark.'

Bree shivered. 'Rosa, you sound positively Gothic!' Then she recalled his words during the ball. 'I think he has something on his mind. A secret.'

'Hmm.' Rosa sat down and poured more tea. 'Lord Penrith is very attractive—I just hope he doesn't turn out to be Bluebeard.'

Max swung up into the driving seat and gathered the reins. *So much for option two—we have a stilted conversation full of undertones that makes us both uncomfortable because of what happened at the ball.* 'Walk on.' The pair moved off sedately and Gregg swung up behind.

Max tried to sort out how he felt and made the un-nerving discovery that his general sense of unease and indecision was worse than before. He wanted Bree, but the thought of marriage was more fraught with dis-comfort the more he contemplated it. He had dragged the locked trunk out of the attic of his memory and forced himself to open it, look at the hurt and shame and anger and fear that he had pushed away so he could get on with his life again. Only now they were out and he was facing them, all the doubt was back.

Drusilla had left him within weeks of their marriage. It was his job to make a marriage, to keep his wife, and he had failed. Was it just that one woman, or was there something about him that was unsuited to matrimony? Dare he risk it again? Dare he risk it with this woman? He was not even sure what he felt for her other than liking, admiration and undoubted desire. Always assuming she did not laugh in his face at the mere thought of it. Bree Mallory did not strike him as a woman likely to be dazzled by a title.

He turned into Bedford Square and then into Tottenham Court Road, heading for the crowded thoroughfare of Oxford Street. 'Any idea of the time, Gregg?' It was too busy to drive one-handed and fish out his pocket watch.

'About three, my lord, I'd hazard.'

Time then to think in peace and quiet at home before Ryder, the man recommended by Lord Lucas, came to discuss his problem.

My problem, Max thought, jeering at himself. *A nice euphemism. I can pretend I have a leak in the roof, or a difficult decision about investments or an unre-*

liable tenant. And a man will come and sort out my problem. Which I should have sorted out years ago.

He was in no better frame of mind at six o'clock when his butler, Bignell, announced, 'Mr Ryder, my lord', and ushered in the investigator.

'Mr Ryder, please, come and sit down.'

'My lord.' One would take him for a superior clerk in his sober, understated clothes and with his quiet manner. But his voice was that of an gentleman, he moved with a swordsman's grace and the grey eyes, when they met Max's, were cool and assessing. From a clerk the scrutiny would have been insolence; from this man it felt like being assessed by a surgeon. It was about as comfortable.

It was also steadying. Max gathered himself mentally and concentrated, much as he would before a fencing bout. 'Lord Lucas recommends you highly.'

'I have been able to be of use to him in the past.' No false modesty or protestations there. 'His lordship tells me that there is a personal matter requiring the highest discretion that you wish investigated.'

'Yes. Ten years ago, when I was twenty-one—just twenty-one—I met a young woman called Drusilla Cornish. She was twenty, the daughter of an apothecary in Swindon. I fell in love with her, and I married her.'

There was a notebook in Ryder's hand—it seemed

to have appeared as though by magic. He jotted something and looked up, a faint smile on his lips. 'I use codes and a shorthand of my own devising, my lord. Your lordship held your present title at this time?'

'Yes. I was the Earl of Penrith, I did marry a tradesman's daughter and, under the terms of my father's will, virtually all my money was in trust until I reached the age of twenty-five, or married with the approval of my trustees. It was every bit as ill judged an action as you are most tactfully not saying.'

'Special licence?' Max nodded. 'And the marriage took place where?' He listened as Max recounted how he had recalled the out-of-the way church in Dorset from a visit to a friend's country estate the year before. 'And her address in Swindon? Her family?'

He told it all, the memory of the dusty little shop coming back so clearly as he spoke that he could smell the herbs and medicines, could see the light glinting on the glass vessels where the sun stuck through the lead-paned windows, could see the vision of loveliness that had seemed to swim out of the shadows like a black-haired mermaid at the sound of the tinny little bell.

'I had toothache, of all the damned prosaic reasons for finding myself in this mess now. I wanted to see my own dentist in London, not submit to some rustic tooth-puller, but I needed something to dull the pain for a day or two. And there she was, serving. Her father was in the back, grinding up some nostrum, her small sister was perched on the end of the counter making up lavender bags.

'I walked in feeling as though some demon were drilling holes in my jaw, fell in love and forgot the pain, all in one glance.' It was surprisingly easy, talking to this dark stranger. Almost he could understand the allure of the confessional. He took a folded paper out of his pocket book. 'Here. I have written down everything I can recall about names and places.'

'Thank you, my lord.' Ryder glanced through it, nodded and tucked it into his own notebook. 'And then?'

'Then I took Drusilla home. I knew my trustees would not approve, but, what the hell—my allowance was a thousand times more than her father earned in a year, we could survive very well for four years. My parents were both dead, my grandmother presided over Longwater. She took one look at Drusilla and told me to say nothing to anyone except the servants.'

'You could rely upon them?'

'Oh, yes, they were old family retainers, every one. They, and my grandmother, set about turning Drusilla into a countess.'

'How well did they succeed?'

'Not at all. She was appalled. She had no idea of what would be expected of her, she was intimidated by the house, by the servants, by my grandmother—by me, once she saw me in my proper setting, as it were.'

Mr Ryder just waited, silently. It was a technique Max used himself and he was wryly amused to find himself succumbing to it. 'If she had loved me, I don't think that would have mattered, but she didn't. I think she had seen me as the equivalent of a wealthy merchant and that was the height of her ambition. She had not expected to have to work for the title and the wealth and the position. I might have been young, and I might have been besotted, but I knew what a countess's duties and responsibilities were.

'She realised that this was not a game and we both realised she did not love me. It took three weeks to reach that point.'

Mr Ryder taped his teeth with the end of his pencil. 'I suppose that there were not grounds for an annulment?' he enquired delicately.

'No.' Max looked back over the years with grim amusement. 'I think you might say that the one place where we were compatible was in bed.'

There was a pause while the investigator gazed tactfully out of the study window and Max consigned those particular memories to a deep, safe, dark, mental cupboard.

'Then she met a gentleman when she was shopping in Norwich. It is the closest town to my country seat. Drusilla enjoyed shopping and Grandmama saw no

harm in it so long as she went incognito. That gentleman was handsome, charming, lived by his wits and
was, as she informed me in the exceedingly ill-spelled
letter she left me, *fun*. She left, taking all those jewels
Grandmama had not locked in the safe.'

'You pursued her?'

'No. I wrote to her at the inn her note had come
from and informed her that I was opening an account
with my bank on which she, and only she, could draw,
and that I hoped she was happy.' He leaned back in his
chair and closed his eyes. 'I never saw her, nor heard
from her, again. Money was taken out, to the limit I
told her I would maintain, for two years. After that it
was untouched and has remained so to this day.'

'The logical presumption would be that she is dead,
or no longer in the country,' Ryder remarked.

'I need more than presumption, Mr Ryder. I need to
know whether I have a wife living or not.'

'Indeed, my lord, I can understand why you feel that
to be desirable. Did you contact her family?'

'No.'

'Make any enquiries at all?'

'None.'

'Why not, my lord? Nine years is a very long time
with, if I may be so frank, the succession to an earl-
dom to be considered.'

Chapter Ten

'Because I had a guilty conscience and because I am unused to failure.' Max had had long enough to work out why he had consigned the problem of his marriage to a locked cupboard. 'Don't think I feel any complacency about my lack of action. But I should never have married her—I took the poor girl completely out of her depth. And having done so, somehow I should have made it work. It may sound arrogant, Mr Ryder, but I am not used to failure.'

'I am sure that is the case, my lord.'

Max paused, tapping the tips of his joined fingers against his lips. 'And the longer I left it, the more difficult it became. I suppose, too, that my damnable pride got in the way as well. I had offered her a golden future and she tossed it back in my face to run off with an adventurer—I was damned if I was going to chase after her.' *Was that at the heart of it? Was that the real reason, and I've been too much of a hypocrite to admit it? Pride?*

'Well, my lord, I think I have enough to commence my investigations. I will write to you weekly to advise you of progress, unless, of course, I make a breakthrough. I will refer to the Countess in terms of a painting that was stolen some years back and which you wish to trace. That should be adequate cover in the event of a letter falling into the wrong hands.'

Ryder stood, tucking his notebook away in a breast pocket. 'Just one more thing, my lord. Did none of her family make any attempt to contact you after the marriage?'

'No.' He looked at the investigator and suddenly that omission seemed as odd to him as it obviously did to Ryder. 'How very strange.'

'Indeed. I believe I will start with them. Good day, my lord.'

Max went to sit at his desk again as the door closed behind Ryder. He felt confidence in the man, both in his discretion and his skill. A few weeks and he would know where he was and how he stood. It was good to have done this at last. For years he had been telling himself that Nevill would make a perfectly acceptable heir. Now he could close his eyes and see the nebulous outline of his own son. The fact that this phantom of the future had only begun to appear since he had met Bree did not escape him.

A son with her blue eyes and his dark hair, or perhaps his brown eyes and her wheaten blonde hair—

either was an attractive thought. And a number of daughters, all like their mother.

Max grinned at his distorted image in the silver inkwell, his spirits lifting from what seemed like an inordinate time in the doldrums. Surely, if one was daydreaming about the number of children one would have with a lady, one was beyond the stage of being undecided about one's feelings? All this needed was very careful timing and complete self-control. And her co-operation, of course. And beyond that, to learn what one had done so very wrong before and not commit the same mistakes again.

By the second circuit of Green Park on Wednesday afternoon with Mr Latymer, Bree had come to the conclusion that she needed at least three new walking dresses if she was going to keep this up. And two new bonnets.

On Tuesday Lord Lansdowne had called and had taken her driving in Hyde Park at the height of the fashionable promenade. She had been acknowledged by a gratifying number of new acquaintances from the Dowager's ball, despite the Viscount's protestations that town was virtually empty of company.

'I wouldn't be up now if it weren't that Grandmama wanted to puff off Sophia's engagement from the town house,' he explained. He moved the phaeton off again after a stop to speak to three of Bree's Grendon cousins who were staying up in town while the fine weather lasted.

'But the Nonesuch Whips are here,' Bree observed. 'At least, enough of you to be having meetings.'

'Mmm.' The Viscount touched his hat to a barouche full of fashionably dressed young matrons as they passed. 'I'm here for Sophia's affair, Greesley's staying on because his elderly uncle, the one who's going to leave him all the money, is threatening to turn up his toes, and Greesley's doing the dutiful. Penrith's up because his suite at his country seat is being redecorated and he's fled from demands to choose hangings—at least, that's his story—and young Nevill's here because Penrith is. Don't know what Latymer's reason is, but once there's a core of us, then it makes it worthwhile for the others and it snowballs.'

'Has Lord Penrith told the other club members about my suggestion for them to drive the stage?' Bree twirled her parasol and tried not to feel guilty about leaving Rosa with a stack of account books. Her companion had protested that she wanted to read them to get a better understanding of the business and had shooed Bree out of the house as soon as Lord Lansdowne had called.

'Indeed he has.' The Viscount was enthusiastic. 'It's what's keeping us all up now, the hope we can get at least two outings in while the weather holds.'

'I really do not understand the attraction,' Bree said

doubtfully, still uneasy that they would try and race. 'I expect you all have beautiful rigs and very fine teams.'

'That's just the point.' Lansdowne caught the end of his whip neatly round the handle in a way that had Bree itching to learn the trick of it. 'We spend the money, but is it our horses and our well-balanced rigs that make us drive well? How do we know? If we take a stagecoach, which, forgive me, is not built to the same standards, and have to take pot luck with teams that are not bred for looks or speed, then the man with the better skills will be obvious.'

'It's more of a challenge, then?' Bree could think of one gentleman who more than lived up to it.

'That's right,' Lansdowne agreed cheerfully. 'Tell me, do you drive, Miss Mallory?' Once she had recovered from the inexplicable coughing fit, Bree was able to assure him that she was capable of managing a phaeton or a curricle, and to convince herself that admitting to being able to handle the reins of a park carriage did not brand her as a hoyden who drove coaches.

She had enjoyed her drive with the Viscount. Then this morning Georgy had arrived in her barouche to ask whether Bree would like to visit Ackermann's Repository with her to chose some prints. It has seemed only courteous to agree, although that made a second day when she would be absent from the Mermaid.

'I'll show Rosa around, settle her into the office,'

Piers had promised firmly. 'You go and enjoy yourself.' Really, if she had not known better, she would have thought Piers and Rosa were in a conspiracy to give her a holiday.

Georgy was intent on buying enough images to make a fashionable print room out of a closet between her dressing room and her husband's, but the necessity to buy what seemed like hundreds of prints from the shop did not distract her from the lure of fashion magazines, a stack of which were now waiting, oozing temptation, on Bree's bedside table.

It seemed strange to have a female friend, especially one as *au fait* with society as Lady Lucas. She seemed to have forgotten that Bree was single and cheerfully chatted of the latest crim. con. scandals, her falling out with her husband over her milliner's bill and her scheme to put him in a better mood by wearing a quite outrageously naughty négligée she had just purchased.

'It is the sheerest pink lawn, with deep rose ribbons and lots of lace, which makes it look as though it is quite decent until one moves and then—*oh la, la!* Charles is going to be beside himself.'

Bree thought of what effect such a garment might have on Max and found the very thought brought a blush to her cheeks. It also brought a very unwelcome tingling feeling in all those places he had kissed and she tried to calm herself by thinking how very unflattering such a garment would be to her complexion in pink. *Deep blue, on the other hand...*

'And how is Dysart?' Georgy demanded, uncannily echoing her train of thought as they sat back in the barouche and regarded their morning's shopping with satisfaction.

'I have no idea. I saw him briefly the day after the ball when he called, but that is all.'

'Really?' Lady Lucas frowned. 'How provoking. I would have thought he would have asked you out driving at least once by now.'

So would I, Bree thought.

'I am convinced you should marry him,' her companion added chattily.

'*What!*' Bree sat bolt upright and shot a glance at the backs of the driver and groom sitting up in front of them. 'I am quite ineligible, even were his lordship interested.'

'Oh, I know I said you had better settle for a younger son,' Georgy said airily, 'but now I know you, I think you would do marvellously for Dysart. You have so much more élan than I could have hoped for—you could carry it off.'

'But I do not want—'

But Georgy was in full flow, although this time she lowered her voice. 'If anyone can mend his broken heart, I am sure you can.'

'His what?' One thing Max Dysart did not appear

to be afflicted by was a broken heart. Anyone less lovelorn she had yet to see.

'They say he fell in love ten years ago and she would not have him, and now he holds the memory of her, for ever frozen, in his heart.'

'That is a horrid image,' Bree said robustly. 'And, in any case, ten years is a long time. Why, he was hardly more than a boy then. Now he's a man.'

'Yes, but ten years ago, he withdrew from society!' Georgy whispered, her voice thrilling. 'In the height of the Season, he vanished off down to Longwater. That must have been when it happened.'

'Well, who was she?' Bree demanded. Max's words at the ball came back: *What would you say if I told you that I had a secret that would scandalise society?* No, it couldn't be that. A broken heart was sad, but not a scandal.

'I have no idea,' Georgy said, breathless with the excitement of a mystery. 'But you can unfreeze his heart…'

'Yuck! I shall do no such thing, even if I were capable of it. And even if it were frozen, which I am sure it is not.'

'Then why has he not married?'

'Because he has not found someone he loves enough.' *And when he does, he is going to court them properly, not promise to take them driving and then forget all about it!*

'You are horribly sensible,' Georgy grumbled. 'Just like darling Charles.'

'Think of the négligée,' Bree whispered to distract her, and was rewarded with a gurgle of laughter and a quick hug.

Now Mr Latymer had called to take her out in his high-perch phaeton. It was a more showy vehicle than Lord Lansdowne's, but she did not feel Mr Latymer's pair was the equivalent in quality of the Viscount's match bays, so honours so far were even.

On hearing that she had been in Hyde Park yesterday, Mr Latymer had offered to take her again, or for her to name her choice, congratulating her when she decided on Green Park. 'So much more tranquil,' he observed, turning in out off the hubbub of Piccadilly and skirting the reservoir with its promenaders.

'This is delightful. I have walked here often, of course, but I had not realised how pleasant it is for driving—so much less crowded than Hyde Park with everyone on the strut.'

'Do you keep a carriage, Miss Mallory?'

'No. Not in town. When we are at home in Buckinghamshire, then I drive a gig.' She regarded Mr Latymer from under the shelter of the brim of her bonnet. He was not as good-looking as Lord Lansdowne, with dark looks which bordered on the sardonic, but he had an edge about him that was quite stimulating, she decided. It wasn't in anything he said, more in the way that he said it. Sometimes he could deliver a compliment with a glint in his black eyes that made her suspect this was all a game to him. It certainly put a girl on her mettle.

'Would you care to drive now?'

'Why...'

'Unless you are unsure about driving more than a single horse.' He made it sound like a challenge.

'Oh, no, I can drive four in—' *Oh, Lord!*

'Four in hand, Miss Mallory? What a very unusual skill for a woman.'

Drat, double drat! 'Farm wagons,' she improvised hastily. 'Only at a walk, of course, for fun, in the summer.'

'Ah, I see. For a moment there I thought you were going to tell me you could drive a stagecoach.'

Bree fought the temptation to look at him and try to read his expression. 'Goodness, what a shocking thing to suggest, Mr Latymer!' She laughed brightly. 'But I would like to try a pair—under your guidance, of course.'

'Certainly.' He pulled up and began to hand her the reins. They both saw her gloves at the same time.

'Oh, bother. I should have worn something more sensible to come out driving.' Bree regarded the almond-green glacé kid gloves ruefully. 'I bought them this morning, and could not resist. But I will surely split or stain them if I try to drive.'

'Why not take them off and wear mine?' Brice Latymer stripped off his gloves as he spoke. 'They'll be too big, of course, but the leather is very fine. They should protect your hands.'

'Thank you.' She really ought to refuse until another day when she could come prepared, but the temptation of the quiet park in the sunshine was too much. 'Oh, dear, I knew I should have bought a larger size.' Bree tugged, but the thin leather clung tenaciously to her warm skin.

'Let me. I think you need to pull finger by finger.' Mr Latymer wrapped his reins around the whip in its stand and shifted on the seat until he was facing her. 'Give me a hand.'

Obediently Bree held out her right hand and sat patiently while he caught each fingertip in turn, tugging the tight leather a fraction at a time. Finally the glove slid off and he caught her hand in his own bare one. 'There, you see? Patience and care.' He began on the other.

It was, she realised, a very intimate act. He was having to sit close, her hand held in his while he used the other hand to fret at each fingertip. He made no move to touch her in any other way, nor did he say anything the slightest bit flirtatious, but Bree was visited by the realisation that he was finding this an arousing experience. There was colour on his cheekbones and his breathing was slightly ragged. She swallowed, her own colour rising.

'Here it comes.' The second glove slid off, the fragile kid insubstantial in his hand. Bree found she could not take her eyes off it; it seemed like a crushed leaf. Latymer lifted her hand and kissed her fingers. 'Such a very hot little hand.'

'Good afternoon.' A deep voice had Bree jerking her hand out of Latymer's grip and sitting bolt upright, her cheeks scarlet. 'Undressing, Miss Mallory?'

She gasped. Of course, it just had to be Max Dysart regarding her with raised eyebrows from the back of a very fine black gelding.

What the devil is she doing, letting Latymer make love to her in the middle of Green Park? He'll be starting on her garters next. Max recognised the look of heavy-lidded concentration—Latymer was hunting, whether Bree in her innocence knew it or not. However, dismounting, dragging him out of the phaeton and punching him, while it would be satisfying, was not acceptable behaviour in public parks, especially as Bree was showing no signs of distress at his actions.

The gelding sidled, picking up his mood. Max steadied it with hands and the pressure of his thighs, without conscious thought.

'Mr Latymer was lending me his gloves as he was

kind enough to offer to let me drive, and I was foolish enough to come in the most impractical ones imaginable.'

Max fought a brisk battle with his own temper, and won. He had made no claim on her—if one discounted a scandalously indiscreet kiss—and he had no right to be jealous if he found her in a public place with another man. But it was damned hard to be rational and fair about this when the other man was Brice Latymer, whom he trusted about as far as he could throw him.

'I was not aware that you wished for driving lessons, Miss Mallory.'

'Hardly lessons, my lord, although I am sure Mr Latymer will be able to give me many useful pointers. Is it not kind of him to remember his promise to take me driving? Lord Lansdowne did as well, and Lady Lucas.'

Hell, I promised to take her driving too! And she's furious that I haven't, Max realised with a flash of insight. *Is that just pique, or is she disappointed?* He should be apologetic that he had forgotten; instead, he cheerfully heaped coals on the flames to see if that produced a reaction.

'Yes, most thoughtful of them,' he agreed cordially. 'You see how much fun you are having since you began to follow my advice, Miss Mallory?' He tipped his hat to her, and nodded to her companion. 'Latymer. Enjoy your drive.' He turned the gelding's head and cantered off towards the park entrance, fully conscious of two pairs of eyes glaring at his back.

'Advice?' Bree was conscious of Brice Latymer's own hostility, even through her own chagrin. There was something between the two men, something she had noticed, but not given any thought to, in the inn yard in Hounslow. Whatever it was, Max had not liked seeing her with Mr Latymer. Infuriating man. It would serve him right if she set out to make him jealous....

'Advice?' Latymer repeated.

'Er, yes. He suggested that I...that I get out more, spend less time at home looking after things.'

'Did he indeed?' Brice Latymer's voice was silky. 'How right he was, of course. But then, Lord Penrith specialises in being right. Now, if you would care to try my gloves?'

Chapter Eleven

The next day brought three invitations to parties from ladies Bree had met at the Dowager's ball, a note from Georgy asking if she was going to Lady Court's soirée, because, if so, could they go together because Lord Lucas would not be at home to escort his wife, and a slim package.

'Goodness, look at these.' Bree pushed the invitations across the breakfast table to Rosa. 'We need more gowns, don't you think? I haven't got anything suitable for full-dress occasions.'

'And I certainly have not. Do you intend to accept them all?'

'I think so. I expect we will get weary of frivolity soon, but it is fun at the moment. So long as you are not finding it too much to go out in the evenings on top of working at the Mermaid.'

'I enjoy it.' Rosa spread honey on her roll and took a bite. 'I am finding it very stimulating, and it is interesting to be working with adults. I do have a list of questions, though, if we could go through them before I go to the office. Unless you need me this morning?'

'No, although we should go shopping, but I do not mind—morning or afternoon are both fine for me.' Bree picked up the package and reached for her bread knife to slit the seals.

'I'll go this morning, then. Did I tell you I have solved the mystery of the fodder bill? Someone had put all the use of oats into the corn column and the… Goodness, what lovely gloves.'

'They are, are they not?' Bree stared at the fine calf-skin gloves, perfect for a lady to drive in, with delicate punch work on the backs and dashing cuffs. They were strong, but as soft as butter when she stroked them.

'Did you order them?'

'No. I think they must be a present.' Bree drew on the right one, flexing her fingers. 'They are silk lined, what luxury.'

'Who from? Oh, look, there is a card.' Rosa caught it up and passed it to Bree.

Max! 'Oh. They are from Mr Latymer.'

'My dear, you cannot possibly accept them. Not from a gentleman.' Rosa ran one finger down the back of the left glove and sighed regretfully.

'Why ever not? I could accept a fan or handker-chiefs, could I not?'

Her companion coloured up. 'Gloves are more… intimate.'

'Whatever do you mean?' Bree pulled on the other glove and smiled appreciatively as she turned her wrist to admire the effect. 'They are hardly underwear!'

'Oh, dear, how can I put this?' Rosa glanced round and checked that the maid was not in the room. 'There is a certain symbolism about gloves. And shoes. You have to insert part of your body into a tight fitting…' She came to a halt, unable to explain further. 'Cinderella,' she added, rather wildly.

Light dawned. 'You mean, like *sex?* Good heavens, I had no idea.' No wonder Mr Latymer was getting hot and bothered and Max had been so frosty when he saw Mr Latymer slowly stripping off her gloves in Green Park. 'How am I supposed to know that?'

'You aren't. I'm supposed, as a good chaperon, to warn you.'

'I'll have to send them back, won't I?'

'I'm afraid so. With a polite note saying you appreciate the gesture, but you are unable to accept articles of apparel.'

'Oh, dear.' Bree sighed and folded the gloves back into their wrapping paper before any butter got on them. The door banged open and Piers bounced in. 'Good morning, Piers.'

'Morning. Good morning, Rosa. Bree, I've finished

all my Latin. I got up early. Now, say I can go down to the Mermaid with Rosa this morning?'

'If you can bounce about like that, and you've finished all the tasks set you, then you ought to be going back to school,' Bree said, feigning severity.

'I'm tired, really.' Piers drooped unconvincingly into a chair next to Rosa. 'I'm just being brave. What's for breakfast?'

'What you see! If you want anything else, then ring for it. Oh, and there's a letter for you.'

'Who from?' Piers forked up the last of the bacon and stuck it inelegantly between two slices of toast.

'Uncle George, I think.' Bree squinted at the handwriting as she passed it over. 'Not his usual tidy hand.'

Piers put down his toast and slit the seal. 'Yes, Uncle George it is.' He read steadily, taking occasional bites of bacon, then stopped eating, his hand still in mid air.

'Piers, for goodness' sake, if you can't mind your manners for me, do think of poor Rosa with your breakfast waving about under her nose,' Bree chided.

'What? Sorry, Rosa. Look, Bree, this is da—I mean, very odd. The old boy doesn't sound himself at all. He rambles on about the farm, not saying anything of any purpose. Then he asks if we are all right and the business is doing well. And then he says what a good thing it is that I am growing up and can manage my half of the company, and that's a great weight off his mind. And then there's something scrawled, which I can't make head nor tail of.' He passed the sheet back and Bree peered at it.

'Neither can I. He's crossed the sheet to save paper.'

Rosa got to her feet. 'I will go down to the Mermaid—you will want to discuss this in private.'

'No, please don't. You are one of the family.' Bree flashed her a worried frown. 'I don't understand this at all. Rosa, can you read this? You might be more used to bad handwriting.'

'It looks like, *never forgive myself.* Excuse me, but is Mr Mallory an elderly gentleman? Could he be becoming confused? It does happen.'

'He is only sixty-five,' Bree protested. 'Oh, dear, perhaps I had better go down and see him.'

'Me too.' Piers perked up.

'Either you are well enough to go back to Harrow or you are still convalescent and must stay here and help Rosa with the business. I can take the Aylesbury stage—Mr Hearn's *Despatch* goes daily from the King's Arms.' Bree frowned and looked at the clock over the mantel. 'It goes at two o'clock, I think. It's only at Snow's Hill at the end of High Holborn,' she explained to Rosa. 'I can go up tomorrow, spend the night and get the morning coach back if it is just a false alarm.'

They all sat looking at the folded letter as though expecting it to speak and solve the riddle of Uncle George's odd ramblings. Rosa gave herself a little shake. 'If we can just go through my list of queries? Then I'll get off to the inn. Do you still want to go shopping this afternoon?'

'Oh, yes,' Bree said with a confidence she was far from feeling. 'I'm sure it's just a storm in a teacup and I can come back directly. If there are any problems, I'll write at once and stay down there.'

They worked through a list of queries about the intricacies of the ticketing system, whether it was worth trying a different printer for waybills, how livestock was priced and why turkeys were not carried— 'Unless dead', as Piers helpfully added—and what to do about the unsatisfactory behaviour of one of the ostlers. Then the others departed, Piers quizzing Rosa about the mystery of the fodder bill.

Bree wandered into the drawing room, sank down on the sofa and regarded the empty fireplace blankly, worrying about her uncle. Should she go down today? *No*, she decided. *He might just have been down in the dumps and there'll be a letter tomorrow saying so. And he'll be mortified if I go haring off down there because of that. I'll give him twenty-four hours.*

But it would be good to have someone to talk to about it. She felt Piers was too young, and she could hardly burden Rosa with family worries, but what if there was something seriously wrong with him? He was unmarried, a reserved, independent type who would hate it if they had to start interfering in his

life, however good their motives and however tactful they were.

If only Max were here. She could talk to him and
he would be sensible and sympathetic and help her
see it in perspective. No, perhaps not so sympathetic
now, not since that stilted visit and the embarrassing
encounter in Green Park.

The sound of the knocker sent her to the window.
There was a phaeton at the kerb, but she did not recognise the horses. Perhaps it was Max.

'Mr Latymer, Miss Mallory.' Peters stood waiting.
'Are you at home?'

'Oh. Yes, yes, I am. Peters, show him in and ask
Lucy to come down, please. He can wait in here. I
just need to get something from the breakfast room.'
After the incident with the gloves she had better be
on her best behaviour, and that included chaperonage.
Bree slipped out of the connecting door and went to
collect the gloves from the table. When she got back
Lucy was perched on a hard chair in the corner and
Brice Latymer was studying the landscape over the
fireplace.

'Miss Mallory, good morning. I see you have received my little gift.'

'Please, sit down, Mr Latymer. Yes, it arrived safely.
The gloves are delightful, but I am afraid I cannot accept them.' She held out the package, but he made no
move to take it.

'But the merest trifle, Miss Mallory, please, relent.' The black eyes held a trace of the heat she recalled from the day before.

'I must insist, sir. I cannot accept articles of apparel.' She continued to hold out the gloves until he had no choice but to get up and take them.

Bree knew she was blushing. Knew, too, that he could see that and that he knew that she knew the significance of the gift. It made her feel decidedly hot and bothered. 'My chaperon is adamant, I am afraid,' she added.

'A pity.' He folded them away into his pocket with a wry smile. 'Perhaps I can persuade you to come for a drive anyway?'

Bree shook her head regretfully. 'I am sorry, but I would be poor company today.'

'My dear Miss Mallory, are you in some distress? What can I do to assist you?' His black eyes were sharp and interested.

'A family matter, sir. A relative who seems…unwell. There is nothing you can do, but thank you for your concern.'

'I can listen,' he said softly. 'Sometimes that helps. Is it a close relative?'

'Yes, my uncle. My late father's brother who lives near Aylesbury in Buckinghamshire.'

'Mmm?' He nodded encouragingly.

'He is the co-owner with my brother of the stage-coach company, and breeds our horses.'

'And Mr Mallory senior is unwell?' Latymer prompted, leaning forwards with his forearms on his knees, sleek and elegant. It all seemed so easy, just to confide in him.

'We had an odd letter from him today. He sounded— I suppose distracted is the word.'

'How disconcerting. His family is looking after him, I suppose?'

'No, he is unmarried. I intend to go down to visit him tomorrow. It is probably nothing, but I want to set my mind at rest.'

'Of course, I can quite see that you would want to do that. Perhaps the burden of the business is too much for him?'

'I do not think it is that. I…I mean, Piers runs the business, although Uncle George owns half.'

'You are obviously concerned and a visitor cannot fail to be a distraction from your thoughts.' He got to his feet and held out his hand. 'Miss Mallory, I will remove myself and hope to persuade you to a drive when you return to town. Good day, and I trust you find your uncle in the best of health.'

Bree said all that was expected and sat down onto her sofa as he left. She really ought to think about what to take tomorrow, and there was Cook to speak to about menus for two days.

'That's what I call a proper gentleman,' Lucy observed, getting up and making her way to the door. 'Ever so good-looking and nice manners with it.'

'Mmm,' Bree agreed absently.

'Shall I pack a bag for tomorrow, Miss Bree? And do you want me to come too?'

'No, I will be fine on the stage, Lucy. If you can pack an overnight bag, please, that would be helpful.' Feeling as though her feet were lead, Bree stood up and went to interview Cook. Pleasant as Mr Latymer was, he was not the gentleman she was yearning to talk to, and the realisation that she had so little control over her emotions was as depressing as anything.

'Miss Mallory!'

Bree looked around, half-expecting to see an ostler from the Mermaid running after her up the crowded pavements of High Holborn. Then she glanced towards the road and saw Max pushing the reins of his curricle into the hands of a groom and jumping down into the traffic.

'My lord, do take a care!' she scolded as he arrived at her side. 'I am sure jumping about like that is not good for your shoulder.' But the sight of him was good for her spirits, however ambivalent her feelings towards him were. Bree felt her heartbeat quicken and she had to struggle to keep the smile off her lips.

'Thanks to the exceptional care I received, my shoulder is almost healed,' he assured her. The memory of his smooth, hot, hard-muscled skin under her palms flashed through Bree's thoughts and she made herself smile politely.

'Excellent.'

'Where are you off to with that bag, all by yourself?' Max demanded, seeing the portmanteau in her hand for the first time.

'Just to the King's Head in Snow Hill to take the Aylesbury stage, my lord. Will you excuse me? It leaves at two and I must hurry.'

'What are you doing, trying out the opposition?' He took the bag from her hand and began to stride along beside her.

'No, just visiting my uncle in Aylesbury.'

'By yourself? On the common stage?' She shot him a look and he tipped his head to one side in rueful acknowledgment that, to her, travel by stage was no particular adventure. 'Let me drive you.'

'In what, my lord?' Bree kept walking briskly as she talked. She had booked her ticket and had not thought it necessary to allow much time to walk the short distance between the two inns. 'Your curricle will take perhaps six hours, almost as long as the stage, and both that, or a chaise, would be equally shocking for me to be seen in.'

'Of course. I was forgetting that you are the respectable Miss Mallory now, not my stagecoach-driving Bree.'

'You made me become respectable,' Bree pointed out, trying not to analyse his words too carefully.

'So I did,' Max agreed. 'So the least I can do is to give you my escort.'

'On the stage? I am in no need of escort, I assure you.' Bree turned into the yard of the King's Head, her eyes automatically assessing the state of the place, comparing and learning. Max was still firmly by her side. 'You will not get an inside ticket, my lord.'

'I will travel in the basket if necessary,' he vowed, turning aside to the ticket office while Bree handed her bag to the guard.

It seemed things were not that bad, for Max emerged with a ticket for the roof. 'But what about your carriage? And your plans? It takes seven hours to Aylesbury—we arrive at nine at night. You must stay over and leave at seven in the morning to get back.' She regarded him helplessly. 'My lord, there is absolutely no need for this.'

'All aboard the *Despatch* for Aylesbury!' The guard began to chivvy the passengers.

'My groom will sort things out—my people are quite used to me taking off with no notice. I fancy another stagecoach adventure. Let me help you inside.'

Bree gave up, let herself be handed in, and wedged herself into a corner seat along with the other five passengers who made for a full inside complement. She just hoped that Max was not too uncomfortable on the roof and that the *Despatch* was not carrying its maximum of twelve outside passengers. It really was no place for a man with an injured shoulder, whatever he said about how well it was healing.

She fretted about him for a while, then came to the conclusion that she could not worry about a grown man as she could about her brother, and let herself enjoy the warm glow of knowing that he was concerned about her.

The disconcerting pang of physical attraction she felt for him had not diminished, she realised, then smiled faintly. She could hardly be more chaperoned than she was now, rattling along, jammed in with five strangers while Max was stuck on the roof. They might exchange a few words at the stops along the way, then she'd be off in a hired chaise to the farm and he would be left to find lodgings in Aylesbury. Tomorrow morning the whole exercise was be repeated.

What did he think he was protecting her against? Highwaymen? It was hardly likely that a full stage, in daylight and with a guard up, would attract an attack.

'Do we stop at Stanmore?' the stout woman opposite her demanded.

'Yes. The second stop,' Bree answered automatically, earning herself affronted looks from the four men in the coach who all obviously thought they were better fitted than a woman to respond. 'The Bell. Then we stop at Watford, Hemel Hempstead, Berkhamsted and Tring. This is a slow coach,' she added.

'I consider it perfectly acceptable,' a thin man Bree decided was a clerk huffed.

'At under six miles an hour?' she retorted.

By the time they pulled into the Blue Anchor in Edgware, Bree felt it politic to step down for a few minutes. She had won a comprehensive argument about speeds, distances and change-times and was well aware that the male occupants of the coach were regarding her with disfavour for her unfeminine assertiveness.

Max swung down beside her. 'Are you all right?'

'Oh, yes. I just wanted the air. How are you? Have you persuaded the driver to give you the ribbons yet?'

'No. He is deaf to my pleas. Shall I offer to kiss him? That worked with the last stagecoach driver I encountered.'

'It did not!' she retorted. 'You did not kiss me until—oh! Stop it, people will hear.' She scrambled back into the coach with a singular lack of dignity and stayed put firmly until Berkhamsted, when need drove her into the King's Arms in search of the privy. Max was standing at the taproom door, a tankard in one hand, when she emerged. Bree marched past with her nose in the air and was mortified by his chuckle.

What with the undercurrent of anxiety about Uncle George, Max's behaviour and her own irritation with herself for caring what he did or thought, Bree was unable to doze and arrived in Aylesbury yawning, stiff and in no mood to deal with importunate gentlemen.

Then she saw Max climbing down from the roof of the coach. He seemed awkward somehow, and when he got down she saw him sway and put out one hand to steady himself. He closed his eyes for a moment and straightened up with an obvious effort. When he saw her watching him, he smiled. 'I'm amazed I can stand up straight after seven hours on that roof.'

'I told you,' she scolded, hastening to his side. 'Honestly, you are as thoughtless as Piers, travelling all that way in discomfort with a bad shoulder, just on a whim.' She glanced round. It was dark, it was becoming chilly, there was a hint of wet in the air and, if he could not secure a room here at the busy Eagle and Child, he would be left scouring the town for lodgings.

'You had better come with me,' she said resignedly, picking up her portmanteau and walking towards the office to secure a chaise for the short drive out to the farm. 'Uncle George has plenty of spare room.'

'Miss Mallory, I assure you I am perfectly all right.' He made to take the bag from her and she wrestled it back, noticing the sudden tightening of his mouth as her action jerked his arm.

'Humour me, my lord. Shall we say I feel the need for some protection for the last leg of the journey?' *Honestly, men! They are so transparent. His shoulder is obviously paining him, but he thinks I haven't noticed. But how am I ever going to persuade him?*

Chapter Twelve

Max bit the inside of his lip to control the grin of triumph that was threatening to give him away. That had been almost too easy. He had hardly needed to do more than flinch a little and move stiffly and Bree had leaped to the conclusion that he needed looking after. 'Thank you,' he said, attempting to sound as though he was having to struggle with his pride to accept, and was rewarded with a sharp nod.

So now they were on their way to her uncle's farm, and Bree thought it was all her own idea.

The notion had come to him out of the blue as she explained her anxieties. It gave him time in her company and it enabled him to find out more about her family. Max might feel more and more sure that Bree would make a wife who would suit him admirably, but he was not about to make the same mistake twice and plunge another woman into a world that was totally alien.

A postilion came out and mounted up; Bree did her

best to lift the bag into the carriage herself, but this time Max won and did it himself, helping her up and settling back on to the worn squabs with a quite genuine sigh of relief. He was conscious of her directing a sidelong look at him from under her lashes, an entirely feminine trick that made his lips twitch with appreciation.

'Tell me about your uncle,' he suggested. 'How will he take you turning up on his doorstep, unchaperoned and with a strange man?'

'Uncle George?' Bree bit her lip in thought. 'Do you know the old tale about the two mice? Well, Uncle George is the Country Mouse and Papa was the Town Mouse. George is quiet, unmarried, a little bit reticent and very hardworking. I do not think for a moment that he will remember that he ought to be worried about my travelling unescorted with a man, although I expect Betsy, his housekeeper, will give me a scold and will watch you like a hawk for signs of decadent London propensities.'

'Such as?' Max demanded, intrigued.

'Getting drunk, pinching the kitchen maid—I don't know *what* goes on in her imagination, but she always seems amazed when we visit and haven't sunk into some slough of moral turpitude as a result of London's corrupting influence.' She brooded a little. 'What exactly *is* turpitude?'

'Let me show you, my pretty.' Max produced a convincing leer and laughed as Bree batted him with her reticule.

'Idiot!' She smiled, reminding him all over again, as if he needed it, that she had a mouth that was made for kissing. 'You are much nicer tonight. You were so stuffy when you called the other day.'

'Was I?' He knew perfectly well he had been. He had bored himself, let alone the two women. 'I expect I was trying to behave with propriety.'

Bree produced a noise that he assumed was the lady-like equivalent of a snort. 'It does not suit you. How is your shoulder now?'

'Much better,' he assured her truthfully. 'Are we there? That was a short journey.'

'Yes, this is it, only a mile of lane to the farmhouse now. There is just the one large house, for both farms. In my great-grandparents' time the land was split into two for two brothers, but they shared the house. It came back together and was split again for my father and uncle. Uncle George will leave his farm to Piers and it will all come back together again.'

'Unconventional,' Max commented. He peered out of the window as the chaise turned right, through high gateposts and into a wide courtyard. The house that stood there was illuminated poorly, but he could see enough to send his eyebrows up. 'That's not so much a farmhouse, more a medium-size manor house!'

'I know. Despite what the Farleighs think, we are

really quite respectable, despite having to work for a living. Thank you.' Max jumped down, flipped the folding step out and handed Bree from the carriage as the front door opened.

'Miss Bree! Why, I didn't look to see you for a few weeks yet.' A comfortably rounded, middle-aged woman held up a lantern and peered at Max. Her expression changed from beaming surprise to suspicion. 'And who might this be, Miss Bree? I don't see your maid.'

'This is Lord Penrith, Betsy. My lord, this is Mrs Hawkins, the housekeeper here.'

'And what are you doing, gallivanting about the countryside with a man, might I ask, miss?' Max tried for an expression of sober reliability and was rewarded with a glare.

Bree hustled the housekeeper inside. 'Betsy, it is trying to rain and we are tired and hungry. Please, let us in before we talk any more.'

They gained the hallway and stood on the stone flags while Mrs Hawkins shut the door on the damp darkness outside. 'Are you married, Miss Bree?' she demanded, turning from this task and wiping her hands on her apron.

'No!' they answered together, with equal vehemence. Max found himself regarding Bree apologetically, while she looked equally abashed at her unflattering reaction.

'Lord Penrith is a friend who very kindly offered to escort me on the stagecoach, Betsy,' Bree said repressively. 'Now, I would like you to make him up a bed in one of Uncle's spare bedrooms, but first, tell me quickly, what is wrong?'

'Wrong? Why, nothing, Miss Bree. What should be wrong?'

'I had such a strange letter from Uncle George, I felt I had to come straight away. Are you sure he is all right?'

'Why, yes, Miss Bree.' The housekeeper frowned. 'He's made some new friends, goes out more than he used to, which is a good thing. He's always been a bit solitary, has Mr Mallory.'

It was on the tip of Max's tongue to ask about these new friends, but he stopped himself. It was Bree's family business.

'Where's your luggage, sir?'

'*My lord,*' Bree corrected, looking harassed. 'Lord Penrith kindly came to my aid at very short notice and has no luggage. He will need to borrow razors and so forth. And a nightshirt. I'll show Lord Penrith to the blue bedroom, Betsy, and you let Uncle George know we're here and find something for our supper, if you would be so kind.'

'Show a man to a bedchamber! You'll do no such thing, Miss Bree. And your uncle's out—I don't know when he'll be back.'

'Out?' From Bree's blank expression Max could only deduce this was a rare occurrence in the evening. 'Well, I'll just have to sit up until he gets in. I do hope it won't be too late because I was planning on catching the seven o'clock stage tomorrow morning. And I will show his lordship to his room, so don't fuss. Lord Penrith is a friend of Viscount Farleigh.'

The mention of Bree's half-brother was obviously a guarantee of respectability. The housekeeper unbent a trifle. 'I'll bring hot water up in a moment, Miss Bree. The bed's all made up, like always, and I ran the warming pan through all the beds only yesterday, so it won't be damp.' She began to make her way towards the back regions of the house. 'Mind you come down directly now, miss!'

'Yes, Betsy.' Bree rolled her eyes at Max and began to lead the way upstairs, lifting a branch of candles off the side table as they went. 'Piers keeps spare razors and things here, although I doubt his shirts will fit you. I'll see if any of Papa's things are to hand.'

'I would not like you to feel you must lend me those. It is my fault I am without a change of linen. I would not put you to the pain….'

'Not at all. They are clean and pressed and really I should be giving them away to a deserving family, but I simply have not got round to it. You are kind to show such sensitivity, but Papa would have hated to see good clothes go to waste.' Her smile was sweet and just tinged with sadness and it made him want to take her in his arms and hold her, gently.

'Bree…'

'Here we are.' She threw open a panelled door before he could act on the impulse and stepped into an antique chamber with an uneven boarded floor, exposed beams in the ceiling and panelling on the walls that glowed richly in the candlelight. Deep blue hangings around the four-poster bed and at the windows explained the name of the room.

She set down the candles on the dresser and went to run a hand between the sheets. 'That's fine. If you could set a light to the fire, I will go and find those things for you. Better if Betsy does not find us in here together.'

'Bree.'

'Yes?' She paused on the threshold, turned and smiled at him. It was enough to overturn all his good resolutions to keep his distance.

Max took one long stride and caught her to him. 'Bree, don't worry.' She quivered in his arms, then, when he did no more than hold her, she sighed wearily and laid her head on his shoulder. 'What is it you fear?'

She shook her head, unaware of the havoc her closeness was creating in him. 'That he is ill, or becoming confused, or that there is some problem with the farms that he is not telling us about. I had better stay,

I think—it was foolish to think I could deal with this in a few hours.' She tipped back her head to look into his face. 'Will you let Piers and Rosa know, when you get back?'

'I am not going back without you.' Max put one hand on her head and turned her cheek back into his chest. That was much safer; if she looked up at him again like that he was going to kiss her, and from the vehemence of her reaction when the housekeeper had asked if they were married, that was unlikely to be welcome. 'And you must try not to imagine things before you see your uncle. He could simply have been having a bad day—the housekeeper has noticed nothing, has she?'

'No, no, she said as much. You are quite right.' Bree let her cheek rest against the soft warmth of Max's linen shirt and closed her eyes. She was being foolish in worrying; Uncle George would be mildly baffled by her descent upon him and everything would be fine.

The comfort of having someone to lean on was unexpected. For years she had been the one leant upon and had accepted it as her lot in life. Now... Without conscious thought she moved her head a little, like a cat butting against a caressing hand. Through the linen she felt the press of something hard and realised it was that scandalous stud. She moved again and felt, rather than heard, his indrawn breath. Max's heartbeat was more pronounced.

What had he said about it? That such things were considered erotic? Touching certainly had an effect. His long fingers slid into her hair, whether just to hold her, or to hold her still, she could not decide. But it brought her to her senses. It was not fair to him to be like this, especially not in a bedchamber and especially not after his reaction to Betsy's embarrassing question had been so vehement. Men's physical responses, she had to remember, were often quite at odds with their deeper feelings.

'I had better go and fetch those things,' she murmured, stepping back. 'Betsy will be along with your hot water in a moment.'

His hands opened, freed her, and he let her go, his smile perfectly bland. But his eyes were dark and intent, denying the soothing message of that smile. Bree found her skin was tingling. 'I won't be a minute.' She not so much left the room, as fled, scurrying down the long passage to the door that led into the part of the house she and Piers owned. Inside Piers's room she leant back against the door and tried for some coherent thought.

For the past few days she had tried to convince herself that Lord Penrith merely wished to pursue an acquaintance that centred around his interest in driving. To believe anything else was to yearn after a relationship that was impossible. Today, on the journey, she had been too irritated by his cool assumption that she needed him to look too closely at her own feelings.

Now, fresh from his arms, she made herself think. She liked him, she wanted him... Bree made herself stop and be honest with herself. Wanted both his company and his friendship, and wanted him, as a man, in her arms and in her bed.

And that was quite impossible. She was not going to take a lover, or be taken as a mistress, and that was that. She had promised herself a love match and she was not going to settle for a few nights of passion. Always assuming that was what Max wanted.

Bree shook her head, more to clear it than to deny her thoughts. When he had kissed her at the ball he had overstepped the bounds of propriety by several long strides. And yet, he had stopped well before things got out of hand, and had done nothing that she had not wanted.

Since then he had kept his distance. Tonight his embrace had been almost one of friendship, if one disregarded that indrawn breath, the beat of his heart, the awareness that she had sensed. It was far from what she imagined the actions of a man seeking an immoral connection would be. And anything else was highly unlikely, given her parentage and his title. It was not as though she was such a great beauty that society would be dazzled by her, as it was by the Gunning sisters, years ago. Nor had she great wealth, that other passport into the ranks of the aristocracy.

The clock down below in the hall chimed. Bree shook her head again, this time with determination. One could hardly stand around like a moonling, brooding. Piers's razors were on the dresser. She began to gather them up, adding shaving soap and a badger-bristle brush, and securing them in a linen towel. She found a neckcloth in one drawer, one of her father's shirts in another and added them to the pile, then sat down on the end of the bed, her burst of practicality ebbing away.

Logic told her that Max was simply acting as a good friend, that he was interested in coaching and had no ulterior motive. The kisses, the hint of arousal when he held her, those were doubtless perfectly normal male responses and she was such an innocent that she was refining upon them too much.

An elder brother to confide in would be helpful, Bree thought with a rueful smile. She could hardly ask Piers how a man might be expected to react with a woman in his arms; the poor boy would be mortified, and she sincerely hoped he had no experience to draw upon.

I could ask Georgy, Bree mused, getting a grip both on herself and the bundle and heading back for Max's room. But how discreet would Lady Lucas be? Would she guess what Bree was worrying about, even if she worded her enquiry in the most general of terms?

'I thought we had agreed that you were not going to worry.' Max's voice startled her so much she almost dropped the things in her arms. She was standing outside the open door of his room and he was just inside it, in his shirtsleeves, neckcloth discarded. 'You are frowning.'

'Oh! No, I was not worrying. Not exactly. I was thinking about something else entirely.' Bree thrust the shaving tackle and clothing into Max's arms and turned on her heel. 'I'll see you downstairs for supper shortly.'

'Thank you.' She had almost made it to the end of the corridor when his voice stopped her. 'Bree? What are you blushing about?'

'I…absolutely nothing,' she said with as much dignity as she could muster. 'I am doubtless red in the face from hanging upside down in the chest in Piers's room looking for a neckcloth.'

Oh, stop trying to fool yourself. She shut her own chamber door safely behind her and stared into the steaming bowl of water Betsy had set ready on the dresser. *You're in love with the man.* If this were a fairy tale, the steam would clear and there would be some message, some guidance, visible in the clear water. All there was in her basin was a rather pretty design of roses on the bottom of the bowl. It was no help whatsoever.

Betsy, who had apparently decided to acquit Max of being a dangerous rake, or at least, to give him the benefit of the doubt, served them a supper of hot pot and vegetables. She refrained from hovering in the dining room, as Bree rather feared she would, instead leaving the door pointedly open.

'I do wish she wouldn't do that,' Bree grumbled as the candles on the long oak table flickered wildly. 'It is creating such a draught.'

'She is ensuring that I am not going to take advantage of you and ravish you while we are alone.' Max helped himself to the buttered cabbage hearts. 'Foolish, of course, I am far too hungry.'

Bree smiled somewhat wanly at the sally. The way she was feeling, it was far more likely that she would do something scandalous than he would. She searched for a safe topic of conversation.

'Where do you get your horses from, my lord?'

He raised an eyebrow at the formality, then his eyes flickered to the sturdy figure of Betsy, coming in with the mustard pot, and he nodded in comprehension.

'From a number of sources, Miss Mallory. Some direct from Ireland—my hunters mainly—others through private sales or at Tattersalls. Do you breed all your own horses for the company here?'

'Mostly, unless we come across something suitable at a bargain price. I have a yen for having all our horses one colour—grey would be smart, I think. No other coach company does that. But Piers and Uncle George think me frivolous for entertaining such an idea.'

'It would be an advertisement. People would clamour to travel behind your match greys.' Max grinned at her. 'But I can't quite make that fit your slogans. You don't fancy chestnuts, do you? The *Challenge Coach Company's Champing Chestnuts* has a fine ring.'

'Chestnuts are too temperamental,' Bree said repressively, finding her sense of humour rather lacking when he chaffed her about the company. She was missing the bustle of the yard, even after only a few days of handing much of her work to Rosa. The thought of cutting herself off entirely was painful. But her involvement with the company was yet another reason why there could never be anything between her and Max.

'You're looking down in the dumps Miss Bree.' Betsy set a large rhubarb pie in front of her. 'There's no need to fret about Mr Mallory, you'll see. I'll just go and get the cream for you.'

'It is only that I am tired,' Bree confessed to Max,

picking up a spoon to serve the dessert. 'I do wish he would come home soon.'

'Why not go to bed after supper?' He accepted a portion of pie and reached for the cream. 'I'll sit up and wait for him and wake you up when he gets back.'

'On the contrary, it is you who should retire and rest. There is your shoulder for one thing, and you are a guest.'

'A self-invited one! But let us both sit up, then. Mr Mallory will come in after a pleasant evening with friends and find us both scandalously asleep on the drawing-room sofa.'

Bree had always liked Uncle George's drawing room, but now she wondered how it would look to Max's sophisticated gaze.

'What a charming room.' He wandered about peering at the walls, crammed with pictures of everything from Great-aunt Emeline to the pig that won the Best in Show at Buckingham three years ago. Piles of books were stacked everywhere, nearly all of them to do with hunting, fishing or horse breeding, and the table was littered with accounts ledgers. 'One could never make the mistake of believing that this room belongs to a married man.'

'Indeed not. I think it must run in the family. Papa was always in trouble with Mama for being so untidy and Piers would revert to this state in two days if I let him, but Uncle George takes no notice of Betsy's nagging.'

She looked around the room. 'Really, I do apologise. I feel I ought to be entertaining you in some way. In fact, there is a piano over there, under all those journals, but I fear it will be sadly out of tune.'

'A hand or two of cards, perhaps?'

'If we can find a pack. Uncle George does not play, but there are probably some in our drawing room.'

'There are two packs here.' Max held one up. 'They look quite new.'

'How peculiar.' Bree came across to look. 'Perhaps he has taken up patience. We will have to play for farthings—any more and I am certain you will bankrupt me.'

'I would not dream of it.' Max lifted some papers off a small side table. 'Shall I deal? We can play for love.'

Chapter Thirteen

They were playing for love and she had won. The cards lay in wild disarray all over the baize table cover; the scores, totalled in Max's rather sprawling hand, showed a clear victory: hers. So she could claim all the love that she wanted, everything she desired, Max was hers...

'Bree! Wake up.'

'Wha—?' She jerked into consciousness and found she was curled up in her chair and Max was looking down at her with an amused expression on his face. The cards were strewn over the table, her own hand all higgledy-piggeldy where she had dropped it. 'Who won?'

'I did.' Max began to gather up the pasteboard rectangles. 'If you mean who stayed awake longest. I think your uncle is home. I heard wheels on the gravel just now.'

'Oh, goodness.' Bree got to her feet, found that her left foot had gone to sleep, and hopped painfully to peer in the spotted mirror. She patted her hair back into something like order and smoothed down her skirts. Max was looking perfectly composed. 'How long have I been asleep?'

He glanced at the clock. 'About an hour. It's half past one.'

There were sounds from the front hall. Bree hurried to open the door. 'Uncle George!'

'Bree? Well, bless my heart, what are you doing here, child?' Her uncle turned from the foot of the stairs and came towards her, a candle in his hand. With relief she saw he looked much as usual, although perhaps his face was a trifle thinner, his hair a little whiter. 'Are you well? Is something amiss?'

'That's what I came to ask you.' Bree reached up a hand to his shoulder and kissed his cheek, cold from the night air. His breath smelt of brandy. 'You wrote such a strange letter, we were worried about you.'

'I did?' He frowned in puzzlement, but followed her as she turned back into the room. 'I don't recall that.'

'Here.' Bree took it out of her reticule and offered it. Her uncle took it, started to read, then coloured.

'That nonsense? I was in my cups, started scribbling some maudlin stuff—I thought I had burned it. That old fool Betsy must have posted it instead.' A movement arrested his attention. 'Who's this?'

'Lord Penrith, Uncle. Max, this is my uncle, Mr

George Mallory.' *In his cups? But Uncle George hardly touches a drop of liquor.*

The men shook hands, George frowning. 'You two are not married, are you?'

'No!' they both chorused again, with such emphasis that Uncle George looked startled. It was really embarrassing the way this household took one look at the pair of them and jumped to that conclusion. Max must be mortified to deny it so vehemently.

'I am a friend of Miss Mallory and her brother,' he said, collecting himself. 'When I discovered Miss Mallory was intending to make this journey by stage with no escort, I offered to accompany her.'

'I see.' George Mallory looked at the cards scattered on the table, then glanced away again. He seemed unsettled, but not, apparently, by his niece's behaviour in sitting up half the night, unchaperoned, with an earl. 'You should be in bed, child. Look at the hour.'

'I came because I was anxious about you, Uncle. If everything was well, I intended to leave again on the morning coach, so there would be no time to speak then.' Bree took his hand. 'I am sorry, I have worried you, arriving like this.'

'There is nothing wrong.' Her uncle fixed her with a direct stare from under beetling grey brows. 'Nothing at all. I can't have you rushing about the place every time I do something foolish. Now, off to your bed with you if you're to be up first thing tomorrow.

I'm expecting you and Piers to stay in a few weeks, aren't I? How is the boy?'

'Much better, Uncle. He sends his love.'

'Better from what?' he demanded.

'From the pneumonia.' Bree regarded him anxiously. 'Don't you recall? I wrote to say he had to come home from Harrow to recuperate.' Out of the corner of her eye she saw Max beginning to edge tactfully towards the door and shook her head at him. He stopped.

'Oh, yes, so you did.' Her uncle seemed to pull himself together, becoming, in the flickering candle- and firelight, someone closer to the vigorous man she had left after her last visit. 'Nothing the matter with me, child. No need for you to stay.'

'Betsy—'

'What's she been saying?'

'Just that you had made some new friends.'

'Aye, so I have. And what of it?'

'Nothing. I am glad.' Bree bit her lip. He seemed fine, if slightly forgetful and somewhat irascible. But perhaps that was simply to be expected with advancing years. 'I will stay if you would like me to, Uncle.'

'No, I thank you. You be off back to London in the morning and keep an eye on that young whippersnapper of a nephew of mine.' He swung round and regarded Max. 'Don't expect I'll see you again, my lord. I thank you for your escort for my niece. Goodnight to you both. I'm off to bed.'

Bree stared at the door as he closed it behind him. 'Well,' she said blankly. 'What did you think?'

Max shrugged. He had walked to the table and was gathering up the cards. 'I don't know him. The cards appeared to worry him, don't you think? Far more than my presence. In his shoes I'd be demanding what the devil was going on with my niece.'

'And he'd been drinking, although he was far from drunk. Perhaps his rheumatism is troubling him. I suppose I had better do as he says and go back to London and Piers and I will take our holiday a little earlier this year.' She broke off and yawned hugely. 'Oh, excuse me! I really must be off to bed.'

Max held the door open for her. 'What do you think, truly?' she asked as he followed her into the hall.

'That he is hiding something. But unless you intend to move in and interrogate him, I am not sure what you can do about it.' Max lit a branch of candles from the one he held. 'My great-aunt became very secretive as she got older. That is probably all it is.'

'Of course. Thank you, Max.' For a moment she thought he was going to say something, then he bent and kissed her, lightly, on the cheek.

'Goodnight, Bree. Sleep tight.'

'There you are! How is he?' Piers demanded as she arrived home half way through the next afternoon, tired, stiff and hungry.

'Is Mr Mallory well?' Rosa set aside a piece of sewing and got to her feet. 'I collect he must be, as you are back so soon.' She tugged the bell pull. 'You look in need of a nice luncheon and a lie down.'

'Oh, yes, indeed I am,' Bree agreed, tugging off her gloves and tossing them and her hat onto the sofa. 'Uncle seems in good health, but, Piers, he had been out, visiting new friends and drinking brandy, which is not like him at all. And he seemed very happy to send me on my way the next morning.' She sat down with a sigh and put up her feet, most improperly, on the fender. 'He says he wrote the letter in a maudlin moment and meant to burn it, but Betsy must have posted it. Max agrees with me that Uncle is hiding something, but goodness knows what.'

'Max? You mean Dysart was with you?' Piers demanded.

'Lord Penrith to you,' Bree corrected. 'He saw me catching the stage and insisted on escorting me. It did his shoulder no good at all, so I felt I had to invite him back to the house.'

Piers, to her relief, appeared to find nothing odd about this, but Bree could feel Rosa's eyes boring into her. She turned and raised one eyebrow with what she hoped was a cool assumption of indifference.

Her companion merely picked up her sewing again and remarked, 'How very gallant of his lordship.'

Braced for criticism or comment, Bree felt curiously

deflated. She wanted to talk about Max, she realised. She could hardly tell Rosa that she was falling in love with the man, but she had at least expected exclamations and discussion, something to give her the opportunity to speak his name. She jumped to her feet. 'I will go and wash and change. That stage was decidedly grubby.'

'Yes, dear,' Rosa said cheerfully. 'That's a good idea.' *Maddening!*

Max sat back in his deep armchair in the book room at the Nonesuch, tapping the folded letter he had just received from Ryder against his knee. It had been short, and couched in the code they had agreed upon. *The originators of the work of art you have lost have moved away. I believe they may have gone to Winchester and I am following that trail. The painting itself has not been seen at its place of origin since it left in your possession.*

Max stuffed the letter into a breast pocket and tried to control his impatience. After all this time it was not to be expected that Ryder would come upon the definite proof he sought in a day or two. He weighed up strolling along to Watier's to eat, as against staying here where the food was less refined, but the company more likely to distract him.

'Dysart, there you are.' It was Brice Latymer.

Max nodded. 'Latymer.' His dislike of the man was

instinctive, but he habitually suppressed it, unwilling to create bad blood amongst club members. Latymer was a poor sport, and had an unpleasantly jealous streak, but it was simpler just to ignore him.

'You were going to give me the direction of that Irish breeder you recommended for heavy hunters.' Latymer dropped elegantly into the chair opposite.

'So I was.' Max fished his pocket book out. 'I have it here, I think—but what's your interest? I imagine you ride too light to be after one yourself.'

'My uncle—the rich, unmarried, one—rides sixteen stone. I thought I'd put myself in his good books with a recommendation. He must be due to remake his will about now. He does it every year.'

'Yes, here it is.' With an inward wince at the blatant greed, Max found the page and made to pass it over.

Latymer stretched out a hand and then hesitated. 'Jot it down for me, there's a good fellow. I don't have a notebook on me.'

Repressing a sigh, Max got to his feet and walked across to one of the writing tables set in alcoves around the wall. By the time he had found a pen with a good nib, scrawled the address and sanded the sheet, Latymer was on his feet studying the portrait hanging over the mantel.

'Prosy old bore that one looks,' he remarked. 'Thanks very much.' He made to go, then half-turned. 'I'm looking forward to that outing you've arranged with Miss Mallory and her stagecoach. Very dashing young lady that, admire her no end.' With a flash of white teeth he was gone, leaving Max glaring after him.

Dashing young lady indeed. He should say something to Bree about Latymer. He turned back to his chair, wrestling with the problem of warning a young lady about a fellow club member when one had no basis for the warning and no standing with the lady. He was trying, damn it, to keep his relationship with Miss Mallory on a very sensible footing for both their sakes, and wanting to punch on the nose any man who mentioned her name was not conducive to that.

Something crackled under his right foot and Max stooped to pick it up. It was Ryder's letter. It must have come out when he pulled out his pocket book. Max jammed it back and strode out of the room. Watier's be damned, he was going to Pickering Place to bet deep in one of the hells over a bottle or two of claret.

'So do *you* actually *drive* a stagecoach, Miss Mallory?' Bree's hand jerked reflexively with the shock, sending a glass of champagne splashing all over a towering arrangement of dried flowers in Lady Lemington's salon.

'What?' she demanded, making Miss Holland, the wide-eyed young lady who had blurted out the question, squeak in surprise.

Lady Lucas had persuaded Bree to come along to the evening reception on the grounds that she would make many new acquaintances who also knew James and his betrothed. As she was determined to do her best to present a conventional front and not embarrass her half-brother, she had to agree it was a good idea.

What she had not expected was to be pounced on by a gaggle of young ladies, very newly out, who had obviously decided that she was dashingly different and that it would be great fun to talk to her. Bree felt rather like a hound she had once observed in the stables being mobbed by a boisterous group of spaniel puppies, all bounce and wagging tails. Like the hound, she was too good natured to snap at them—until Miss Holland's question.

'Only Mr Mallory was telling us all about the stage-coaches and how he can drive.' Miss Holland, and several of the girls, cast lingering glances at Piers, who was deep in conversation with several of the Nonesuch Whips and blissfully unaware that his profile was attracting the attention of susceptible young women. 'And we've seen you driving in the park, you do it ever so well, and it seems so dashing to drive a stage-coach...'

Bree could feel herself becoming flustered, and struggled for composure. It was the effect of a guilty conscience, she knew full well. If it had not been for that scandalous drive, which had so nearly ended in disaster at Hounslow, she would probably have been quite happy to admit that she had taken the reins once or twice, in a purely private setting. Now she felt so self-conscious about it that she could hardly choke out the denial.

'Of course I do not. That would be a most scandalous thing to do,' she began, aware, even as she spoke, that she was protesting too vehemently.

'No lady would do such a thing,' a smooth, faintly amused voice added at her elbow. Brice Latymer fixed the gaggle of girls with a smile that was half-reproof, half-flirtation and which reduced them all to simpering giggles. 'You have quite put poor Miss Mallory to the blush. Run along and bat your eyelashes at Mr Mallory and no doubt he'll tell you exciting tales of highwaymen.'

They fluttered away, too bashful, Bree was glad to see, to go to talk to Piers. 'Oh, thank you, sir.' She turned to him with a heartfelt sigh. 'It would be such a trial for my half-brother if that sort of rumour got about, and it is so difficult to deny without sounding over-emphatic.'

Mr Latymer tucked her hand under his elbow and steered her in the direction of the refreshment room. 'Of course it is,' he agreed, holding out a chair for her and snapping his fingers at the waiter. 'Champagne. And lobster patties, I think, unless you would care for a sweetmeat?'

'No, lobster would be delightful.' Bree began to ply her fan.

'Of course, it is particularly difficult to deny when it is the truth,' Brice Latymer said so smoothly that for a second his words did not penetrate.

'I…you…whatever do you mean, sir?' She hoped she was sounding suitably outraged and feared she was managing only to be guiltily flustered.

'I mean no criticism, Miss Mallory. You drive a pair with exceptional skill for a lady. The way you take up the ribbons and the way you attack turns and gateways makes me think you have experience driving something much bigger—and you do have the vehicle to hand, as it were.' He tipped his head on one side and regarded her with a twinkle. 'Not that I would dream of making that observation to anyone else, I assure you.'

'I…' Bree made a decision. 'My father taught me to drive four in hand, privately, on our land. My brother Viscount Farleigh would be horrified if it were known, and it would make me seem so fast.'

'It will remain our secret, and you need have no fear that I will tease you about it.' He let his hand rest lightly on hers as it lay open on the table and Bree felt a flood of relief wash through her. Reflexively she let her fingers curl into his; he squeezed and released hers. 'Now, let us talk of other, safer matters until those delightful roses in your cheeks fade a little.

'How is your uncle, the one you were so concerned about the other day?'

'I went to visit him, and it seemed to us...' She hesitated, aware of the slip, then decided he would assume she had gone with Piers. 'It seemed that there is something strange about him. But there is nothing I can put my finger on. We will go and stay for several days in a few weeks' time. That will give us a better chance to observe him.'

Their refreshments came, and after a glass of champagne, and a delicious patty, all accompanied by Mr Latymer's sprightly commentary on their fellow guests, Bree felt decidedly better. He might be a little waspish, and she suspected he was probably not safe company for very young ladies, but she found Mr Latymer refreshing.

'I gather our picnic expedition to Greenwich Park on Saturday has been confirmed,' he observed, raising a finger to the waiter who was passing with a tray of delectable sweetmeats and nodding encouragement to Bree as she took one.

'Yes. Our spare coach is free that day, and I have a new team I am rather pleased with.' They just happened to be chestnuts, by happy coincidence rather than deliberate planning, and she smiled to herself at the thought of Max's ridiculous slogan. *Champing Chestnuts* indeed!

The day itself had been arranged by dint of the exchange of exceedingly formal and impersonal notes. *Lord Penrith presents his compliments to Miss Mallory and begs to enquire if she and Mr Mallory are able to join the Nonesuch Whips with one of their equipages on Saturday 10th September for a picnic expedition to Greenwich Park. If it is not convenient to use one of their own conveyances, he begs the pleasure of their company as his guests...*

If it had not been for the invitation, Bree would have concluded that Max was avoiding her again after that strangely intense journey into Buckinghamshire. At least, for her it had been intense—for him, she had no idea. Max's thoughts about her, his motives, remained a mystery.

'Miss Mallory, Latymer.' *Max.* She had conjured him up just by thinking about him. Bree suppressed the foolish, superstitious thought and managed to plaster a polite smile on her lips.

'My lord. I had no idea you were here this evening.' *Or else I would have spent the entire day in a foolish state of dither over what to wear, how to do my hair, what I would say to you.* She was aware of Mr Latymer's cool gaze upon her and strove for composure. 'May I recommend the lobster patties?'

'I find I have little appetite this evening, Miss Mallory,' he rejoined politely and she realised that his eyes were not on her, but were clashing with Mr Latymer's.

'I am looking forward to the picnic on Saturday,'

she said brightly. The atmosphere had changed; if she had not known that the sky outside was clear and the stars twinkling she would have thought thunder and lightning were imminent, her skin prickled so.

'As am I, Miss Mallory. May I hope you will do me the favour of travelling in my drag?'

'I had just invited Miss Mallory to travel in mine,' Latymer interjected. *Had he? Did he ask me while I was daydreaming about Max?*

'I will travel out with Mr Latymer and home with Lord Penrith,' she declared brightly, then realised she had succeeded in satisfying neither man. She ought to feel flattered that they were bristling over her—rather, she felt a stab of something not far removed from fear. Their antagonism was real, not the joshing rivalry of friends.

'I was first in this matter,' Mr Latymer said tightly. 'You do not like to yield point, do you, Dysart?'

'I never yield what is mine,' Max said tightly. 'Miss Mallory, until Saturday.'

'My lord.' She nodded politely, her stomach tightening with tension. *What is his? Just what does* that *mean?*

Chapter Fourteen

The small household at Gower Street was in turmoil, a state which neatly mirrored Bree's own state of mind. She had spent two days attempting to put her thoughts and emotions into some kind of sensible state and was aware of failing miserably.

Rosa was managing her work at the Mermaid magnificently, which had the effect of making Bree feel that her own nose was thoroughly out of joint. In this, at least, she understood her own feelings. She had believed herself indispensable and had found that she was not, a discovery that was a salutary lesson.

And she was not yet comfortable with her newly acquired leisure and her status as a slightly shady member of the *ton*. If truth be told, she found most of the parties dull, shopping soon palled and she had found no close friends amongst her new acquaintances other than Lady Lucas and Mr Latymer.

Bree grimaced, knowing that her long habit of reticence and self-sufficiency was holding her back from making new friends. In time, no doubt, she would learn to confide and share.

But what did she feel about Max? *No.* She stopped that line of thought and corrected herself. She knew exactly what she thought of the Earl of Penrith: she was in love with him, fool that she was.

What does he think about me? Now that was the real question. Goodness knows, was the honest reply. Lust? Friendship? Mild liking? But what explained the fact that he would drop everything to travel in thoroughgoing discomfort on the roof of a stage just in order to keep an eye on her? Or that he would kiss her very comprehensively in the course of an evening, and then subject her to a dull afternoon call and formal invitations to what should be a very informal event?

The spare coach, gleaming from top rail to wheel hubs, stood outside, causing a minor traffic jam in Gower Street and enormous entertainment for every street urchin for blocks around. The chestnuts were, indeed, champing at the bit, and she had a nasty feeling she was going to receive confirmation of the generally held belief that horses of that colour were flighty and unreliable.

William Huggins, an enormous nosegay stuck in the buttonhole of his many-caped greatcoat, sat on the box. He was good-naturedly flicking away urchins with his whip, making them shriek with delight as the whip-point snapped just behind their skinny buttocks without making more than a great deal of noise.

Their most experienced groom was up behind, the yard of tin polished until it gleamed, and the domestic staff were packing the last items into not one, but two, bulging picnic hampers.

'Raised pork pie, gooseberry tart, a pound of butter—don't squash that!—the ham's in that cloth...' Cook scurried about, checking things off her list while Piers supervised the stowing of a keg of ale, a half-dozen bottles of wine and jugs of Cook's celebrated ginger ale and lemonade.

The arrival of Brice Latymer's drag, all gleaming dark blue lacquer, brass rails and with a team of handsome greys, put the finishing touch to the chaos in the street. Bree was aware of her neighbours' curtains twitching, the heads of curious staff poking up out of service areas and even one or two front doors opening surreptitiously.

'I had better go with Mr Latymer,' Bree said to Piers. 'At least that will help unblock the street. Now, you know where we are all meeting up in Green Park?' She tipped back her head to look up at Huggins. 'You understand? You yield the ribbons to whichever of the Whips they decide, and you take over his drag unless he has brought a second driver, in which case you sit up behind with Pratt.'

'Aye, Miss Bree, whatever you say, though it's much

against my better judgement. I just hope they can all drive as well as his lordship.' *His lordship* was, no doubt, Lord Penrith.

'I don't think anyone can match him—except you, of course,' she added hastily. 'But they are all very good drivers. And you'll let Piers take the ribbons as well.'

'Aye, Miss Bree.' The coachman jerked his head towards Latymer's drag. 'That one know what he's doing?'

'I hope so, Bill.' Bree grinned, relaxing into familiar banter with her oldest friend. 'He'd better, starting off right under your nose!'

Max circled his drag in behind the array already drawn up just inside the park. There were ten, twelve when Latymer and the stage joined them. He had drawn up a list of drivers to take turns with the stage and had extracted the sworn word of all of them not to race—or face his wrath.

Now as they gossiped and joked, tossing friendly insult from box to box, he thought about the letter he had just received from Ryder.

It seems more than probable that all of those responsible for producing your art work perished in an epidemic of smallpox, which ravished Winchester seven years ago, the enquiry agent had written. *I am in the process of checking all the parish registers in the city—it may be that this will lead directly to the fate of the article in question.*

In other words, Drusilla probably perished with her family. It would explain the total silence. He shuddered inwardly at the thought of that horrible disease, struggling, yet again, with the knowledge that his own easy release from this coil meant the confirmation of his wife's death.

A rise in the volume of noise around him jerked Max back to the present. Latymer's drag, dashing behind its match greys, came through the gates to join them, and, behind it, the *Cheltenham Challenge*, driven with an emphatic flourish by a burly coachman he recognised, entered the park to a long blast on the horn.

To a man the Whips applauded and the coachman, every inch the showman, took a bow. Max grinned, his dark mood forgotten, and waved to Piers, perched up on the box, serious in his many-caped greatcoat. He waved back, suddenly looking more fourteen than seventeen.

Then he saw Bree looking out of the window of Latymer's drag and it was as though something had sucked the air out of his lungs. 'Sir? My lord?' Gregg, who had remained silent beside him throughout his brooding abstraction on Drusilla, sounded mildly agitated.

'What?' Max pulled himself together and looked at

his team, who were sidling uneasily. His right hand had clamped down on the reins, quite unnecessarily. He lifted it off, steadied them with his voice. 'Sorry, Gregg, I wasn't concentrating.'

'Not to be wondered at, my lord,' the groom re-marked with the familiarity of a man who had known his employer since he was learning to ride. 'The young lady makes a right lovely picture in that blue garment. A pelisse, is it? Goes a treat with Mr Latymer's paint-work.'

'Mind your tongue,' Max snapped, caught himself, and added ruefully, 'She does, doesn't she?'

'Are we expecting an announcement in that direc-tion, my lord?'

Gregg was one of the servants who knew about Drusilla. 'Possibly. It is not something I would wish talked about.'

'Certainly not, my lord. Do you think I'm a pick-thank, to be gossiping about your business all over?'

'No, but take care, all the same. There's a lady's reputation to consider.'

'Aye, my lord. We'll be off then.'

Viscount Lansdowne had drawn first drive with the stage and changed places with William Huggins, who was grinning like a youngster at the prospect of driv-ing the viscount's blacks. Piers stayed up on the stage. Max could see him earnestly explaining the foibles of the team to Lansdowne. A likeable lad that, he would enjoy having him as a brother-in-law. He caught himself up; it was too soon to think like that, far too soon to be able to make any commitment to Bree.

Bree leaned back in the comfort of the drag and listened with half an ear to Rosa's enthusiastic comments on the vehicle. Other than the space taken up by Mr Latymer's contribution to the communal picnic, they had the interior to themselves.

'It is so lavish,' Rosa commented, running a palm over the well-stuffed, tightly buttoned cushions. 'This is best serge, and I am sure he has had it dyed to match the livery.' She began to rummage about, playing with all the fittings. 'Look at these door pockets, and what are those cords in the ceiling?'

'For gentlemen's hats.' Bree roused herself from gazing at the landscape in a sort of daydream. 'The brims fit under the parallel cords and the hat hangs down.'

The drag lurched and she peered out of the window with more attention. 'Mr Latymer is not as smooth a driver as his lordship.'

'Which lordship?' Rosa kept her face straight, but Bree sensed she was being teased.

'Lord Penrith. I have not driven in a four in hand with any of the other gentlemen.'

'Of course. Silly me.'

Bree narrowed her eyes at her companion's teasing,

but made no comment. From wanting nothing more than to discuss Max Dysart the other afternoon, she felt she could hardly bear to mention his name, such was her state of unsettling preoccupation with him.

The stops to enable the various gentlemen to take over the stage made the journey to Greenwich longer than it would normally be, but finally they arrived at the sloping parkland with the Observatory perched above them and the palace below.

Bree and Rosa allowed themselves to be handed out of the drag and on to the close-cropped turf, smiling in delight at the view that spread out before them over the Thames. Servants clustered round, lifting out the picnic hampers from the various vehicles and carrying them off to the spot where the meal was to be taken.

The drivers set down their passengers and then moved the drags on to various patches of flatter ground. The grooms began to unharness the horses and lead them off under the shade of the trees where an impromptu horse-line had been set up with hay nets and water buckets.

'It is all very well organised, Mr Latymer,' Bree commented as he led her and Rosa over to a spot where they could watch without being caught up in the bustle.

'We usually bring the same grooms, and the servants come on ahead with rugs and cloths and so forth. Everyone knows the routine.' They watched in companionable silence while the last hampers were lifted out and carried away to the picnic area. 'There now, nothing left to do but enjoy ourselves,' Latymer observed.

'I see we are not the only lady passengers,' Rosa commented. 'Look, Miss Mallory, there are the Collins sisters, and is that Lady Harrison I can see over by the oak tree?'

'Do you mind if we stroll over and greet our acquaintances, Mr Latymer?'

'Not at all, Miss Mallory. Perhaps you will give me the pleasure of pointing out some of the landmarks to you after luncheon.'

With that agreed, the ladies made their way down the slope to join the small group who were finding cushions and rugs and making themselves comfortable.

'Miss Mallory, do join us!' The three Collins sisters waved and Bree strolled across, leaving Rosa chatting to Lady Harrison, her daughter and her companion.

'The gentlemen have all deserted us.' Miss Collins, the eldest of the three and a pretty red head, laughed. 'They always do, of course. I do not know why I am surprised. They would like us to think they are engaged in earnest discussion of matters of substance, but we know they are only talking about horses and prize fights.'

Bree found a cushion and settled down between

Miss Jane and Miss Catherine. 'You came with your brother?' She followed their gestures to where the men stood round the stagecoach, all in vigorous discussion with William Huggins. 'Oh dear, do you think they will spare us any of their attention with such a distraction?'

'Well…' Miss Collins pouted comically '…I am used to being cut out by that spiteful cat Augusta Harrison, but I've never been ignored for a red-faced man with three chins before!'

'Ah, but that red-faced man is Bonebreaker Bill,' Bree explained. 'It is not every day you have the opportunity to talk to a legend.'

'And he works for you?' Miss Jane asked.

'For my brother,' Bree said firmly. 'Oh, look, the gentlemen are coming to join us at last.'

They were straggling down the hill, still intent in discussion of the stagecoach, as was obvious from their hand gestures. Bree watched and waited. Max was heading directly for them. She caught his eye, smiled and felt the curve of her lips freeze as he nodded pleasantly and went to sit on the rug next to Lady Harrison.

'Humph,' Miss Catherine observed inelegantly. She lowered her voice to a conspiratorial whisper. 'Do you think Lord Penrith is having an affair with Lady Harrison? They do say her husband's hardly ever at home.'

'Why ever should you imagine such a thing?' Bree

demanded. She knew why she felt so snappish, but what she did not know was why she had so confidently expected Max to come to her side. *As though we belong together.*

'Well, they do say that his heart was broken, years ago, which is why he has never married. So I expect he has lots of lovers.'

'Really?' That was what Lady Georgy had said. Bree knew she should not be gossiping, not about such a subject. It was like sucking a sore tooth: painful but irresistible. 'What happened, to break his heart?'

'No one knows, or at least, if they do, they are not telling unmarried girls. It is very mysterious. But he is so eligible and you would think he'd want to marry for an heir, wouldn't you? So there must be something in it.'

'Nevill Harlow's his heir, isn't he?' Miss Collins turned large green eyes towards Nevill, who was sprawled inelegantly under the shade of a lime tree in earnest discussion with Piers. 'I did think he was rather young, but if he's going to be an earl one day, perhaps he's more interesting than I thought.'

'I am sure Lord Penrith will marry sooner or later,' Bree said, squashing the subject. 'Look, they have finished setting out the picnic. What a wonderful spread.'

The young ladies got up and strolled over to admire the combined contents of all the hampers. Footmen were setting out piles of cushions and rugs under trees and a trestle table had been set up for the drinks.

'Allow me to find you a comfortable cushion and fetch you a plate, Miss Mallory.' It was Max, with his disconcerting habit of appearing at her elbow when she least expected him.

'Thank you, my lord. I must confess to being very sharp-set. Do you always feast so lavishly?' She sank down on to the cushion Max found for her and looked up at him, narrowing her eyes against the sunlight that filtered through the branches.

'The picnics are generally excellent,' he admitted. 'Although it can vary—they are best when we have several ladies with us. When we eat at inns it is usually good. Now, what would you like?'

For you to sit down next to me and tell me how you feel about me, and not sit and flirt with Lady Harrison, that is what I would like. 'Oh, anything—a nice mixture of what is there. Surprise me if you can,' she said lightly as other ladies were escorted to the surrounding seats and they were no longer alone.

Bree was completely inexperienced with the rituals of courtship, and half the time she was convinced that Max felt nothing for her than friendship. Then he would say something, or she would catch his eyes on her, and a strange shiver of awareness would pass through her as though they had exchanged a thought, or an emotion. Did he feel it too? Or was she just fooling herself that there could be anything between an earl and the daughter of a yeoman?

Or was he working up to making an improper proposal? She did hope not. Strangely, despite the fact that in her heart of hearts she knew they had no future as man and wife, and despite feeling certain that she was in love with him, Bree felt not the slightest fear that she would succumb to such temptation if it were offered.

The memory of Max's kisses were like some tale she had read over and over—utterly familiar, imprinted on her memory, but unreal all the same. Her body still stirred when she thought of them, but she was confident that this physical temptation could be resisted, if it ever came again. It could lead nowhere and she was not such a fool as to throw her hat over the windmill for a few moments of passion. She knew that, for her, a loving marriage was the only relationship she would accept.

'Miss Mallory?' He was back, a plate in each hand and one of the footmen behind him holding glasses. Bree smiled her thanks and accepted her plate, expecting Max to sit beside her. But he handed the second plate to the person at her side. 'Lady Harrison. I hope you both have a pleasant meal.'

Bree stared after his broad back as it retreated down the slope to the next group of diners. 'Oh.'

She had not realised she had spoken aloud until

Lady Harrison remarked, 'Did you expect Lord Penrith to join us?'

'No. No, of course not.' *Protesting too much...* 'Why should he?' That was not much better, implying there would be no reason why he would wish to take luncheon with Lady Harrison.

'Penrith is not much given to the company of young ladies,' the older woman observed, with a sideways smile at Bree's carefully blank face. 'He takes great care not to entangle himself.'

'Very wise, I am sure,' Bree responded sweetly. 'After all, I am certain he can find plenty of married ladies to *entertain* him. Shocking, of course, but such is society, I gather.'

Lady Harrison's expression acquired a touch of acid. 'That is a bold observation for a young lady in the marriage mart to be making about her elders.'

'But I am not on the catch for a husband,' Bree corrected politely. 'I have no expectation of making a match, so I find myself freer to call a spade a b—' she caught herself just in time '—a shovel.' She forked up a little kedgeree with composure. 'This is truly excellent.' But her eyes rested on the familiar head below her.

Bree passed the rest of the meal in silence. Lady Harrison, affronted, turned her shoulder, and Rosa had become absorbed into a group a little farther along. She had scanned the area before she sat down, had seen Bree in apparently harmonious conversation with Lady Harrison, waved and left her to it.

This gave Bree ample opportunity to review her own sharp tongue and lack of discretion, the unreliability of certain gentlemen and the folly of love. It could not be said to improve her digestion.

'Miss Mallory, might I suggest a short stroll before dessert?' It was Mr Latymer. She was so glad to see him that she scrambled to her feet with unladylike speed.

'Yes, I should like that, thank you.'

'There is a most excellent vantage point, just around here.' Brice Latymer waved a languid hand towards a stand of trees. 'The views to the river are delightful.'

Bree cast a look down the slope to where Rosa sat, deep in conversation. She should not really go wandering off alone with a man, but this was Mr Latymer, for goodness' sake, and surely it was not much different from driving alone with a gentleman in the park, an unexceptional activity.

The clump of trees was thicker, and larger, than she had imagined. And there was no view, merely a glade opening up. She turned, puzzled, and suddenly apprehensive.

'Miss Mallory.' Mr Latymer took her hand, making her jump. 'Bree. You cannot be unaware of my feelings for you.'

'Mr Latymer!' Bree tried to tug her hand free and

found it held tight. In fact, the movement brought her closer to him. How had she ever thought his gaze friendly and bland? It was hot, fierce and, she groped wildly for a word, *greedy.* 'Mr Latymer, please let me go. I have no idea what you are referring to.'

'Do not be so coy. Marry me.'

'No! I mean, I am conscious of the honour you do me, sir, but I do not feel that we should suit.' *There, that was what one said, was it not? Now he will let go, bow and remove himself.*

But Brice Latymer had not read the same stories that Bree had, or if he had, he showed no inclination to follow the script. He pulled her hard against him, bent his head and took her mouth. Instinctively Bree tried to scream and found that all she had done was to open her lips to him and to his tongue. It was every bit as horrible as she had imagined, before her experience with Max had shown her how pleasurable kissing could be. It obviously depended totally on the man doing the kissing.

'Stop it!' She managed to wrench her mouth free, only to be jerked back and held against his body, which was hard, hot and very obviously aroused. 'I do not wish to marry you, sir! Let me go!'

'Tease,' he said breathlessly. 'You know you want it, want me. You've given me enough encouragement, damn it.' She tried to push him away, but for all her strong wrists she found she was helpless. 'Marry me.

I know about horses, I'll help the business, I'm not too proud to marry trade.'

'No!' This time there were no polite words to soften her refusal. 'Let me go!'

'Not until you're ruined.' He was panting with the effort to hold her, but for all her struggles he was still too much for her. 'Another ten minutes in here and you'll have to marry me, Bree Mallory, whether you want to or not.'

Chapter Fifteen

'Where is Miss Mallory?' Nevill asked. All through the meal Max had been aware of her presence behind him, of her gaze on his back. Instinct told him she was not pleased to be deserted. This conclusion produced a certain smug male satisfaction at the thought that she cared, but he was riding his emotions on a tight rein with Bree. All his instincts told him that he was free to hazard his fortune with her. All his judgement and caution warned him against making that assumption, or to exposing her to speculation and gossip. If he were wrong about Drusilla, the consequences would be awful.

'Behind us, just up the slope with Lady Harrison,' he said lazily. But even as he spoke he knew he was wrong. She wasn't there, that sensation of being watched had left him. Max rolled round on to his elbow to look up the hill. There was no sign of Bree.

'She has probably gone into the ladies' retiring carriage,' he murmured, nodding towards the vehicle with its drawn blinds that had been set up for the comfort of the ladies, who could not be expected to vanish into the surrounding shrubberies as the men could.

Nevill blushed. 'She isn't. I glanced that way just now and Miss Collins was entering it.'

'Why do you want to know?' Max rolled over until he was facing up the slope and could survey all the scattered groups. A sense of unease gripped him, which was ridiculous; they were in the middle of a civilised English park, surrounded by friends.

'I wanted to ask her if I could visit their breeding stables. I asked Mallory, but he said his sister was a little concerned about their uncle's health and might not agree.'

'Yes, she is anxious about him.' Max got to his feet and climbed up to where Lady Harrison was sitting, spotting Rosa admiring someone's sketch book as he passed. 'Did you see where Miss Mallory went?' he asked, as Melinda Harrison favoured him with her cool smile.

'She went off with Latymer, about five minutes ago.'

'Alone?'

'As far as I can see. That young lady is a sad romp.'

'In which direction?' He was not going to waste time defending Bree's good name, or asking why a supposedly responsible matron had let her wander off unchaperoned with a man; time for that when he was assured that she was safe and sound.

Lady Harrison waved vaguely towards the east. 'That way, I think.'

Max strode off, his eyes scanning the ground ahead as the grass sward curved around, out of sight behind the big stand of trees. Surely she would not be so imprudent as to actually enter the woodland?

The sound of a scuffle ahead made him break into a run; as he rounded the bend he found himself in a small clearing in the side of the wood. Bree was hard up against a tree, Latymer holding her and kissing her, despite her frantically kicking feet.

Max heard a snarl, realising with a jolt that it was coming from his own throat. He was across the clearing without being conscious of moving, then his hand was on Latymer's shoulder. He heaved the other man back, turned him and let fly with his left fist.

Latymer sprawled on the ground at his feet. Across his prone body Max met Bree's wide eyes. The pupils were almost black, her face white, her hair disordered and her bonnet fallen to the ground. Very slowly she slid down the tree trunk until she was sitting on the short grass, her eyes never leaving his face.

Max found he had stopped breathing and drew in a deep breath. Then he saw that the neckline of her bodice was dragged down, that the delicate upper swell of her breast was exposed, and this time he had no trouble knowing where the snarl was coming from.

'Max!' It was Nevill, hanging on to his arm. 'You can't hit him, he's down.'

'That can be remedied.' Max stooped, seized Brice Latymer by the neckcloth and hauled him, choking, to his feet. 'Have you any objections if I kill him now?'

'You must not.' Nevill, with more courage than Max knew his cousin possessed, was hanging on to his arm like a pitbull terrier. 'You will have to call him out,' he stammered. 'I'll be your second.' He looked as white as Bree, and as though he were about to cast up his accounts.

Max released his grip on Latymer's neckcloth. 'Name your friends.'

Brice staggered back, clutched a low branch for support, and croaked, 'I apologise. Completely. Miss Mallory...' He turned to Bree, who met his gaze squarely. Her eyes were chilly, although her lower lip quivered. Max wanted to hug her. 'My feelings got the better of me. I apologise a hundred times over. My behaviour was inexcusable.'

'*What?* You have the brazen nerve to even attempt to apologise to the lady after mauling her like that?' Max felt his fists clenching. 'Name—'

'You cannot.' It was Nevill again, tugging at his sleeve. 'You really can't, Max, not if he's apologised.' He frowned, biting his lip. 'Can you?'

'No one I've called out has ever apologised before,' Max admitted, glaring at Latymer in furious frustration. 'But you are probably correct, not if the lady accepts his apology.' He looked across at Bree. 'I cannot imagine for a moment that she will find it acceptable.'

'Someone said to me, quite recently, something that is apropos to this situation,' she said. Her voice shook a little and he forced himself to stand still and not to make matters worse by going and dragging her into his arms in front of witnesses. 'Let me see, what was it?' She frowned. 'Oh, yes. *It is a sad fact that a lady, incautiously without chaperonage, may find herself kissed, or worse.* Not that I am excusing Mr Latymer's behaviour, but I should have been more cautious.' She shot Latymer a hard look. 'I accept your apology, sir, but I hope never to find myself in a position where I have to exchange a single word with you, ever again.'

'You are most generous, Miss Mallory.' Latymer was red in the face, his usual pose of cool, languid indifference shattered. 'Believe me, it was the passion of the moment, the effect of your—'

'Latymer, if you are not out of my sight in one minute, and out of this park in ten, I will call you out for being a chicken-hearted coward in front of the entire club.'

Latymer bent to pick up his hat and walked away without another word, his gait stiff, the back of his neck crimson.

'Nevill, go and find Miss Mallory's companion.' Max hardly dared move to touch her. He was so angry that he was afraid that if he did, if he felt her tremble, he would go after Latymer and kill him.

'No. No, please do not tell Rosa.' His heart ached at the courage it must be taking for her to keep her voice steady and to smile reassuringly at Nevill. The lad was shaking with reaction now, appalled to his chivalrous core by what he had seen.

'Mr Harlow, would you be very kind and find Miss Thorpe and tell her that I have taken a walk with Lord Penrith to see a good view of the Thames? It will be the truth, it is what I thought was going to happen when I agreed to walk with Mr Latymer. I will tell her what happened later, but I do not want to have any—' Her voice wavered and she got it back under control with a visible effort. 'Any fuss,' she finished, rather desperately.

'Of course.' With a job to do that did not involve the hideous etiquette of the duel, or the sight of a lady battling tears, Nevill rose to the occasion with aplomb. 'I will see if Miss Thorpe has had any dessert yet, and if she has, I will see if she would like to take a stroll in the opposite direction.' He bowed, with all the formality of the ballroom and strode off, pausing at the edge of the clearing. 'And if Latymer hasn't gone, I'll see that he does.' He marched off, a young knight, ready to do battle for a lady's honour.

'Oh, dear,' Bree said faintly. 'He isn't going to get into a brawl, is he?'

'No,' Max assured her. 'Latymer will be gone too fast for that.' He wanted to go to her, hold her, kiss away the taste of Latymer's mouth on hers, smooth his palms over every bruise on her body. And he knew if he did that he would reveal his feelings for her as clearly as if he had handed her his soul to read.

He could not be in any doubt now: he loved this woman, he wanted to marry her and he had to protect her. Max drew in a deep breath. He could do this. He could fight his own feelings, do the right thing, take her hand and help her to her feet, escort her to the ladies' retiring carriage so she could put her dress to order, splash water on her face.

'Max.' Bree's voice quavered, her face crumpled, then she had it under control again. Her determination not to give in to tears tore at his heart. 'Max, please, just hold me.'

He could fight himself, but it seemed he could not fight her. Max went to her side, took her hands and lifted her to her feet. Bree smiled at him fleetingly, then simply slid her arms around him, under his coat, and leaned into his body with a tired sigh as though she was coming home after a long journey. His arms went round her, held her tight, and with a sigh that echoed her own, he laid his cheek on her tousled hair.

'That's better. I feel safe now.' She gave a shaky chuckle. 'I was an idiot. You are being very forbearing in not telling me so.'

'You were an idiot,' Max assured her gravely. *And so am I.* 'Bree, we really ought to get back.'

'Who will miss us?' She seemed quite content to hold a conversation with his top waistcoat button. 'Mr Harlow will distract Rosa. Everyone will be having a rest after luncheon, or strolling about admiring the views.'

Max lifted his head, found her chin and tilted her face up so he could look at her. 'And they'll be coming round that corner at any minute to find you in my arms.' *Just don't kiss her...*

'Oh.' She looked up at him, her shock temporarily forgotten in her concern. 'That would put you in an awkward position. I am sorry to be so thoughtless. Max, I really do not feel ready to go back. Is there somewhere we can sit, just for a little while, so I can compose myself?'

There was his drag, parked, as far as he could calculate, just beyond the edge of this copse. One might as well be hanged for a sheep as a lamb.

'Yes, of course. My drag is just through here.' He gently disentangled himself. 'I think you had better put on your bonnet and try and reorder your bodice.' Bree gave a gasp, tugged at the wayward neckline and restored herself to modest order. Max handed her the bonnet, then, when it was tied in place to hide the worst of the damage to her *coiffure*, tucked her hand under his elbow and began to walk back. 'If anyone comes, faint.'

'What?'

'Faint. You strolled this way to see if there was a view. You saw an adder. You screamed, I heard you, rushed to your side and am just escorting you back. If you faint, then that will cover up any amount of disorder to your gown and hair.'

'And what were you doing in the woods when I screamed?' Bree was sounding far more like herself now.

'That is the sort of question no lady asks,' Max said repressively and was rewarded with a gurgle of laughter that choked off as she struggled for control.

'I am sorry. I would have thought I could deal with something like that with ease, but I feel so shaky. It is truly feeble of me—I send young bucks to the right-about every day at the inn.'

'Why should you not feel shocked and distressed?' he asked brusquely. 'When you trust someone you do not expect them to attack you, or to betray your confidence. Snubbing young fools in a crowded inn yard is quite different from dealing with a determined attempt on your virtue, I would have thought.'

'True,' she agreed sadly. 'I thought he was my friend, which only makes it worse. Did you know he was…unreliable?'

'I have never liked him, and it is mutual. If I had

thought you in the slightest danger from him, I would have warned you.' *Could I have guessed? Should I have said something? That incident with her gloves in the park...* 'Here we are. Would you like to sit inside and compose yourself and I will go and fetch you a drink?'

The drag presented a safe wall between them and the open slope. Max opened the door and flipped down the step. Bree let herself be handed in, then turned, clutching his hand. 'Max, please don't go, just sit with me while I tidy my hair and find some balance.'

With a sensation that he was about to step off a cliff, Max followed her in and pulled the door shut. The solid shutters of the drag's windows were closed. He found the strap for the one on the side facing the wood and ran it down six inches, letting in enough light to show him her face.

Her big blue eyes were wide in the gloom, her mouth full, trembling as she smiled at him. Bree untied her bonnet, laid it on the seat next to her and began to unpin her hair. It was the stuff of his fantasies, of the heated dreams that had woken him, sweating and rigid with desire, for nights after their first encounter. In the stage, her unravelling plait had transfixed him. Now, helpless, Max watched the golden silk slide free, down, over her shoulders, and knew he was lost.

* * *

'Do you have a comb? I have just realised I left my reticule on the rug.' Freeing her hair, the routine of unpinning it, beginning to gather up its weight in her hands, was strangely soothing. She was a fool to be so feeble about this, Bree told herself. It was not as though she were some sheltered miss.

It was that kiss that had so revolted her, polluting the lovely memory of Max's lips on hers, turning something wonderful into something sordid and disgusting and violent. Max had given, Latymer had tried to take.

'Yes. Here.' Max held out a comb and she took it, their fingertips touching. His hand trembled, just faintly.

'What is it? Max?' Bree tossed the comb on to the seat beside her and caught both his hands in hers. His eyes glinted in the half-light, his expression was tense, focused.

'Your hair.' He freed one hand and reached out to touch it, just the very ends of it. 'I dream about your hair.'

Instead of answering, she lifted her hand, the one still holding his, and pressed his palm against her hair. 'Touch it then.' It seemed to enchant him. She did not understand, but she knew she wanted his hands on her, somewhere, everywhere. Her reservations, her certainty that she wanted nothing but marriage, wavered, shook under the impact of the reality of his closeness.

Max froze, then his hands slid into her hair, cradling her head. They were so close, opposite each other in the carriage, that her knees slid between his.

'Bree.' His voice was husky. 'Bree, I want to behave every bit as badly as Latymer did. I want to kiss you. I want to more than kiss you. Do you understand? You should not be alone with me. I should never have brought you here.'

They were not the words of love she dreamed about, and knew she would never hear from him. But they were words of desire. Max wanted her. She wanted him, loved him, and knew there was only one way she was ever going to have him. It went against everything she had been brought up to respect, it could ruin her if anyone ever found out. But suddenly she knew with utter conviction that she wanted it more than anything in the world, other than to hear him say *I love you.*

'Yes, I understand,' she said steadily. 'I understand what you want, and I want it too.'

'Bree.' His hands tightened in her hair. 'Bree, think what you are saying. If I am not careful you could be ruined. I could get you with child—'

'Then be careful,' she whispered, twisting her head to bring her lips against his wrist. Under the sensitive swell she felt his pulse, wild, hard, demanding, and knew she had to answer it.

'God. Bree—' Max did not move, as she had expected, to take her into his arms. Instead he just looked at her and in his eyes she could read a vast indecision. It seemed alien in someone as assured, so strong. It was as though he were weighing up a monumental choice. 'Damn it, ten years,' he murmured, so softly she was not certain she had heard him correctly. 'I *must* be free.'

Before she could puzzle any more he leaned towards her and took her lips. Her previous experience had been so limited to his kiss on the terrace and, just now, Brice Latymer's assault, that she would not have expected to be able to read anything into a kiss.

But this, she realised quite clearly, was a claiming. He wasn't rough, but he left her in no doubt that if she was thinking about any other man, then that was a mistake, because she was his.

She was crushed against his body, although quite how she got there she was not sure. Her mouth was open to him, his tongue was possessing her, thrusting, making it quite clear how he wanted this embrace to end. Bree shifted until she could lock her arms around his neck, and surrendered to the demand he was making.

Her own tongue, it seemed, knew how to respond. Gradually the fierce, possessive pressure eased and he let them both breathe. Daring, Bree nipped his lower lip, gently, and gasped as he responded by drawing her own lip into his mouth and suckling it with tantalising slowness.

Every part of her thrummed with desire, with a sort of abandon which she would have thought quite alien to her nature. But in Max's arms she was transformed into another creature altogether, someone she did not recognise, someone who lived only to be here, with him, like this.

He released her mouth and began to lick and nip his way down her neck while his fingers made short work of the hooks at the back of her bodice. Impatient, beyond shyness, Bree pushed at the lapels of his coat. He shrugged it off, then, his fingers tangling with hers, unbuttoned his waistcoat and tossed that to one side.

Bree wrenched at his neckcloth, pulled it free, dropped it just as her own bodice slid down, revealing her breasts, shielded only by the fine camisole. Max went still, his right hand cupped, just cradling the swell of her left breast. She should have been shy, blushing at his touch, but all she could do was to glory in the look in his eyes. He made her feel beautiful, desired, worshipped.

He bent his head and licked first one nipple, then the other, with the very tip of his tongue. The heat and wetness through the fine fabric made her gasp, shocked beyond belief at the effect of such a concentrated touch. The aching heat shot through her body, pooled in her belly, made her shift her hips in restless arousal and arch her back to bring his mouth closer.

He stroked the camisole down until she was naked to the waist, smoothing his palms, warm and slightly rough, over the curves of her breasts, his thumbs finding the sensitive points and tormenting them into hard, aching nubs.

Bree fumbled for his shirt buttons, began to free them, hardly able to focus over the waves of sensation Max was inflicting on her. 'Oh!' The skin of his chest was hot, smooth over hard muscle. Hair tickled her palms, then her questing fingertips found his nipples, and that tantalising stud, and rubbed experimentally.

They tightened under her caress as hers had done under his infinitely more experienced touch. His groan startled her more, giving her a glimpse of the power she had over him. She might be inexperienced, but he desired her, and she could give him pleasure.

'Witch,' he murmured huskily in her ear, making the fine hairs shiver along her hairline. 'Tell me what you want.'

'I want you to make love to me,' she gasped, 'for ever.'

Chapter Sixteen

'Rest assured, I intend to make love to you for as long as is humanly possible, Miss Mallory,' Max assured her, his attempts at a formal response somewhat spoilt by a gasp that was part laughter, part passion. 'I cannot promise eternity.'

She realised that his hand was sliding up her calf under her light muslin skirt, beneath the fine linen petticoat and shift, up to her knee where he paused, tickling gently around the soft back, his fingers tantalising on the silk of her stocking. Bree gasped against his neck, spreading her palm flat on his chest, pressing against the tautly erect nipples and the flat pectoral muscles.

Was he going to go higher? She shifted restlessly in his embrace. He had said he would be careful. What did that mean? What did he intend to do? Could he possibly calm the raging, restless fire that was making her want to beg and plead?

Max's hand found her garter, played for a second or

two with the warm flesh that swelled around its taut-
ness, then slid up the inside of her thigh.

'Ah!' She wanted to go limp and rigid in his embrace, both at once. She wanted to open her legs wan-
tonly and yet she wanted to arch up, press herself
against him. Confused, Bree buried her face in his
shoulder.

'Open for me, sweetheart.' His fingers were nudging intimately. Blushing, stifling her gasp of shocked
pleasure against his bare skin, Bree let her legs relax,
felt his fingers slide up into the hot, damp, intimately
secret part of her. It was torment, exquisitely embarrassing torment, and then his index finger touched
part of her that had her bowing up against the curve
of his palm.

He was waiting for her reactions, she realised hazily.
He knew exactly what he was doing, how she would
respond. He was playing her like a violinist playing
an instrument. He knew the music; she could only try
and sight-read.

'Oh, so sweet,' he was murmuring against her hair,
his lips gentling her neck, her ear, her cheek, all he
could reach as she burrowed into him, too shaken to
let him see her face. 'Let me in, love.' That questing
finger slid inside her, making her gasp louder. Restless, her head began to move on his shoulder until he
was able to capture her mouth. His tongue slipped between her lips as a second finger sheathed itself gently.

His thumb found the aching point that seemed to be the focus of all the sensation that screamed through her, and something began to build, a tension that racked her, demanding release.

Somehow, with some fragment of will she did not realise she possessed, Bree managed to focus. 'Max.'

'Mmm?'

'Max…oh!…Max, what about you?' Against her hip was the very obvious evidence of his arousal. Bree slid her hand between them and brazenly cupped it around the hard, hot swelling. One handed, he wrenched at fastenings, freed the fall of his breeches, and Bree found she was grasping hot satin over iron, heated flesh that throbbed under her grasp. She could not see, but she could feel, had enough room, just, to move her hand.

'Harder.' He gasped, resting his forehead against her head as she did as he told her, but his own relentless caress of her body did not stop. 'Move your hand up and…oh, God! Yes, like that.'

Cramped, thralled, racked with an almost unbearable tension at war with her desperate desire to pleasure Max, Bree surrendered utterly to sensation. Something was coming closer for her, and, she could tell from his breathing, for Max.

Now, now, a voice in her head screamed and the tension exploded, shatteringly, destroying thought and sight, leaving a pleasure that was almost pain, and the realisation that Max was with her, his own body reaching the release she had brought it.

'Oh,' she breathed softly. He had shifted her slightly in his arms and she slowly began to come back from wherever the ecstasy had cast her. Hazily Bree realised that Max was using his long shirt tails to deal with the evidence of his own release, while still cradling her gently.

'Are you all right, sweetheart?' He tipped her blushing face up to his and kissed her, lightly.

'Mmm.' She nodded, speechless with love and delight and shyness.

'I know you said to make love to you for ever, but I do think we ought to rejoin the others....'

Bree blinked at him, then sat up with a muffled shriek as reality slapped back the warm clouds of sensuality. 'I had forgotten where we are!'

'I rather thought you had.' Max dragged on his shirt and tucked it in, then lifted his cravat with a grimace, before beginning to tie it.

Bree smoothed down her skirts and struggled to fasten her bodice. Luckily the hooks were few and easy to reach over her shoulder. She tugged the bodice about until it sat smoothly and found Max's comb where she had dropped it on the seat. The only thing to do with her hair was to braid it tightly and bundle it under her bonnet.

Max, his coat on, was managing to look relatively

respectable, although his neckcloth would have shamed Piers's worst efforts. They looked at each other in silence for a long moment, Bree feeling the curling tendrils of satisfied passion and aching longing knotting in her stomach. She wanted to stay there, hold him, linger over the moment. The air was disturbingly musky, sending little messages of arousal through her nerves.

'What is that scent?'

'Sex,' Max said bluntly. 'Love making,' he amended more gently, reaching out to touch her flushed cheek with one fingertip. 'It is a good thing you are travelling back in this drag and not anyone else.' He opened the door cautiously and looked out. 'The coast is clear.'

'But Rosa! What is she going to think?'

'I'll leave the door open. Either she won't know what it is, or she'll assume someone has taken advantage of the empty carriage—but she won't know who.'

'I'll be looking so guilty, she'll guess,' Bree said glumly, taking Max's hand and jumping down.

'Do you feel guilty?' Max peered round the side of the drag, without waiting for her answer. 'Look, see that group just on the fringe of the wood? If you cut across the corner, down that little path, you can join them without them noticing where you've come from. They've got a telescope and they're looking at the view.'

'All right.' Bree picked up her skirts and began to

walk towards the path, then turned back. 'And, no, I do not feel guilty.'

'Neither do I, and I should. Bree, we won't be able to talk again today, not as I'd wish. I'll come and see you tomorrow.'

He was gone before she could respond. *What will he say tomorrow? Will he want to make me his lover? Can I? Should I? He won't feel he has to offer for me, surely?* She stopped dead, appalled at the thought. She had as good as begged him to make love to her, convinced that marriage was out of the question. But what if he felt honour bound to offer it? *I will have to refuse. I must be strong enough to do that*, she told herself as she slipped into the fringes of the group clustered around a telescope.

Then she recognised the bonnet in front of her. Rosa. Of all the bad luck, the one person in the party who could be guaranteed to recognise that this Miss Mallory was not the same person who had set out so blithely that morning.

With the uncanny ability to spot wrongdoing that Bree was convinced all teachers possessed, Rosa turned and looked at her. Her eyebrows lifted, but all she said was, 'Miss Mallory, do come and see this wonderful view.' As Bree passed her, Rosa added brightly, 'Oh, my goodness, do stand still one moment, there is a spider just gone down the back of your gown.'

The other ladies moved sharply away, the gentlemen averted their gaze, and Rosa rapidly undid the hooks on the back of Bree's gown and did them up again. 'There,' she said. 'All safe now.' She bent close. 'And in the right holes this time,' she hissed in Bree's ear, her expression promising a close interrogation, all the way home.

'Nevill.' Max emerged just behind his cousin who was standing, arms crossed, gazing belligerently out across the park.

'Latymer's gone, but I am keeping an eye out in case he tries to sneak back, the cur.' He curled a magnificent lip, which drooped ludicrously as he took in his cousin's appearance. 'What on earth have you been doing?' he demanded. 'Have you seen the state of your neckcloth?'

'Give me yours,' Max demanded.

'What?'

'Your neckcloth. Don't tell me you haven't got a Belcher handkerchief in the pocket of your greatcoat. Put that on instead.'

'But, damn it, Max, it isn't the sort of thing you wear when ladies are about,' he protested as Max propelled him ruthlessly towards the stagecoach.

'You're young, you are coaching-mad, they'll excuse you.' Max was unsympathetic.

'Oh, all right.' His cousin rummaged in a pocket

and came out with a red handkerchief, lavishly spotted with white. He unwound his own neckcloth carefully and handed it over to Max.

'Thank you,' He squinted in the panes of the stagecoach-door window as he arranged the still-crisp muslin. 'How's that?'

'Better than yours looked. But what on earth have you been doing? It was perfectly fine, even after you hit Latymer.' He stared at Max's impassive face, the thoughts chasing themselves across his countenance with vivid clarity. Max gritted his teeth and kept his face bland.

'Oh, Lord,' Nevill said sympathetically. 'Did Miss Mallory cry all over you? It's awful, isn't it, when they do that? I can recall Janey when she last got upset over some beau or other that Mama forbade her to see. She wept buckets. Flattened my neckcloth and made my shirt all soggy. I don't think I handled it very well, looking back. I think you have to pat them on the shoulder and go "there, there" or something.'

He panted after Max as he strode back up the hill. 'I'm glad she didn't cry all over me. Miss Mallory, I mean. I'm sure you looked after her much better than I would have done.'

With his cousin heaping coals of fire on his conscience, Max scanned the park. Everyone was gathering at the picnic spot again, the servants were packing up the hampers and folding rugs and the grooms were beginning to harness up the vehicles.

And there, chatting with apparent composure to the Misses Collins, was Bree, Rosa at her side. He veered off towards his drag, wanting to give Bree as much time as possible to gather her composure before confronting her again.

Tomorrow he would see her, tell her everything and reveal the uncertainties that lay ahead. He realised he had no idea how she would react, either to his declaration, his offer or his story.

He knew her too well, deep in his heart, to believe that she had gone into his arms expecting to trap him into marriage. She said that she wanted him, and wanted his lovemaking, with an innocent honesty that had held no calculation. She had trusted him not to go beyond the bounds of what was safe for her, and, thank Heavens, he had controlled the need to take all he wanted of her.

Honesty forced him to acknowledge that was partly because he dreamed of taking her on his own wide bed, seeing the swathes of her hair spread out on the dark green silk coverlet, watching her eyes on him as he loved her into ecstasy…

'My lord?' Gregg was standing patiently beside the off leader.

It was said that no man was a hero to his valet. Max had a feeling that that applied equally to head grooms. 'Have I been standing here long, Gregg?' he enquired mildly.

'About two minutes, my lord. You didn't say anything, but you had an odd smile on your face, sort of dreamy.'

'Thank you. I am not sure I wanted such a vivid description of my doubtless ludicrous appearance, though.'

Gregg grinned. 'No, my lord, sorry, my lord. Are we ready to go?'

'Yes.' Max swung himself up onto the high box. 'Miss Mallory and Miss Thorpe are over there.' He gestured with his whip. 'Go down, present my compliments and enquire if they would find it convenient to leave now.'

'Aye, my lord.' The groom touched his forehead and strode off. Max gathered the reins, brought his team up to their bits and watched the other drivers doing the same. He did not want to catch Bree's eye, not yet while that contact might undermine her composure. He had no illusions about how shaken she was feeling. He could not recall feeling this mixture of delight, uncertainty and anticipation since the time he lost his virginity to a willing and cheerfully experienced dairymaid, or since the first time with Drusilla.

No. Max steadied the leaders, who were becoming restive, and thought back into the past. This was not how it had been with his wife. With Drusilla there had always been that faint, nagging feeling of something not being right. At the time he had put it down to his own conscience pricking him for making a clandestine marriage; now he saw only too clearly it was an instinct of wrongness about the woman herself and his own feelings. He should have listened to it then. He should listen to his heart now.

Voices beyond his right shoulder brought him back to the present. 'There you are, ladies.' It was Gregg, ushering his passengers into the carriage.

'Thank you.' Rosa Thorpe's clear and pleasant tones. Nothing from Bree. Max found he was tensed, waiting for her voice. The realisation shook him with something that was almost resentment: he was being dragged from his comfortable state of emotional neutrality. He was having to feel again, and with that came the potential for hurt.

Gregg climbed up and settled down beside him. 'All tight and snug, my lord.' Max touched the wheelers with his whip and joined the cavalcade of coaches making their way back to London.

Bree sat very upright in the drag. Both window shutters were fully down, sparing nothing of her expression from Rosa's steady scrutiny.

'Well?'

'Well, what?' the ex-governess asked with a half-smile.

'Well, aren't you going to ask me about why my gown was done up wrongly?'

'If you want to tell me, I am sure you will. I am not your guardian, Bree, I am your employee.'

Bree flushed. 'You are my friend, and just now it feels as if you are my conscience.'

'You have a perfectly good one of your own, I am certain.' Rosa was smiling now. 'I may not be your conscience, but I can be your confidant. Or not, as you choose.'

'I very foolishly went for a stroll with Mr Latymer.' Rosa's smile faded. 'He attempted to kiss me. No,' she corrected herself, 'he did kiss me, he was trying to force himself on me, he demanded I marry him and he threatened to ruin me so that I had no choice.'

'Oh, my dear!' Rosa reached out and took her hand. 'I was unforgivably lax. I should have been keeping an eye out. I should have gone with you.'

Bree shook her head. 'I knew where you were, I just did not believe there would be a problem. I had not the slightest suspicion I could not trust him.'

'But what happened? Your gown—'

'That was not Mr Latymer.' Bree gritted her teeth and pressed on—confession was supposed to be good for the soul, wasn't it? 'Max and his cousin Mr Harlow found us. Max hit Mr Latymer—'

'Excellent!'

'He knocked him down and called him out, but Mr

Latymer apologised to me, very fully. He was over-come by his emotions, it seems.' Rosa snorted. 'Quite. But I felt I had to accept the apology, otherwise Max would have fought him.'

'Oh. Disappointing, for I am sure Lord Penrith would have given him a very salutary lesson. Still, there was always the risk of scandal, or an accident, so I suppose it was best avoided.' She frowned. 'How long did this cowardly attack take? For him to have undone your gown…' She hesitated. 'But, no, you said that was not him.'

'Um, no. Latymer did not do that.' Rosa's eyebrows soared. 'I was feeling very shaken. I asked Max to let me recover here, in his drag. I asked him to stay and keep me company. One thing led to another.'

'Indeed? How much of *another*?'

'Not that much,' Bree hastened to assure her. 'More than kissing, though. Quite a lot more,' she added in a burst of honesty.

Rosa brooded for a moment. 'He has made you a declaration?'

'No. No, he said he will call tomorrow, that we must talk. Rosa, I am not a suitable wife for him, not in his position, and I most certainly do not want to entrap a man into marriage just because things got out of hand when he was trying to comfort me.'

'Poppycock! If Lord Penrith was intending to com-fort you, that's what he would have done. He isn't a green lad like his nephew. He knows exactly what goes on between a man and a woman, and how he is going to feel and react, and he is perfectly capable of keeping things within bounds if he wants to.'

'I suppose so.' Bree twisted the cords of her reticule until they knotted and sprang free of her fingers. 'But he did not take advantage of me. I wanted him to make love to me, and if he had wanted to he could have seduced me utterly. And he didn't. I am definitely still a virgin,' she added earnestly.

Rosa's lips twitched. 'I am glad to hear it. I have no wish to spend days anxiously watching the calendar!' She pondered while Bree gazed out of the window and hoped her blushes were subsiding. 'You know, I think Lord Penrith has sent you a very clear message. He did make love to you and yet he behaved with restraint and consideration. I think you may expect a perfectly honourable offer of marriage, my dear.'

'But I cannot. That would be dreadful.' Worse even than if he made her an improper proposal.

'Why?' Rosa demanded. 'You have some highly eligible connections.'

'When Mama remarried, James's grandfather took him away from her and hardly allowed contact again, so shocked was he at the match. James treats us as an embarrassment he can barely trust not to disgrace him and even Lady Georgiana thinks I should aim for a younger son. She did say something the other day about Max, but I think her enthusiasm for matchmaking is getting the better of her.

'And,' Bree pursued relentlessly, as much to school her own wild fantasies as to convince Rosa, 'we are in trade. It isn't even as though I sit at home like so many merchants' daughters, behaving genteelly and avoiding all contact with the business. I have been running it.'

'I agree with everything you say. But Lord Penrith is a powerful man with his fair share of arrogance,' Rosa observed. 'I imagine that what he wants, he takes, and to hell with the consequences.'

'Then I must make even more of an effort to do the right thing.' Bree tried to find some inner tranquillity by watching the passing scene, but it could not hold her attention. 'You know, Rosa, there is some mystery about Max. This afternoon he murmured something, just before he…just before. He said something about ten years and being free.

'You don't think he made some vow of celibacy after the incident that people whisper about? They do say his heart was broken. And at the ball he asked me what I would say if I knew he had some scandal in his life.'

'A man like that, in his early thirties, will almost certainly have attracted some scandal along the way, I would have thought,' Rosa pronounced.

'James excepted.'

'Yes.' Rosa's smile tugged at the corners of her mouth. 'It is hard to imagine your half-brother indulging in anything reprehensible. But the remark about ten years is odd, I agree. I cannot imagine Lord Penrith remaining celibate for ten days, let alone ten years. Not with that mouth, those eyes. He is a man of very well-developed passions, I would judge.'

'Rosa!'

'I am not blind, am I?' her companion enquired with dignity, which was somewhat spoilt by the twinkle in her eyes. 'Your Max Dysart is a man of experience and I would judge his wife will be a fortunate woman.'

'Not that I am likely to find out,' Bree murmured. And whatever else he felt, he did not love her—if he did, surely he would have said so in the course of that passionate encounter?

Chapter Seventeen

'Lord Penrith, Miss Mallory.'

Bree bit her lip and glanced down at the simple lines of her muslin morning gown. She had been determined not to dress up and look as though she was expecting a proposal from an earl; now she worried that she was insultingly underdressed.

'I must go and write to my aunt,' Rosa announced, folding the *Morning Post* and laying it to one side. 'I will say good morning to his lordship on my way past.'

'Don't go!'

Rosa sent her a look compounded of affection, exasperation and encouragement. 'Show his lordship in, Peters.'

'Yes, Miss Thorpe.'

Her companion disappeared on the heels of the footman, leaving Bree with the sensation that she had been cast adrift.

Rosa's voice carried clearly from the hallway. 'Good

morning, my lord, what a pleasant day we had yester-day. I do thank you for it.'

'Good morning, Miss Thorpe. It was my pleasure, and of course the Whips are indebted to Miss Mallory for arranging the coach.'

They were chatting just outside the door while she sat there in the grip of panic, feeling as though she were about to have a tooth pulled or worse.

'Do go in, my lord,' Rosa said brightly. 'I have a little errand, but Miss Mallory will be delighted to receive you.'

The door, which had been left ajar, opened and Max came in, closing it behind him. 'Good morning, Bree. *Are* you delighted?' His voice was deep and gentle and lightly teasing.

'Of course,' she responded brightly. 'Good morning, my lord. Please, do sit down. Would you care for some coffee? Rosa will be back in a moment.'

His expression was politely disbelieving. 'I think we are safe for some time, and no, thank you, I am not in need of refreshment.'

'Oh.' Bree found she was perched on the edge of the *chaise* and made herself sit back and arrange her limbs with rather more grace. 'I had a delightful day yesterday. I so enjoyed the drive and the picnic.'

'And the rest of the day?'

'Not the encounter with Mr Latymer, disgusting man. I must thank you again for rescuing me. I am intending to write to Mr Harlow today to thank him also for his support.'

'And no doubt the drive back was delightful?'

'Indeed it was. I have to say that you drive far more smoothly than Mr Latymer, my lord.'

'Thank you.' Max inclined his head gravely to acknowledge the compliment. 'Which leaves us with just one part of the day to discuss.'

'Yes.' Bree made herself keep her head up and not seek refuge in looking at her clasped hands. 'I...I acted very improperly and I am most grateful for your restraint in not taking advantage of my forward behaviour, my lord.'

'Will you please stop calling me *my lord* every sentence?' he demanded.

'No. I do not think I will, my lord. I have allowed myself to get into the way of addressing and treating you with undue familiarity. I am sure it contributed to what occurred yesterday.'

'Ah. So you characterise that incident in the drag as improper, forward and the result of undue familiarity, but you feel I did not take advantage of that undue familiarity, do you, Miss Mallory?' His voice was very quiet and calm. Bree found she had wrapped the ribbon that trimmed her bodice into a tight knot round her thumb. It hurt.

'Yes.' She disentangled her thumb, frowning down

at the crumpled dark blue satin as though its wreck was a matter of the utmost importance.

'Would you be surprised to know that my friends consider me adept at keeping my temper under control? That I am, in fact, renowned for that control and that they try, on occasion, to make me lose my temper for a bet? They do not succeed.'

'I am not surprised, my lord. I saw you lose your temper yesterday, but you very soon had your emotions under restraint.' Her own emotions were threatening to escape, either in a fit of hysteria or a demand that he leave at once before she said anything rash, like *I love you.*

Max got to his feet with a suddenness that took her completely by surprise. He covered the space between them in one long stride, took her firmly by each arm, just above the elbows, and hauled her to her feet.

'Well, observe me about to lose my temper, Miss Mallory, because I assure you, one more *my lord* out of you, one more attempt to dismiss what happened yesterday as the result of some kind of foolish imprudence on your part, and I swear you will experience the full force of it.'

She was very firmly held, although Max was not hurting her. She wondered hazily what would happen if she screamed, or struggled. She ought to feel afraid after the way Brice Latymer had manhandled her yesterday, but she was not. All she felt was warm, agitated in a deliciously arousing sort of way and anxious, although she was not certain about what.

'What are you going to do?' Her mouth was quite dry, her knees were rapidly turning to jelly and she was fleetingly grateful that he was holding her so very firmly, or she rather thought she would melt in a puddle at his feet. 'My lord?' she added, casting a match on the kindling.

'This,' he growled, and yanked her close to his chest, bent his head and kissed her with a ruthless efficiency that had her whimpering against his mouth. She wanted to hold on to him, but her arms were trapped by her side.

'Now.' Max set her back from him as abruptly as he had kissed her. 'Will you stop this nonsense? What happened was the result of something strong and important between us. Are you telling me you do not recognise it?'

'No. No, I'm not. Max, will you please let go of my arms?'

'What?' He looked down at his hands as though only just aware that he was gripping her. He opened his hands as though she were hot. 'Hell. Am I hurting you?'

'No, but it was stopping me doing this.' Bree reached up, curled her arms round his neck and kissed him, as softly as his kiss had been hard. 'No!' She stepped back, holding up a hand to hold him where he was, and took refuge behind the *chaise*. 'I know how I felt, what it meant to me, but I cannot think straight while you are holding me.'

'Good.' His eyes were dark, intense and thrilling. 'I don't want you thinking straight while I am kissing you.'

'But we cannot keep doing that,' Bree said, amazed to find her own voice steady and reasonable. 'It is scandalous behaviour.'

'Yes. Yes, it is.' His voice changed, flattened. Bree sensed the energy draining out of him to be replaced with something akin to resignation.

'Bree, come and sit down. I promise not to pounce on you again.'

Cautiously she came round the side of the chaise and perched on the edge, relaxing a little as Max sat opposite. He was just too big to be looming over her in the feminine sitting room.

'Bree. I came here intending to ask you to marry me.'

'Oh. Oh, Max, I was so afraid you would feel you had to ask.'

'And I was expecting you to say just that.' He leaned back in his chair, regarding her thoughtfully over clasped hands. 'You are going to repeat all this nonsense about your father's family, about being in trade, about managing the company, aren't you?'

'Yes, and it is not nonsense,' she said stoutly.

'Bree, you have enough good connections to satisfy even my grandmother, and that is saying something. You have beauty and intelligence and charm and courage. You would make a magnificent countess.'

He means it. The dazzling prospect hung before her, then the sense of his words registered. 'You *were* intending to ask me? I *would* make a magnificent countess?'

'There is something I must tell you. Something I thought I could say nothing about until I was certain it was resolved. And then I let my feelings get the better of me, and I have ended up compromising you.'

'It was equally my fault,' she retorted. *So that is why he says nothing about love. He has compromised me, so he feels he must make the best of it and marry me.* 'And I am not ruined, nobody knows but us, and Rosa, so there is no need to feel obligated in any way.'

Damn, she is convinced I feel I must *propose to her.* Max wrestled with his conscience. He had come intending to throw all caution to the wind, to tell Bree he loved her, that he wanted to marry her. But as he had looked into those wide, trusting eyes, he knew he could not risk binding her to him, that to do so was less than honourable. And to tell her that he loved her risked drawing her in dangerously close. She already liked and trusted him, he knew she desired him. But love was a step too far to hazard, and, if they could not marry, it was better if only one of them were nursing a broken heart. He deserved that it was he.

'Bree, I have been married before. I may still be married.'

Max saw the colour drain out of Bree's face, leaving only spots on her cheekbones as though someone had pressed rose petals to the skin. Even her lips seemed to have paled.

'You were married, and now you do not know if you are or not?'

'Yes. I was married ten years ago. My wife, Drusilla, left me only weeks later. Let me tell you it from the beginning.'

He began to speak, managing to keep his voice dispassionate as he recounted the story. Bree's eyes never left his face, but as he spoke she curled up into the corner of the *chaise*, her feet tucked up under her skirts, her arms hugging a cushion for unconscious comfort.

Doggedly he continued the tale, trying to explain, when he hardly understood it himself, why he had left it so long to find his errant wife.

'Why did you decide to trace her in the end?' she asked. Her colour had come back, her gaze on his face was less intense, her arms around the cushion more relaxed. Max realised with an overwhelming sense of relief that she was not going to reject him out of hand for what had happened.

'I became restless to have the matter settled, to

know where I was.' He smiled at her. 'Nevill is a fine young man, but I found I wanted a son of my own to succeed me.

'I engaged an enquiry agent, a man called Ryder. He has been seeking for her. Now he believes he knows what happened to her family—they died of smallpox in Winchester, seven years ago.'

'Poor souls.' Bree's instinctive reaction, the distress in her voice, caught at his heart. 'And you do not know if she, Drusilla, died with them?'

'Yes, I do not know. Ryder is still searching, but the registers are unclear. There was an epidemic in the city, the parish priest was taken ill too, record keeping was a shambles.'

'So you may be a widower, but you cannot tell?'

'No.' *What do I hope for? Not for Drusilla to have died of that hideous disease. Just for the impossible, just to never had made the mistake and married her in the first place.* 'It seems likely, but how can I be sure? I have no idea how she came to be parted from her lover. I will probably never know, unless I find her alive.'

'Oh, Max.' Bree leaned forward, caught his hands in hers before he could stop her. He found, prudence be damned, that he needed her touch. 'I am so sorry. What a truly terrible thing, not to know. What will you do now?'

'I think I need to go to Winchester, to join Ryder

and see if we can find some witness to what happened to the family, who died, who lived.'

'And what then?' She was pale to the lips, but composed, her chin firm without a tremor. *Thank God, she is not as affected as I feared. It is just desire and friendship on her part, she does not feel as I do.*

'If she is alive, then I will seek a divorce.' He ignored Bree's shocked intake of breath. 'If she is not, then I will return and ask you again to marry me. If it is to be a divorce, then I cannot say how long it will take. It requires a private Act of Parliament. Will you wait for me, Bree?'

'No. No, I will not, *you* cannot. Max, you do not have to marry me. You have married once, out of your class, and see what became of it. I am wrong for you, I know it. Do you want to set another tragedy in train?' She released his hands with enough force to throw them apart and was on her feet before he could catch her to him.

'Do not touch me, Max. We do not seem to have the self-control that we should. You must not marry me, even if you are free to do so now. I cannot tell you what to do if you still find yourself married, that is for your own conscience, but you must not divorce her for any thought of marriage to me.'

Bree turned to face him, spots of colour on her high cheekbones, her mouth trembling. He found he had no desire to kiss it. He had expected shock; he had not expected such a comprehensive rejection of his suit. *But I love you!* No, he could not say that now, it was too late, it would sound like an attempt at emotional blackmail. *I have lost her.* Nothing mattered in the face of that realisation, nothing in the world.

'I think you had better go, Max,' she said steadily. 'I appreciate very much your gallantry in offering for me after what happened yesterday. I cannot say I regret it, although I know that I should.' A fleeting smile twisted the corner of her mouth. 'I wish I could keep you as a friend, but I do not think it wise, do you? Not after this—'

'Bree! Are you in? Oh, yes, so you are.' It was Piers, out of breath and urgent, something clutched in his hand. 'Look at this! Betsy has written us a letter.'

'What?' Bree twitched the paper out of his hand. Max could see that the interruption had upset her precarious balance. 'Betsy?' He saw the focus come back into her eyes and was perversely, savagely glad that he had unsettled her to that extent.

'It is Uncle George,' Piers said. 'I can hardly make out her handwriting, but something is very wrong—we must go.'

'Yes. Yes, of course we must. Let me think. It is too late to catch a stage. We had better hire a chaise.'

'Take mine.' Max put all the authority he could muster into the statement, not knowing whether she would respond to it at all. Bree turned to him, the resolute lines her face had settled into swept away by a warm smile.

'Max, thank you. You are such a good friend. I should not accept I know, but I am going to.'

Is that what it has come to? That I am her good friend? I can make her happy with the loan of a chaise, it seems. She can break my heart with a smile. A little while ago I would have been content with friendship. Now the very word is coals of fire when I want so much more.

'Think nothing of it. I will have it sent round at once.'

Chapter Eighteen

Bree leaned back in the corner of the chaise and brooded on Max and his proposal. In her daydreams she had pictured a future together; now she knew that what she had done in refusing him was right and that dream had gone for ever. His loss would not hurt only her. Piers's enthusiastic acceptance of a man whom he already seemed to regard as a superior older brother was giving him the male guidance he had so long lacked.

Her life was changing out of all recognition from how it had been before James's betrothal, yet all of it seemed meaningless now. Could she go back to her old life? It did not seem possible.

She sighed as familiar landmarks slipped past. 'Nearly there. Uncle George is going to be surprised to see us. Do you think Betsy told him she had written?'

'I'm still trying to read this letter.' Piers squinted at it, turning it towards the chaise window. 'She says something about him drinking and playing cards at the Queen's Head.'

'Well, I knew about that,' Bree pointed out, butterflies chasing round her stomach. 'But it didn't seem excessive.'

'But something new has happened.' He brought the page almost to his nose. '*Won't forgive himself* and *Master Piers* is all I can make out—it looks as though a drunken spider has been all over it with its feet in the inkwell.'

'Never mind, we'll know in a minute. We're here.'

Bree jumped down as soon as the step was lowered. The housekeeper came to the pealing of the bell, only to gape at the smart carriage and the liveried postilions.

'Lord love us, Miss Bree! You got my letter then, thank the good Lord.' She bustled forward, wiping her hands on her apron. 'I've been that worried. And Master Piers, bless you. What's all this about being poorly? They don't feed you properly at that school of yours. You come along with me—'

'Betsy.' Bree cut in with the skill bred of long familiarity with the housekeeper's conversational style. 'Please see to it that Lord Penrith's postilions are looked after.' She looked up at the men and gestured to the stable-yard arch. 'The stables are round there. Tell them that you brought me and you need lodging.

When the horses are settled, come to the kitchen door and Mrs Bryant will find you something to eat.'

As they touched their hats and took the chaise away, Bree swung back. 'Betsy, we came as soon as we got your letter, but we cannot read your handwriting. What has happened to our uncle? Where is he?'

'In his study, Miss Bree. He hasn't been right for days, that's why I wrote. He's been awful quiet all day today, brooding like. I don't know what's the matter with him, not properly, but he keeps saying he has betrayed Master Piers, or some such thing. He had a visitor again last night, stayed late, into the small hours.'

'We'll go and see him, thank you, Betsy.' Bree led the way down the flagged passageway as the housekeeper bustled off in the direction of the kitchen. 'Perhaps he is unwell? A brain fever? That might account for saying strange things about you. Perhaps that was the doctor last night.'

'Staying into the small hours?' Piers queried reasonably as she tapped on the planked oak door.

'Uncle, it's us, Piers and Bree. Do let us in.' Silence. Bree lifted the latch and pushed. The room was gloomy with only one candle lit against the gathering dusk. A figure was slumped at the cluttered desk. As they came in George Mallory pushed back his chair and gaped at them. Bree saw, with a sinking sort of dread, that he was unshaven and that his hands were trembling.

'I was writing to you. Trying to. To you both. Oh, Bree, lass, Piers, my boy, I've done a dreadful thing. Your father would never forgive me.' He dropped his grizzled head into his hands.

'Uncle, don't…don't say that, it can't be that bad. Come, we will sit down and you can tell us about it.' She pressed him back in his chair, suddenly very conscious of the feel of his shoulders under her hands. He was losing weight, ageing, when he had always been ageless to her. She felt full of dread. 'Piers, light some more candles.'

The older man flinched at the light and Bree realised she could smell stale brandy on him. 'Tell us, we'll help,' she said, desperately hoping it was true.

'I've lost my share of the company,' George blurted out, so suddenly she could only stare at him, waiting for the words to make sense. 'Gambled it away. Lost it at cards.'

'Oh, bloody hell.' Piers sat down with a thump. 'Who to?'

His uncle did not answer him directly. His eyes were fixed on Bree. 'I got to playing cards, a few nights a week, down at the Queen's Head. Same men—I was there every night. I found I enjoyed it, lost a bit, drank too much. Then I found it was difficult to stop and I was losing more. Nothing too much to manage, though.' His voice trailed off.

'Is that when you wrote the letter that brought me

here the other day?' Bree asked gently. *How could he have lost as much as half the company is worth?* She fought her impatience and let him tell the story at his own pace.

'Yes. Tried to stop going down there in the evenings, but I went again, night before last. Got to talking to a gentleman, a real London swell. He bought me a drink or two, we played a hand. I won.' Bree's heart sank. It was all to obvious where this was going.

'I won again, and again. I felt a bit bad about it, to tell you the truth, so I asked him back for supper— the food's not up to much down at the Queen's Head.'

'And you played some more, and began to lose?'

'Yes. He said he'd come again last night, give me a chance to win it back. I lost again, and when we added up the IOUs—Bree, it was everything I have and more.'

'So he said he'd take your share in the company?'

'Yes. I offered him all my horses, all my cash, asked for time to raise the rest, but he said no. All he wanted was the *Challenge Coaching Company*. He knew all about it, called it by name.'

'Where is he now?' Bree got to her feet, a hard determination settling over her. Who this sharp was and how he had come to be there, preying on her uncle, she could not fathom, but he was not going to get away with it.

'Down at the inn. He's leaving tomorrow—I was

writing to warn you to expect him at the Mermaid with his lawyer.'

'I will go and see him and buy it back.'

'We have that much money?' Piers stared at her.

'No.' Bree stared into the candlelight, wrestling with her conscience. For herself she would not dream of it, but for Piers's future she was prepared to sacrifice both pride and principle. 'But I know a man who has.

'I will ask Max. What's the alternative?' she demanded in the face of Piers's gesture of protest. 'To go to a moneylender? Or to James?'

'James would never agree,' her brother said positively. 'He does not approve of the business, and we would never convince him how important this is.'

'I will ask Max to lend it to Uncle—it will have to be repaid.' George Mallory was too sunk in gloom to take in what she was saying—the brief discussion seemed to have gone over his head. 'Piers, stay here with Uncle.'

'You cannot go off to a common inn by yourself to meet a strange man. I'm coming too.' Piers clattered at her heels as she strode down the hall, and out of the front door. Bree did not argue: Piers's tall frame and fierce indignation were too much of a comfort to have at her side.

It took only twenty minutes to have a pony hitched to the gig and to drive the quarter mile to the Queen's

Head, sitting next to the church in the little hamlet. 'What's he doing here, this *gentleman*?' she asked. 'A London swell, Uncle said. It is hardly the place for a sharp to find pigeons for the plucking.'

'Perhaps he came for a reason, deliberately to find Uncle,' Piers speculated. 'But who? Why?'

Bree shrugged. Speculation would do them no good. She flicked the reins around the hitching bar outside the inn and swept inside. 'Good evening, Mr Tanner. You have a gentleman staying here? He dined with my uncle the other night.'

The publican came out from behind his counter, his expression puzzled at the tone of her voice. 'Aye, Miss Mallory, he's taking his supper in the back parlour. Private like,' he added as Bree headed off in the direction he pointed.

She did not trouble to knock, sweeping in to confront the man who looked up in surprise as the door banged back. He laid down his knife and got slowly to his feet, a wary smile on his face.

Bree's stomach performed a slow flip. 'Brice Latymer. I should have guessed.'

'Mr Latymer?' At her side Piers stared. 'What are you doing here?'

'He is taking his revenge, I suppose,' Bree said with loathing. 'At the picnic he made advances to me. I rebuffed him. Lord Penrith and Mr Harlow threw him out. I imagine his pride is severely dented.'

Latymer was warily keeping the table between himself and the Mallorys, a wise precaution as Piers lunged forward, fists clenched. 'You bastard! I'll call you out. How dare you touch my sister!'

'Piers, no.' Bree held his arm and he subsided, his lanky frame quivering with anger. 'I want to know how he knew about Uncle.'

'You told me, my dear. Don't you recall confiding your worries about poor Uncle? I thought then it might come in useful, and how right I was.'

'How despicable you are,' Bree observed. 'Do you save every morsel of gossip, every hint of weakness, every possibility for advantage on the off chance that you can profit by it?' It was strange, but she felt quite cold and controlled, as though she was dealing with a reptile, not a human being at all.

'Of course.' He smiled and she wondered how she had never before seen the cold that lay behind his eyes. 'I was not born with a silver spoon in my mouth like your lover Penrith. I have had to make my own way by my wits.'

Bree ignored Piers's growl at Latymer's description of Max, but the significance of the words had not escaped her. 'So that is what it is—you are jealous of the earl. I turned you down, he called you to account.' The flush on the man's cheekbones betrayed him. 'I imagine he is your superior in every way one can name,' she said contemptuously. 'I will buy the company back from you.'

'And I will not sell it.' Latymer moved back from the table, his lean elegance incongruous in the modest inn parlour. His expression was venomous as he picked up an ebony cane that was propped against the fireplace and began to twirl it. The flash of the silver mountings fretted at Bree's nerves. 'I will not sell for any amount you might name.'

'How do you expect the company to function, split like that?' she demanded.

'Poorly, I imagine,' he drawled. 'It can run to rack and ruin for all I care—it cost me nothing to acquire my share. Of course, my dear, you could marry me and then we'd all be one happy family and I'll be as anxious as you that it runs well. What do you think? You may have found my proposal not smooth enough for your tastes, but we could deal well together.'

'You disgust—' Bree did not finish the sentence as Piers pulled free from her grip on his arm.

'She is not marrying you, you are going to be dead!'

'Piers.' Bree cut off the boy's tirade with a sharp word. 'Mr Latymer, I would not marry you if you professed undying love and crawled over hot coals to my feet. You are a treacherous, spiteful, vindictive, two-faced liar. You will hear from our lawyers. Come, Piers.'

'They won't find a crack in it, my dear. Your uncle's

in his right mind. This was a gambling debt between gentlemen.'

'Gentlemen!' Piers snarled, lunged back towards the table and was brought up short by the point of a long steel blade at his throat.

'A swordstick.' Bree, her heart in her throat, reached out a trembling hand and took Piers's arm, pulling the boy back towards her. Latymer made no move to come round the table after them. 'I should have guessed you'd use a coward's weapon. But do not worry, we are both unarmed, and we are leaving.'

They walked out of the inn, arm in arm for support, too shaken to say anything until the pony was making its way back to the farm. 'Bree, he'll ruin us. We cannot run the company with half of it in hostile hands,' Piers stammered. 'If he won't sell, any amount of money from Lord Penrith will not help.'

'We are going back to London tomorrow morning,' Bree said. 'And we will ask Max for help. He will know what to do.' She shook the reins and the reluctant pony lumbered into a trot. 'Now we must do our best to lift Uncle's spirits. Put a brave face on it, Piers—like you did just now. I was so proud of you.' And so scared for him. Whatever happened, she had to keep him away from Brice Latymer.

Max sat back in his chair, studying the fan of cards in his hand. Across the table in the best private parlour that the Sun in Splendour in Winchester could boast, the man who called himself Jack Ryder did the same.

A fire crackled in the grate, the remains of an excellent supper had been cleared away and a rare Bordeaux gleamed ruby light in their glasses.

He felt, strangely, calm. It was not at all how he had expected to feel after viewing the unmarked plot that held the remains of Drusilla's family in the corner of the small church of one of the city's outlying parishes.

With Ryder he had found the verger and they had dragged the registers out of their cupboard in the vestry and pored over them. As the agent had told him, the entries during the epidemic that had ravaged the city were scanty and ill written.

'Vicar was taken with it,' the verger explained. 'He lived, although his wife died. The sexton and I, we did our best with notebooks and scraps of paper, but we were burying that many, sometimes we forgot. We're not lettered men, my lords.' He rubbed a gnarled hand over his face. 'It was a terrible time, that it was. Bitter bad.'

'Here is what I found before.' Ryder pushed a register towards Max. 'See. Fifteenth of May, *The Cornish family, 3 souls.* But which three?'

'I can see if I can find the old notebooks,' the verger offered. 'I gave them all to Vicar, once he was up from his sickbed. He read the service over all the graves then, and filled in the registers, best as he could. He was in a right state, though, still weak himself, and his wife just gone.

'They'll all be in here, I suspicion,' he mumbled, pulling out a battered chest. 'Aye, there you are.'

The two men had looked at the jumble of scraps of paper, battered notebooks and pieces of old parchment, all covered in blotched and pot-hooked handwriting. Ryder dug in his pocket and handed the verger a coin. 'A jug of ale and three tankards, if you'll be so good. This could be a long business.'

It had taken them three hours before they found the notes relating to that day in May 1807. Max spread the page out on the table. 'Buried Mr Matthew Cornish, apothecary, Mrs Letty Cornish his wife, Drusilla Cornish his daughter, spinster, of Eastcheape, dead of the pox, 15th day of May,' he read. 'We must put this under lock and key here and go and see the vicar. Will you swear before a lawyer where it was found?'

'Aye, I'll do that,' the verger nodded. 'It's my handwriting too, I'll swear to that as well. We'll put it in this cupboard here, all safe and sound.'

After they had seen the vicar, a thin, tremulous man with pockmarked cheeks, and had made arrangements for an attorney to come to the vestry next day, the verger guided them to the gravesite. Max had stood there a long while, the flowers he had brought held loosely in his hand, his eyes unfocused as he thought of his wife. Then he had put down the flowers with the sense of having found an answer to an unspoken question, and asked the old man for the direction of a monumental mason.

'What name will you have put on the stone?' Ryder asked, striding beside him through the drizzle.

'Her own, with her parents'. She did not want the marriage—I will not force the name on her now.' The stone mason's work shed was dusty, dim and noisy, but somehow the act of doing something was curiously soothing and he left with the sense of having come to the end of a book and of having closed it, completed.

Now, in the warm comfort of the inn, he was enjoying the sensation of matching his wits against someone he could not read at all. The play was about even, they were winning almost turn and turn about, yet there was something in Ryder's game that made Max suspect he was more than the excellent card player he appeared to be.

Max played an ace and took the hand. 'May I make an observation that may appear insulting, without the risk of being called out?' he enquired, watching the other man's hands as he dealt.

Ryder glanced up, smiled and returned his attention to the cards. 'You may, my lord.'

'You play like a sharp, yet I would swear you have neither played to lose, nor to win unfairly, this evening.'

Ryder raised one eyebrow. 'You have a good eye,

my lord. I can play booty...' he glanced up to make sure Max understood the cant phrase '...to draw the pigeons in, and I can rook them royally when I have them. You are the first man I have ever played against who has called me, my lord—and that when I was playing fair.'

'Call me Dysart. That is my name, although I might hazard a guess that Jack Ryder is not yours.' Max picked up the cards he had been dealt and fanned them out.

'It is part of it.' The other man made his play, then drained his glass. 'I should say that I have never cheated for personal gain, only in the course of my work—and where it was deserved.' He reached for the bottle and refilled their glasses. 'After today, is there anything further I can assist you with?'

'No, nothing, I thank you. I shall make sure Lord Lucas is well aware of how much you have assisted me. I would prefer it if you sent your accounting directly to me, marked for my personal attention. My secretary is not aware of this enquiry.'

Ryder nodded. 'It will be done. You are travelling direct back to town tomorrow?'

'Yes.' Max grinned, his thumb caressing the Queen of Hearts in the cards fanned in his hand. The consequences of their day's discoveries were beginning to sink in. Surely, with the proof that he had been a widower for seven years, he could win Bree round? 'Oh, yes. I have a lady to see. Are you married, Ryder?'

'I have not that felicity,' the other man replied, straight-faced. 'But I wish you good fortune.'

They travelled back to London together, Ryder amusing himself by teaching Max some of the sharper's skills. They were still chuckling over Max's attempts to palm aces as they came through the front door of his town house and were confronted by an agitated butler.

'My lord! Miss Mallory is here without a chaperon!' He saw Ryder behind Max and froze into an expression of mortified dignity at such a lapse on his part before a visitor.

'Outrageous, Bignell, I shall have to marry the lady, I suppose.' Max sighed, tossing his hat to the footman. 'Ryder, come and meet Miss Mallory.'

He pushed open the salon door and strolled in, only to be brought up short by the sight of Bree's white, strained face and Piers, coiled like a spring under tension, at her side. 'Max! Thank goodness you are back. I am so sorry, coming here like this, but we need your help so badly. You will never guess what that toad Latymer has done.'

'If he has laid a finger on you—' His insides were suddenly hollow as the memory of Bree struggling in Latymer's arms came flooding back. He grasped her by the shoulders as he searched her face, his light-hearted mood swept clean away.

'No, not that, although he had a swordstick at Piers's throat. Max, he has cheated Uncle out of his share of the coach company.'

Behind him Max heard Ryder clearing his throat. 'I'll just—'

'No, Ryder, don't go, we may need you.' He took Bree's arm and guided her back into the room. 'Piers, are you all right?'

'The bastard—' the boy began.

Max held up a hand. 'Not that language in front of your sister.' Bree growled, making Max's lips twitch. He imagined she would have a stronger word for Latymer. 'This is Mr Ryder, who acts in confidential matters for me. Tell us what happened.'

'Mr Ryder.' Bree nodded politely, sat down on the nearest sofa and swallowed, obviously marshalling the facts. Max listened, trying to control his fury as the tale unfolded. 'He thinks he has us over a barrel,' she concluded. 'He says that a gambling debt between gentlemen could not be challenged legally, and I expect he is right. My uncle is of sound mind, no one coerced him into playing, he admits that himself. He signed IOUs.' She turned troubled blue eyes on Max. 'I am sorry, Ma…my lord. I could think of no one else to advise us. James will not have the slightest sympathy.'

Inside, somewhere beyond the fury, Max felt a warm glow building. She had come to him, trusted him to help her. Despite what she had said, her protests, he knew she felt more for him than she would admit.

'Your uncle could default,' Ryder observed dispassionately from where he stood near the window. With a fraction of his attention Max noted the way he had automatically taken up a position where he could scan the street. The man was dangerous.

'And have Latymer spread it far and wide that he did so?' Bree demanded. 'My half-brother is about to marry the daughter of the Duke of Matchingham. Piers and I are already considered something of an embarrassment. Latymer will know how to make a scandal out of this.'

The agent cleared his throat. 'Dysart, have you played Latymer? How good is he? Does he cheat?' Ryder's questions brought a grim smile to Max's lips—he could see where this was heading.

'He plays moderately well, not as well as I do. I have never suspected foul play, although he would not dare to try it, I suspect, not in the club. Against an inexperienced player, slightly fuddled with drink—I can imagine nothing more likely.'

'Then we have him,' Ryder said, a slow smile curling his lips. 'All I need to do is to lure him into a game, somewhere public, then either catch him cheating, or create the illusion that he has. As the price of our silence he hands back all the IOUs and any documents from Miss Mallory's uncle.'

Max watched Bree's face as she listened. He loved the way she tipped her head slightly to one side as she concentrated, and the focus of those incredible blue eyes on Ryder's face. 'That sounds a wonderful plan—except, where are you going to catch him?'

'I wouldn't be surprised if he doesn't turn up at the club,' Max observed. 'He has the brass neck to do so. He knows Nevill and I will keep quiet so as not to bring your name into it, he knows I won't call him out now he has apologised. He has no reason to suppose you would bring your uncle's problems to me.

'Now, all we need to do is to introduce Ryder as a guest. If you don't mind letting him into the secret, I'll ask Lansdowne to do it so there will be no connection with me.'

'I'll wait to hear.' Jack Ryder nodded pleasantly to the Mallorys. 'A pleasure to meet you. Dysart, you know where to find me.'

Max saw him to the door then came back into the room. 'I'm sure you must be busy, Piers,' he observed.

'No.' The lad beamed back. 'That's a great plot to snare Latymer, I wish I could see what happens.'

'Piers,' Max said with more emphasis and a jerk of his head towards the door. 'I am convinced that Miss Thorpe is in need of a discussion about company business after your absence. I will see your sister home.'

'Oh. Oh, right. Yes, I'll be off then.' He grinned cheekily at Max as he strolled out. 'Is this worth a driving lesson?'

'You can drive my Hanoverians,' Max assured him. 'Just go!'

Chapter Nineteen

Bree emerged from a vengeful daydream of Brice Latymer being exposed as a cheat in front of the entire Nonesuch Club to find herself alone in the room with Max.

'Where has Piers gone?'

'I bribed him to leave us alone. Are you all right?' Max came and sat next to her, pulling her snug against his shoulder before she could protest. It felt so good to lean into the solid strength of him.

'I am fine now, thanks to you.' With a determined effort she sat up and moved along the seat, putting a safe distance between them. It had been so easy to slip back into that intimate closeness with him. 'Is Mr Ryder the enquiry agent you have engaged to trace your wife?'

'Yes.' Max looked down at his clasped hands, then up to meet her eyes. She realised, fear pooling in her belly, that she could not read his expression, but that he was about to say something momentous. She should have given up all hope of marriage to him, she knew that, but it still felt as though her fate hung in the balance.

'Has he found her?' Her voice shook, just a little.

'Yes,' Max said again. 'We both did. Bree, she died, in Winchester, with her family, just as Ryder thought. We found the verger who recorded the details and have a sworn affidavit.'

'Oh.' Bree felt the tears filling her eyes. 'Oh, poor woman. And poor you. How was it in Winchester? Or would you prefer not to speak of it?'

'Sad. But, strangely, good. I felt able to say good-bye to Drusilla. At last I know the worst. I have ordered a headstone for them, paid the sexton to keep the grave in good order.'

They sat in silence for several minutes, the soft tick of the clock the only sound in the room. Bree tried to sort out her feelings and found she did not know what to think, how to feel, only that the temptation to turn into Max's arms was almost overwhelming.

'Oh, God. Bree.' Max reached out for her, took her mouth with a savage intensity that fired her blood, swept away her tenuous self-control. Instinctively she knew what it was, this fierceness. He had contemplated death, stood by a graveside, now he wanted to reaffirm the fact that he was alive, that she was here, in his arms.

Max's hands swept over her, restless, seeking. Now

her body knew what his wanted and responded to him, arching against him as her fingers clenched hard on his shoulders. Now she recognised and understood that hot, liquid feeling inside her, the gathering knot of tension, so low down.

'I want you so much.' His voice was ragged against the soft skin beneath her ear. His mouth moved on the column of her neck, his lips nipping painlessly until suddenly he bit, very gently, against the pulse.

Bree gasped. 'I want you too.'

'We should not.' He did not sound overly convinced by this virtuous intention.

'Yes,' Bree agreed shakily, ruining the effect by experimentally nipping the tendon beneath his right ear. Max rolled her over until she was lying full length on the *chaise*, his weight on her. Cautiously Bree moved her legs so he was cradled between her thighs. In this position his arousal was unmistakable, rousing an equally fierce reaction in her. 'Oh!' Her lips lifted to him of their own accord. 'This is more comfortable than the drag.'

'A bed would be more comfortable still.' The front of her bodice was fastened by a number of tiny mother-of-pearl buttons. Max seemed intent on opening them with his teeth while his hands were wreaking havoc with her hair. 'We should not,' he repeated, his voice muffled by the fabric of her chemise.

Bree tried to think thoughts of self-control while

writhing under the impact of his tongue—hot, wet—through the thin fabric. 'Yes.' His mouth closed round her left nipple. 'Aah! I mean *no*, I agree, we should not.'

Silence and a complete lack of movement. Bree raised her head enough to squint down. Max had his chin propped in her cleavage and was regarding her quizzically.

She prodded him. 'Stop it, you make me want to giggle, looking at me like that.'

He snorted and rolled off her to stand by the *chaise* and offer her a hand to sit up. 'That was not my intention, Miss Mallory. I fear you are sadly lacking in romance.'

'I fear I am sadly amiss in leading you on,' she confessed, buttoning up her bodice with fingers that shook slightly. The lawn of her chemise clung damp to breasts that seemed strangely heavy. 'I should not be alone with you without a chaperon.'

'I will sit over here and behave myself while you do something about your hair.' He steepled his fingertips and watched her over them. 'What is that Herrick said? "A sweet disorder in the dress kindles in clothes a wantonness… I see a wild civility do more bewitch me than when art is too precise in every part."'

'That is so romantic. I hadn't heard it before.' Enchanted, Bree turned from the overmantel mirror where she was rebraiding her hair. 'Do you enjoy poetry?'

'I only started reading it when I met you.'

'Oh. Oh, Max, that's the loveliest thing anyone has ever said to me.' Bree knelt down beside his chair, her hands on his knees. 'Max, I cannot regard what just happened. We are both emotional, both upset.' She sat back on her heels as his hand wandered round to stroke the back of her neck. 'Stop it, Max! If you start that, goodness knows where it will end.'

'I know where I would like it to end. Bree, we need to talk again. What I discovered in Winchester changes everything.'

He saw the cloud come over her expression, cursed her scruples, cursed himself for not knowing whether to go slowly with her or press her to agree to marry him.

'Not now. Max, I am too confused by all of this, too worried about Uncle to give you an answer, at least not an answer that I have thought seriously about. Will you give me until this wretched business with Latymer is over?'

He made himself smile and saw the relief in her eyes. 'Then you must be off home, because you are far too much temptation here. I'll ring for the chaise to take you back.'

'Thank you. And thank you for not pressing me

about something which I know you feel, honourably, you should pursue.'

I love you, that is all and it is everything. He almost said it, then caught himself. To press a declaration of love on a woman who was anxious, tired and uncertain was asking for the answer he least wanted.

'I really should go and write to Uncle, tell him not to worry,' Bree added. 'You will let me know as soon as there is any news, won't you?'

'It's likely to be at three in the morning,' Max said, pulling the bell cord to summon Bignell. 'Wouldn't you rather wait until a civilised hour?'

'No.' Bree tucked her hand into the crook of his elbow as he escorted her to the door. 'I want to know as soon as possible so I can drink to his disgrace.'

It took three days before Max, Ryder and Lansdowne could set up their trap. Max spent each evening in the Nonesuch Club card room, enduring a certain amount of sly chaffing. Somehow a rumour was spreading that he was enamoured of a lady. No one was so rash as to allude to it directly.

'I have not seen Miss Mallory recently,' Lord Huntington remarked with a casual air, pausing by Max's table to cast a knowing eye over the fall of the cards.

'Miss Mallory is visiting relatives I believe,' Max responded quellingly. Bree had agreed to stay at home and not risk running into Latymer. 'Her brother said something to that effect when I was talking to him about another outing for the Whips with the stage-coach.'

On the third evening, when he was beginning to wonder if he had overestimated Latymer's arrogance, Nevill appeared at his table. 'I say, Dysart, I need to speak to you urgently.'

Max finished his hand and followed his cousin into the book room. 'What is it?'

'That bounder Latymer has just strolled in, bold as brass. He should be thrown out.'

'Not by us.' Max took him by the shoulder. 'We cannot make a scene without bringing a lady's name into it. Treat him with the indifference he deserves.'

'I hadn't thought of that.' Nevill scowled. 'It goes against the grain tolerating the swine, but, as you say, we cannot risk compromising a lady.' He marched out, looking noble. Max tugged the bell pull, then scribbled a note while he waited for a footman.

'Take this to Lord Lansdowne's house with all speed. It is essential it reaches his lordship personally.'

He sauntered back into the card room to choose his ground. His former place had been taken; he found another with a group just arrived and settled down to play.

Latymer came in, paused in the doorway and scanned the room. Max, watching him in a convenient mirror, saw there was heightened colour in his cheeks and that he looked about him with a nervous intensity. But no one paid him any attention beyond a nod when he caught someone's eye, so he came right in, found a chair at a solitary table and signalled the waiter for a drink.

Max bided his time, glancing occasionally at the clock. As it struck twelve Lansdowne entered, Ryder at his side. They paused close by Latymer's table. Max could just hear his friend's voice. 'If you would like a drink, just tell them to put it to my account. I'm sorry to abandon you the moment we get here, but I've some rather urgent business—I'll be back within the hour. Do you care to play? I could introduce you...'

'No, I thank you.' There was a slight hesitancy in Ryder's voice that had Max suppressing a smile. 'I'm not a great card player. I enjoy it, of course, but I don't play in clubs, just socially. I'm sure I'd be a complete bore as a partner for anyone here.'

He settled at a table close to Latymer and began to look around with a kind of shy curiosity that made Max wonder if the man had ever been on the stage. Was Latymer going to take the bait?

Ryder shifted in his seat, caught Latymer's eye and said, 'This seems a very pleasant club. I am staying with Lord Lansdowne for a few days and he was kind enough to bring me as his guest.' He appeared to feel he had said too much without an introduction, and subsided awkwardly.

Max could not hear Latymer's response, but within five minutes the two men were sitting at the same table and Latymer was offering the cards to Ryder to cut.

By the time Lansdowne came back there was a small pile of money in front of each man. The viscount took up position, leaning negligently against the wall just behind Latymer, his eyes on the play of cards as though patiently waiting for his guest to finish.

Nevill stopped by Max's table and he caught the young man's arm. 'Go and talk quietly to Lansdowne. Watch the fall of the cards. Do nothing, take your cue from him.'

The pile in front of Latymer grew; in front of Ryder it diminished. Soon he was scribbling notes and pushing those across the table. Suddenly, following a discard by his opponent, he froze, looked at his own hand, at the discards and said in a puzzled voice, 'I say, that's damned odd.' He spoke so low that Max almost had to lip read the words.

'Quiet,' Lansdowne said softly, taking a step forward, gripping Latymer by the sleeve and bringing him to his feet. 'Come with me.'

With Nevill on his other side they hustled Latymer out. 'He's a bit the worse for wear,' Nevill said brightly as someone looked up. 'Castaway, don't you know?'

Max laid down his cards and excused himself. 'My cousin may need a hand.'

In the book room Lansdowne was confronting Latymer across a table on which lay the ace of spades. 'Fell out of his sleeve when I shook it,' he said grimly.

Ryder, still perfectly in character, stammered, 'My God! I couldn't work out what was wrong—I mean, I don't play all that much, but I'm not as bad as all that. Yet I couldn't get the slightest edge after the first few hands. But in a gentleman's club! I never dreamt…'

'You lying sharp!' Latymer swung round, his face livid.

'How dare you insult my guest,' Lansdowne snapped. 'I've a mind to call you out.'

'And you won't get out of *this* by apologising,' Nevill said with satisfaction.

Latymer sank down onto a chair and looked at the faces surrounding him. 'So that's what this is about. Miss Mallory…'

'Miss Mallory has graciously accepted your apology, and if you mention her name once more I will ram it down your throat. No, it is not about that.' Max sat down opposite him. 'It's about your most recent bout of sharping in Buckinghamshire. I want all the papers, every IOU—and I want a document from you admitting that you obtained a half-share in the *Challenge Coaching Company* by fraudulent means. And then we will let you go and won't tell the polite world that you were caught trying to rook a gentleman in the Nonesuch Club's card room.' He sat back. 'Well?'

'Damn you to hell.' Brice Latymer stared back, white to the lips. 'You'll ruin me.'

'Only if you do not do as I ask. We are all prepared to turn a blind eye if the half-share in the company returns to its proper owner.' Max dug in his card case. 'Here is the direction of my attorney at law. You will call upon him tomorrow, return all the paperwork and sign an affidavit disclaiming all rights to the *Challenge Coach Company.* Or you will never set foot in any polite gathering in London again.'

With a snarl Latymer snatched the rectangle of pasteboard and flung out of the room. Behind him four gentlemen collapsed into library chairs and let out a collective *huff* of breath.

'Will someone please tell me what is going on?' Nevill asked plaintively.

Bree was fast asleep when she was roused by Lucy. Pushing her frivolous lace nightcap out of her eyes, she struggled up in bed. 'What is it?' Over the maid's shoulder she could see Peters outside her door, his livery pulled on anyhow and his nightcap askew on his head, obviously forgotten.

'Lord Penrith and another gentleman are here. They insist you'll wish to see them, whatever the hour, Miss Bree.'

'Lord Penrith? Oh, thank goodness.' She rubbed her eyes. 'At least, I hope it is good news. Peters, rouse Mr Mallory. Lucy, hand me my wrapper, then fetch Miss Thorpe. I shall go down.'

'In your wrapper, Miss Bree?' Lucy looked scandalised as Bree scrambled out of bed and slipped her arms into the frivolous confection of lace and satin that she had acquired from the same place as Lady Georgy purchased her own lingerie.

'That is why I asked you to fetch Miss Thorpe, Lucy.' Bree tossed the words back over her shoulder as she ran downstairs. The drawing-room door was open. Inside, Max and Mr Ryder were standing before the almost dead embers of the fire. 'What happened?'

Both men gazed at her, their mouths dropping slightly open. Under any other circumstances this would have been flattering; just now Bree was too anxious for flirting. 'Well?' she demanded.

'Very well.' Max appeared to recover his equilibrium before his companion. 'He will be visiting my attorney tomorrow to hand over all papers and to sign documents denying any claim on the company and admitting he played foul.'

'Oh, Max, thank you!' Bree ran forward and hugged as much of him as she could manage.

'I collect that Mr Ryder has also been wonderful,' Rosa said drily from the doorway. 'Miss Mallory, might I suggest that we offer the gentlemen refreshment?'

Bree let Max go, suddenly conscious of what she was doing and the spectacle she must be presenting. She had rejected Max's suit, and knew she should do so when he pressed it again. She must not forget herself.

'Mr Ryder, how wonderful that your clever scheme has worked. I do thank you, both for myself and Piers, but most of all for my uncle. The relief is enormous.' The footman was hovering in the doorway. 'Peters, for goodness' sake, take off your nightcap and fetch the decanters for the gentlemen. No, on second thoughts, fetch the champagne and enough glasses for all of us—we have a famous victory to drink to.'

She sat down, sweeping her flounced skirts into order as though they belonged to a ball gown. Across the room she could see Max's lips twitching appreciatively, but kept her face straight, anxious not to disconcert the rather austere Mr Ryder. Peters staggered back with a loaded tray.

'Excellent. Lord Penrith, would you do the honours?'

Max went and took the bottle. 'A fine year. You have a notable cellar, Miss Mallory.'

'I won it in the coaching inns' Christmas lottery,' Bree confessed. 'Our cellar here is a disgrace.' She watched, her heart brimming as the frothing liquid filled the glasses, then took her own from Max and lifted it in a toast. 'To our gallant rescuers.'

Chapter Twenty

Max waited until eleven the next day before calling. He wanted Bree rested, calm and, with any luck, alone. He achieved the first and the last, but he was not sure about how calm she was when he was ushered into the sitting room.

Bree was sitting at her desk, piles of paper all around her, chewing the end of her quill while she stared into space. When he came in her eyes flew to his face and she coloured up, giving him hope that she had been sitting daydreaming about him.

'Hello.'

She sat still, regarding him solemnly, then she smiled and got to her feet. 'Max.' She came towards him, let him take her hand and drop a kiss onto her cheek, but she drew away almost immediately and went to sit in one of the chairs before the fireplace.

Max dropped into the other and crossed his legs, sitting back to give her the space she seemed to need.

There was a sense of withdrawal, of distance, that was new about her; she had made up her mind, he could see that.

Bree folded her hands carefully in her lap. He was going to ask her to marry him, now he knew he was free to do so, and she had to tell him, again, that she could not. His first marriage, to a woman far from his world, had been a disaster. She was closer to that world, but perhaps could see even more clearly than Drusilla ever had what a gulf still yawned between them.

Mama had been cut off from her family for the crime of marrying a respectable yeoman farmer. She, the offspring of that *mésalliance*, was closely related to a major business enterprise, enough to tar her thoroughly with the dreaded label of *trade*. Even with a half-brother of impeccable *ton*, she would always be the outsider, but at least now she was accepted while she walked that fine line. To presume to marry an earl would be, she was certain, considered shocking. And Max would spend his entire time defending his wife against snubs and slights.

And that was just the start of it. What did she know of the sort of life he lived?

'Bree?' She jumped and realised that she had let her mind wander right off. 'Bree, stop sitting there thinking of all the reasons why you should turn me down.' He was smiling, but she could see the tension in him.

'I'm sorry.'

'Might I at least ask you first?'

'Yes, of course.' She was irredeemably unsuitable, everything proved it. *I cannot even hear a proposal of marriage without making a* gaffe.

'Bree, do you think I am asking you to marry me because I compromised you at the picnic?' It was not what she had expected him to start by saying and she frowned, trying to work out what to reply.

'Well, yes. There can be no other reason, I am so very unsuitable for you.'

'Really?' Max raised one dark brow. 'Now there I must beg to differ. There is one reason above all why I wish to marry you, Bree Mallory, and that is because I love you.'

Bree simply gaped at him. 'Love? Me? But you never said.'

'It is a little difficult trying to persuade one woman that you love her while confessing that you may, or may not, be married to another. I realised what an impossible situation it was once I had started, but I could hardly not say anything after the picnic.' She found it impossible to speak, simply staring at him and the wry smile that curved his lips. 'I have no excuse for what happened in the drag other than overwhelming passion. I knew I loved you, I knew I wanted you, yet I could not tell you.'

'You love me?' The words came out as a croak.

'Yes.'

She sat staring at him, silenced by his calm certainty. 'You…' They were the words she had been dreaming of hearing Max say to her. She must be dreaming. She got her breathing under control to try again. He was watching her, that smile still twisting his lips, and she realised he was apprehensive too. It was true. 'Me?'

'Yes. I love *you*, Bree Mallory. That is why I want to marry you. That is why I would want to marry you even if you were Bill Huggins's daughter. It is just fortunate that you aren't, so we will not have that particular obstacle to overcome.'

'Bill's disapproval?' Bree ventured. Her heart was beating hard, she still felt unsteadily as though the floor was not quite level, but she was beginning to hope.

'Society's disapproval.' Max leaned forward and reached for her. She held out her hands and found them enveloped in his. They were large, warm and very comforting. The unsteady feeling began to vanish. 'Max. I love you too.' She blinked, her eyes suddenly blurred with tears. 'I never thought I would be able to say it. I love you.'

He lifted her hands, still within his, and pressed his face into them, coming to his knees in front of her. It was such a spontaneous, unexpected reaction that she gasped, looking down on the dark, bent head.

She could feel the faint prickle of stubble against her palms despite his close morning shave. She could feel the brush of his lashes, the heat of his breath.

'Max? Max, darling?' He looked up at that, making her colour at being caught uttering such an endearment. There was laughter in his eyes, which were no longer dark and intense. Laughter and tenderness and relief.

'That's all right, then,' he said prosaically, making her own lips twitch at his teasing. Then he straightened up, caught her in his arms and settled her on his knees. 'Ah. Now that is better, now I can kiss you properly.'

As if his kisses before had not been proper kisses, Bree thought, giving herself up to the sensual slide of his lips over hers, the slow intensity of the kiss, the heated promise of his tongue, thrusting and claiming. With a sigh of complete abandon she curled into him, careless of crumpled skirts or the bows coming undone under Max's exploring fingers.

He could have taken her there on the *chaise*, she realised hazily when he finally released her mouth and stilled his wandering hands. An involuntary murmur of complaint escaped her lips and Max chuckled. 'I want to spend the next hour with you on my knee, kissing us both into insensibility, but I suppose we should remember where we are.'

'I suppose so,' Bree agreed reluctantly. 'Max. I love

you so much, but are you certain I will make you a good wife? There are so many reasons why I am unsuitable.'

'You will never be a pattern-book countess,' Max said thoughtfully. 'I think you would be utterly miserable if I tried to make you one. But then so would I, because what I want is *you*, with your intelligence and your courage and your lack of convention. You will be a perfect countess, but you will be *our* perfect countess, not someone else's ideal of one.'

'It was why I thought I should say *no*, before I realised you loved me. But if you feel like that…'

'We could try being conventional in all the things that do not matter to us,' Max suggested with a grin. 'I know, I'll start by asking your brother's permission to make my addresses to you.'

'Piers?' Bree tried to imagine it. 'He would die of embarrassment!'

'No, James. I can be very pompous, which he will enjoy. We should do things in style, don't you think?'

'He won't know whether to be furious or gratified.' Bree laughed, tickling his ear with her breath. 'He has no control over me, of course, but he will like to be asked. Then he will start thinking about how little I deserve such an honour—it will give him a headache for a week.'

'You are a cruel woman.' Max tightened his arms around her and tried to come to terms with being unconditionally happy. It felt extremely strange. 'Bree, where would you like to be married from? Have you a hankering after a big society wedding in town? We'd need to wait until the start of the Season to get a really good crowd.'

'Oh, no! Must we wait that long?' Her slender frame wriggling in his lap as she sat up to look at him was wreaking wonderful havoc with his willpower. 'And I would like to be married from home in Buckinghamshire, with Uncle George to give me away, and just a few people there.'

Max found he was hardly listening to what Bree was saying, his attention was so riveted by watching the effect on her eyes of the rapid progress of her thoughts and emotions. There were flecks of darker blue amidst the bluebell colour, her pupils contracted, then opened wide. Then something obviously worried her and the irises themselves seemed to darken.

'But should you not be in mourning? I had not thought of that. I have no idea of what the mourning period would be under the circumstances. And when it is over, perhaps you would not wish for a quiet country wedding. I am sorry, Max, I am so dazed, I am not thinking sensibly.'

He had not thought of mourning. 'No, I am not going to don blacks for a year, the time for that is long past. I mourned Drusilla when she left me, I made that last journey to find her and I said goodbye, but I am not going to reduce the time you and I have together by one minute more than I have to.

'And a quiet country wedding would suit me. We can go from the farm to Longwater, my estate in Norfolk, for our honeymoon.' He made a mental note to explain firmly to the Dowager Countess that it would be just the time for her to make a prolonged trip into town.

'Max.' Bree uncurled herself fully and sat up, still perched on his knees. 'Will you say anything about your first marriage to anyone? I will not mention it unless you wish.'

'No.' He thought about it, then shook his head. 'No. I will not make a secret of it—after all, it will have to be on the licence, even though I will obtain a special one—but we will let old history lie and not mention it unless we have to. Tell your family and Miss Thorpe, of course.'

He found, watching her, that it was impossible to believe that she truly would be his, that he could love, was loved in return. 'Bree?'

'Mmm?' She was fiddling with the narrow frill of his shirt as though she wanted to attack the buttons.

'Will it take you very long to buy your bride clothes, do you think?'

'Ages.' She sighed deeply, her lush mouth turning down disconsolately at the corners. 'I will have such a long list. So much shopping. And then there are all the preparations to make, even for a small country wedding. Oh, I should say at least three.'

'Months?' Max demanded, standing up and scooping Bree off his knee and on to her feet as he did so. 'You want me to wait *months*?'

Bree looked up into his stormy face and laughed from pure happiness. 'I was teasing you, Max. Three weeks. It is a ridiculously short time, of course, but I can't bear to wait.'

'Little witch! I seem to have lost my sense of humour as far as you are concerned. I want you so much. I love you so much.'

'Show me.' She reached up, curling her fingers around his lapels and tugging. 'Show me.'

His mouth, leisurely and confidently sensual, slid over hers, seeking and finding, teasing and caressing. Bree snuggled closer, stood on tiptoe and reached up to play with the hair at the nape of his neck. His skin was so soft there, yet the muscles beneath were so hard, it fascinated her. Everything about his body fascinated her and she just wanted to explore.

When he released her mouth, more so they could both breathe than for any other reason, she murmured, 'You make me feel very wanton.'

'You make me feel like picking you up and taking you straight upstairs to bed,' he said huskily. 'What do you think?'

'That it is very tempting—and that we must not.

Think what a bad example to the servants, let alone Piers. And Rosa would chase you out with the carpet beater.'

The sound of someone fumbling with the door handle sent Bree flying back to the *chaise* to perch primly on the edge while Max strode over to the fireplace to admire the rather dull landscape that hung over it.

Rosa entered. 'You see,' Bree observed, 'we are both terrified of her.'

'I beg your pardon, my dear?'

'I was just observing to his lordship that you are an excellent chaperon.'

'As we all know, that is far from the case.' Miss Thorpe fixed Max with what was obviously intended to be a reproving stare.

'But, my dear Miss Thorpe, I must disagree. Is it not the sole aim and intent of a chaperon to ensure her charge makes the best possible match?'

'Why, yes, but—'

'But Miss Mallory and I are to be married.'

'Married? Oh, how wonderful! Oh, Bree, my dear—' Rosa kissed Bree, spun round, hugged Max, went pink the moment she realised what she had done and sank down on the *chaise*, clutching her charge's hand in hers. 'I am so happy for you both. When? Where? How much time have we to prepare?'

'In three weeks' time, I hope. And in the country,

from the farmhouse with Uncle George to give me away. I must go down there tomorrow.'

'In my chaise,' Max interrupted. The look he sent her made her feel protected, sheltered, infinitely cared for. He was going to have to learn that she was too independent to be treated like spun glass, but just now it was purest magic. 'I'm not having you jaunting about on the stage again.'

'No, Max, if you say not.' The twinkle in his eyes made it quite clear he could see through this meekness.

Three weeks seemed both an eternity and the most fleeting of moments. It was an age if one was aching to be in the arms of a tall, dark-eyed gentleman. It was no time at all if one was attempting to organise a 'quiet' country wedding.

Piers found himself shuttling between Aylesbury and London with lists, supplies of linen and china and increasingly frantic questions and instructions from both directions.

Rosa divided her time between assisting Bree and reorganising the coaching company office to her own satisfaction. She drove the staff to new heights of efficiency by lightning raids upon all parts of the yard and created lengthy lists of her own for when Bree was away at Longwater.

'I presume his lordship will expect you to cease

your involvement with the company after your marriage,' she observed, looking up from her notes on a review of timetables.

Bree was startled. 'Of course he won't!' Would he? They had never discussed it. Bree saw a wide moat of misunderstandings opening up in front of her. Just as she had realised she could not flaunt the association with the company once her relationship with James was so well known in society, she knew she would have to be even more discreet once she was a countess. But a complete break? It was unthinkable.

Just how dictatorial would Max be as a husband? He was unconventional now. He accepted her independent behaviour, although there were increasing incidences of him trying to shelter her. But how would things change when they married?

For the first time Bree felt a stir of anxiety on her own behalf about his first marriage. He had expected certain standards, certain behaviour from Drusilla that she had not been able or willing to comply with, and in the end she had fled. Just how understanding and supportive had Max been? Chilled, she forced her attention back to Rosa's suggestion about a new route to King's Lynn, but the unease persisted.

Max entered the Gower Street house that morning to find Peters and Lucy in the hallway struggling with a number of large trunks and Rosa halfway up the stairs with an armful of gowns. A maid he had not seen before rushed into the hall balancing a stack of what appeared to be flimsy undergarments, saw Max, gave a faint shriek and dropped them, confirming his guess. Of his betrothed there was no sign. Max regarded the frivolous bits of nonsense with interest, then smiled at Miss Thorpe.

'Good morning, ma'am.'

'Lord Penrith, good morning.' The companion managed to look as composed as was possible, given that a peer of the realm was standing in the front hall with chemises and corsets strewn around his booted feet. 'Miss Mallory is in the sitting room.'

'I will remove myself then. I assume there is nothing I can do to help?'

'Nothing, I thank you. Maria, stop whimpering and pick those things up so his lordship can move.'

He pushed the door open and stood quietly watching Bree working at her desk, unaware of his presence. He felt the love washing softly through him like ripples of water at the sea's edge. It was so new, this feeling of tenderness, of possessiveness, of desire tempered with the knowledge that this was for ever.

Then Bree looked up and saw him and smiled and he was across the room, pulling her out of the chair and into his arms so he could look down into her face and just marvel at his own good fortune.

Her body tensed a little in his embrace, she turned

her face so that his lips found her cheek and not her mouth and her eyes held a hint of anxiety.

Max guided her to one of the armchairs and urged her to sit, taking the one opposite at a distance from which he could study her face. Ten days until the wedding—perhaps, despite her passion in his arms, she was becoming apprehensive about the wedding night. Or perhaps it was just that she was overworked and tired.

'I have brought what I promise is positively the last version of my guest list,' he said, pulling it from his inside pocket. 'I have annotated it with notes on who will be travelling from where, and who needs rooms. That last, I am glad to say, has not changed since the previous list.'

'In that case, we will be all right.' Bree nodded briskly. It did not appear to be the practical issues that were worrying her. 'Uncle George can put up all those members of my family who will be staying over in his half of the house. All of yours can stay in either my and Piers's half, or at the Eagle and Child in Aylesbury. I have engaged the Queen's Head in the village for the extra servants.'

She took his list and scanned it, giving Max the opportunity to watch her more closely. She was losing weight, he thought, anxious that he was leaving too much on her shoulders.

'If this is final, then I will write to Betsy and we

can make the firm lists of everything needed. I think the biggest problem is chairs and trestles for the wedding breakfast, but we can borrow from neighbours. I thought of holding it in the great barn, as we do for Harvest Supper.'

'It is very unconventional,' Max observed. He was delighted by the idea. Bree's face fell.

'I thought I had told you about that. Do you think it too informal? Only I do not know where else we could accommodate so many places.' To his horror he thought he could detect a gleam of tears in her eyes. 'I should have thought. Is it too late to have it in London after all?'

Max jumped up and knelt beside her chair, taking her hands into his—they were cold, her index finger was red from the indentation of the pen and there were ink splashes on her hands. He lifted them in his clasp and kissed the sore finger gently.

'My darling, it will be wonderful. You had told me about it. I love the notion, the guests will love it. If I had not thought it would work, I would have said something days ago.' She smiled shakily. 'You are working too hard. You must let me help. My grandmother will be in town soon. She will be delighted to assist.'

The shutters came down over Bree's brilliant blue gaze and she smiled politely. *So that's it.*

Chapter Twenty-One

Max regarded Bree's carefully neutral expression. 'I would not wish to trouble the Dowager,' she said politely. 'Although of course she will want to make sure everything is done correctly.'

'If we wish to get married on a Thames wherry and then set off on our honeymoon in a gypsy caravan, that is just what we shall do,' Max said robustly. 'Grandmama has nothing to say to it. I just thought that she might be able to take Miss Thorpe's place on occasion when you are shopping, or visiting, so Miss Thorpe can get on with helping you with some of the organising.'

'Yes, of course, that would be very kind, but I do not wish to impose.' Still she did not seem reassured.

'Are you dreading her ruling the roost when we live at Longwater? She has announced her intention to move to the Dower House before the wedding—did she not write to you to tell you?'

'Yes, of course, it was a very kind letter.'

'Mmm.' Max regarded her quizzically. 'And you are wondering just how far away the Dower House is, and how many times a day she will be over saying things like, "I see you have moved the épergne in the Chinese drawing room. It has been there since 1066"?'

'They didn't have épergnes in 1066,' Bree said, a reluctant smile lifting the corners of her mouth. 'And, yes, I suppose I am rather dreading it.'

'There is no need—I give you my word she will not interfere. She has told me she intends not to set foot over the threshold except at your invitation.'

'Oh, no! But it is her home. I could not possibly expect that,' Bree protested. 'It is just that I am not used to being a countess and I expect I will make all kinds of hideous mistakes and I was lying awake all last night wondering if I did the right thing. I should have refused you and then you would have married a suitable young lady who is used to such things.'

'So that is why you have bags under your eyes.' Max smoothed the faint dark shadows with his thumbs.

'I don't have bags,' Bree protested, the smile back again.

Max sat back on his heels, studying her. 'What do you think the duties of a countess are?' he asked eventually.

'Um…to direct the households, take care of the dependents of the estate, to entertain the earl's friends and associates, to do good in the local communities, to keep the earl happy. Oh, yes, and to produce an heir,' she added with a blush.

'I believe that covers it,' Max said. 'I think you can do all that, don't you? Keeping the earl happy is, of course, of paramount importance, and the production of the heir is also a consideration. How many children would you like?'

'I hadn't thought.' Discussing it was making her deliciously flustered. Max wondered how much longer he was going to manage to refrain from kissing her.

'I have given it some thought, I must confess. I realised I was falling in love with you when I caught myself speculating on whether they would have a mixture of our colouring, or whether the boys would be blue-eyed and blond and the girls brunettes or the other way around.'

As she had when he had told her about the poetry, Bree's face lit up. Max wondered why she was finding it so hard to believe he was truly in love with her. But how to convince her?

'I don't mind what colouring they have,' she confessed. 'But I would like perhaps four.'

'Then four it is. What is it, Bree? You are still worried, aren't you?'

'Will you expect me to cut all links with the company? I know I should, but it has been so important to me, and Piers is still at school, and it is vital for his future...'

'Hush.' He pulled her into his arms and kissed her until he could feel all the resistance and tension drain out of her, then set her back in her seat before temptation got the better of him. 'You can carry on just as you are now, my love, only promise me you will not try to drive a stagecoach again.'

'I promise. Oh, Max, I am sorry to be so anxious, only I know how difficult it must have been before, to marry a wife so much out of your circle. I don't want to be a problem to you.'

'And at three o'clock in the morning you wonder if I put so much pressure on Drusilla that it drove her away?' He had been half-expecting this, but it still hurt to see the doubt in her eyes.

'At ten o'clock this morning actually, in broad daylight,' she confessed ruefully. 'Max, I love you and I trust you and I am having silly pre-wedding vapours. I wish it was all over and we could just run away somewhere. I am not going to let your first marriage come between us, I swear it.'

He leaned forward to cup her cheek with his hand. He had felt on such firm ground with Bree that to have felt it shake, even a little, reminded him how precious she was to him. 'If ever you want to know anything about it, ask me. I will not speak of it unless you do, but you can ask anything, tell me any worry.'

Bree turned her cheek against the warmth of his palm, feeling the calluses from riding and driving, the sensitive fingertips that seemed to know exactly which part of her body to caress. Calm seeped through her and she smiled at herself for her worries.

'Thank you, I promise I will do that. Max, do you realise that in ten days we will be married?' She bent forward, kissed him lightly and got to her feet.

'It had not escaped my notice.' Max moved to her desk and began to mend her pens with the little pearl-handled knife that lay by the standish. 'I have not yet got to the pathetic stage of working out how many hours it will be before I can carry you over the threshold at Longwater though.'

She had a sudden vision of the future. Of Max, perhaps with a touch more grey at his temples, standing just as he was now, mending a pen, and herself, her belly swollen with their child, sitting looking up at him, and somewhere the sound of other children laughing.

It was so vivid that it took her a moment to come to herself when Peters coughed.

'Yes, Peters?' The footman was standing in the doorway, looking perplexed.

'A lady—' He corrected himself. 'A female person has called, Miss Mallory, asking for you.'

'Who is it?'

'She would not give her name, Miss Mallory. She has no card and she is heavily veiled.'

'Not a lady? Is it someone come to speak to Cook about a position?'

'No, Miss Mallory. She's not *quite* a lady, if you know what I mean. But she's not a servant, I don't think. Her gown's quite respectable.'

'Well, show her in, Peters.' Bree turned to Max with a shrug. 'I had better see what she wants. Perhaps it is someone collecting for a charitable organisation.'

'Your visitor, Miss Mallory.'

The woman stepped into the drawing room and stood quietly facing Bree while the footman closed the door behind her. Max remained where he was, behind her line of sight, and she gave no sign of noticing there was anyone else in the room. Her gown was a drab merino with a modest line of braid around the hem, worn under a dark green pelisse. She was wearing a bonnet with a small poke, entirely covered by a thick black veil of the kind worn for deepest mourning. It covered her face and hung down below the level of her chin.

'Good afternoon,' Bree said, trying not to show how disconcerting the blank screen of the veil was. 'I am Miss Mallory. How may I assist you?'

'I hope I may assist you,' the woman said, raising her gloved hands to the hem of the veil. 'I hope I may be in time to prevent you marrying Lord Penrith.'

She lifted the veil and for a moment Bree could not quite realise what she was looking at. Then she saw a pair of wide green eyes under arched black brows, a sweetly curved mouth and a face that was completely destroyed by the most hideous scarring she had ever seen. There was not a part of the skin untouched by the ghastly pits and craters. Bree knew what it was, she had seen smallpox scars before, but never anything so dreadful as this.

'You…'

'I am Lady Penrith.' The soft voice with its hint of West Country burr seemed to echo in Bree's head. 'I am Max's wife.' She was aware of Max moving, as though released from a trance; she saw the woman turn and see him and heard her say, 'Oh, Max! Darling, why did you not come for me when I wrote? Why did you abandon me?' And then the echo in her head turned into the sound of a rushing wind, the room went dark and she slipped to the floor in a dead faint.

Bree came to herself in her bedchamber, Rosa by her side. 'Rosa, what on earth happened? I have had the most dreadful nightmare.'

'No, you have not,' her companion said bluntly. 'Bree, there is no easy way to say this. That woman downstairs maintains that she is Lady Penrith. Max appears to accept it.'

'But Drusilla is dead. Max went to her grave, he is having a headstone made.'

'Apparently there has been some mistake.'

'And they are both still here?' It was a nightmare, a waking one. It was so frightful that Bree simply could not comprehend it.

'She will not go until she has spoken to you. She will not go with Max, she says she does not trust him. Piers and I discussed it and decided we can hardly have her bundled out of the house onto the street.'

She doesn't trust him. The woman's words echoed in Bree's head. *Why did you abandon me?* Bree sat up. 'I will go down and speak to her.'

'Max wants to come to you. He asked to be told the moment you regained consciousness.'

'I will see her first.' Bree went to the washstand to splash cold water on her face.

'But, Bree—'

'I will go downstairs. It would not be proper for him to come up here. He is a married man.' The room seemed to tip a little as she said it, but she gripped the edge of the washstand with wet fingers until she had herself under command again. 'How is Piers taking it?'

'He is stunned, we both are. Bree—Max cannot have known she was alive. He seems as shaken as the rest of us.'

'Whether he knew or not, the fact remains that she is. At least we found out now and not after the wedding.'

'How can you be so calm?' Rosa was staring at her.

'What is the alternative?' Bree enquired baldly. 'Hysterics?'

In the hallway Piers was pacing back and forth, his fists clenched. 'Bree.' He ran to the foot of the stairs and put his arms around her. 'Bree, if he knowingly deceived you, I shall call him out.'

'Oh, bless you.' She allowed herself the weakness of resting her head against his shoulder for a moment. 'That won't mend matters, my love. Stay here with Rosa.'

She tapped on the drawing-room door and went in.

Bree had not known quite what to expect on the other side of the door. What she found was Drusilla seated on the *chaise*, her bonnet, veil and gloves discarded, and Max standing on the other side of the room. If they had been speaking, they had stopped at her knock, but Bree felt instinctively that they were two people who had rapidly found themselves unable to communicate.

Max looked at her, the pain in his eyes so acute that for the first time the realisation of what she had lost hit her. It was as though she had been in shock and someone had slapped her face to bring her out of it.

Hastily she averted her gaze, covering up her reaction by making rather a business of finding a chair and sitting down. 'Have you rung for refreshments? A cup of tea, perhaps?' *The English answer to any disaster*, she mocked herself.

'Thank you, tea would be very nice.' Drusilla smiled faintly, her wonderful green eyes wide and guileless.

How does she manage it? She is confronting her husband after ten years and a terrible tragedy and yet she seems as composed as though they had parted an hour ago. Bree began to wonder if Drusilla was perhaps not very intelligent, or that she had so little imagination or empathy that she simply did not comprehend the havoc her reappearance was causing.

'Would you be so good as to ring the bell for Peters, Ma...Lord Penrith.' Rather desperately she turned to Drusilla. 'Have you had a long journey to get here?'

'It took me all day yesterday. I have been living in Portsmouth. I stayed at the Bull and Mouth last night, then I went to find Lord Penrith. I stood in the square, watching, not daring to go in. But I knew I had to see you—I had read the gossip columns all about the marriage. Then he came out and I followed in a hackney. I enquired of the girl delivering milk and she told me who lived here, so I knocked.'

She told the tale as though reciting from a book. Bree was left with the impression of a young girl, forced to perform her poetry lesson in front of adults, not a woman of almost thirty. *Nerves, poor thing*, she reproved herself. *How would I manage?*

'Your arrival is timely,' she said, seeing the involuntary grimace on Max's face as she said it. 'We would have sent out the invitations tomorrow.'

'Indeed.' He moved forward and sat, taking a chair so the three of them formed the points of a triangle. Bree was visited by the fancy that he had been waiting for someone to come in before he was willing to move any closer to his wife.

'So, what have you decided?' she asked briskly. If she let herself weaken, think of anything other than the practicalities of this hideous situation, she was going to fall apart.

'Nothing,' Max said. 'We have been rehearsing the circumstances of our…parting, and what has occurred since.'

'Might I know these circumstances?' Bree enquired. 'I feel I have some legitimate interest.' *I am sounding hard and brittle.* She could hear her own tone and hated it, but it was the best she could manage. It was better than hysterics and reproaches.

'You know the start of it. Bree, I would spare you this, but it is better that you hear it all, ask whatever questions you have. As I told you, Drusilla met a man, shortly after our marriage, and ran away with him. I organised funds for her and after some years they stopped being drawn upon. I heard nothing more.'

'I wrote to you!' Drusilla burst out. 'I wrote to the town house and to Longwater. I wrote and told you I had left Simeon, that he was cruel to me and I couldn't bear it. I told you I was ashamed to take your money any longer and that I wanted to come home, to beg your forgiveness. And you ignored me.'

Her hands twisted together in her lap as she spoke, then, in a gesture of despair, she held them up and let them drop back, palms down. They were white, smooth, perfectly untouched by the frightful scarring which had wrecked her face. Bree glanced down at her own hands. She kept them carefully, yet the lines of the tendons showed under the skin, there was the odd freckle, a tiny scar on one knuckle. This woman was older than she, and yet her hands were whiter, plumper, without freckle or blemish. Whatever she had been doing for ten years, it had not involved any form of manual work.

'I never received your letters, as I have just been telling you,' Max said evenly.

'You must have done,' Drusilla retorted. 'I do not believe you. But that is in the past now. I knew I could not trust you to help me, I was resolved not to live on your money, so I went back to my parents.' She turned to face Bree, the light from the window highlighting the dreadful mask of her face. 'The Countess of Penrith earned her living serving behind the counter in an apothecary's shop, a pretty tale, is it not?'

Bree could not answer the bitterness directly. She could not believe Max would lie, and yet, why would he not receive letters? Mail to peers of the realm did not go astray, and more than one letter had seemed impossible. Unless Drusilla was lying. Unless Drusilla was not who she claimed.

'I suppose,' she said, directly to Max, 'that you are entirely satisfied that this is your wife?'

'Oh!' The other woman gave a strangled sob, and buried her face in her handkerchief.

'That hair, those eyes, her voice—all as I recall from that very first meeting,' Max said, his gaze on the bowed black head. 'And she knows things that only my wife would know.'

Drusilla raised her face from the handkerchief revealing a tear-streaked visage. Bree felt a pang of guilt at doing this, but it was her life, her happiness, her lover, all were being snatched from her.

'I know about a certain *ornament* on his body,' Drusilla said viciously, then, as Bree felt her face colour, added, 'and so do you, I see, so that does not convince you it requires marriage to become that intimate with Max. Do you want me to tell him, in front of you, where we first made love, what he said to me? I can describe the nightgown I wore on our wedding night, I can tell you about the boathouse on the lake at Longwater and one endless night—'

'Enough,' Max snapped, his tone the first clue that he was as close to losing control as Bree felt herself to be. 'I believe you. Bree, we must accept it, I am married.'

'You sound as though you wish I were dead,' Drusilla said.

'I stood at your graveside,' Max retorted. 'How do you think I feel? Whose grave was it in truth?'

'My sister's. We all caught the smallpox, they died, all three of them. I do not know how I survived. I wish I had not! The register was not made up properly. I went to look. There were so many people dying in that outbreak, it was no surprise. I was about to tell the verger, then I saw my own face reflected in a glass and I could not bear it. I was alive—now I had the chance to vanish altogether.'

'I am sorry,' Bree said shakily. 'I do not wish to add to your troubles with my own…feelings.'

The other woman turned her head away, apparently overcome again, this time by the sympathy in Bree's voice. In cruel contrast to her face, her nape was as white, tender and unscathed as her hands. The black glossy tendrils of her hair curled in stark contrast to the flawless skin.

'How have you lived since then?' Max asked, his voice softer.

'I sold the shop and I went to Portsmouth. I make my living as a milliner.'

'And what now?' Bree asked. 'What do you want now? To return to your husband?' *Husband, husband, if I say it enough I will come to accept it.*

'No!' Drusilla's response was instant. 'Never. I do not trust him now he knows I am alive.'

'For God's sake!' Max sprang to his feet. 'Do you fear that I will murder you? Of all the outrageous, unfounded—'

'You abandoned me before. I almost died.'

'How was I to know? I never had your letters.' He turned on his heel and strode to the window, his back to them. Bree could almost feel the tension in him as he strove for control. 'What do you want?'

'A little house somewhere I can live retired. Enough money for comfort. Is that so much to ask? There is a cottage *ornée* in the park at Longwater that would do very well.'

'Is that before or after the divorce?' Max asked quietly.

Chapter Twenty-Two

'Divorce?' Bree's eyes flew to his face. 'No, Max, you cannot! Not, not when she has been so...ill.'

'My wife left me after only days of marriage to live as another man's concubine. She took my money, made every attempt to cover up her whereabouts until now when she can be assured of my very close attention to her demands.' He spun round to face Bree, his face dark with anger. 'She puts that look on your face, that hurt in your eyes, and you tell me to be kind to her?'

'Max, I cannot marry you. And I do not believe you really could bring yourself to obtain a divorce. *I love you*,' she burst out. 'And I know the man I love is not someone who could do that to a woman he once loved. Imagine the scandal, the talk. She cannot defend herself, not now.' She found she was on her feet, uncaring that Drusilla was sitting feet away. 'I love you, and I am right, am I not?'

'I love you too.' Max reached out for her and drew

her into his arms. 'I love you, I would die for you, and, yes, you are right. I cannot divorce her.'

Bree let herself stand within the circle of his embrace for a long moment, then slowly drew away. That was the last time, the last embrace. At least she had the satisfaction that they were doing the right thing. That seemed a hollow consolation.

'What now?' she asked Drusilla when she had control of her voice again. 'Where will you go while things are being arranged? To the town house with Lord Penrith?'

'No! I have told you, I will not stay with him, not in the same house.'

Max looked so furious that Bree spoke before he could let rip with what he was so obviously feeling. 'Stay here.'

'What!'

'But, Max, what else can we do? She will not go to you, she can hardly stay in a hotel with one tiny bag and no maid and you cannot send her on to Longwater until you have warned the Dowager and arranged for the cottage. This is the most discreet way.'

'So you house my wife while we set about cancelling our wedding?'

'I suppose so.' Bree shrugged resignedly. 'Max, unless you and Drusilla want to talk further today, I suggest I show her to her room and she can rest until dinner. I would be grateful if you could call tomorrow morning and we can discuss what to do about cancelling the preparations for the wedding when we are both a little calmer.'

'Very well.' His eyes were troubled, but he managed a smile for her, the tenderness in the curve of his lips, a caress. 'I will call at ten. Goodbye, Drusilla.'

His wife turned a shoulder on him, he shrugged and went out leaving Bree staring at her unwelcome houseguest. Drusilla looked up at her suddenly. 'Do you hate me? You must wish I was dead. Do you really love him? You can't, can you, not a pompous aristocrat like him?'

'Pompous? Max?' Bree stared at her. 'He is anything but that, and, yes, I do love him. I do not hate you and I do not wish you were dead—I just wish you had never met him, that is all. But you did. And I do not understand how you can misjudge him so.'

'You wanted to marry him—have you met that old dragon of a grandmother?'

'No, not yet.' Bree went to the door, anxious to get Drusilla upstairs before she vented the whole of her pent-up feelings.

'She's worse than he is. Must do this, must do that. Talk like this, pay attention to that. It was like being at school. Dr…dreadful.'

That wasn't what you were about to say. 'Come upstairs and rest,' Bree said firmly, to disguise her own puzzlement. The longer she was in this woman's company, the odder she seemed. *Of course she does*, part of her contradicted. *You've had a shock, she's taking the man you love from you. You cannot expect to like her!*

Silent now, Drusilla followed Bree upstairs to the spare bedroom next to Rosa's room. 'Here you are. I will send my maid up. Let her know if there is anything you need.'

She closed the door and wandered downstairs, wondering vaguely why she was not in the throes of violent hysterics. 'Years of having to cope with whatever comes along, I suppose,' she murmured out loud as she reached the hall, only to find Rosa waiting anxiously.

'What did you just say?'

'I was explaining to myself why I was not in the throes of strong hysterics,' Bree said wryly. 'I have settled my betrothed's wife in the spare bedroom, by the way. She is staying with us, as she cannot bring herself to be with Max.'

Rosa's face was so expressive of her feelings that Bree found she could laugh—a little. 'I'll explain quickly on the way down to the basement. I need to send Lucy up to her.'

Her rapid explanation was enough to strike Rosa dumb by the time they pushed open the door and went into the kitchen. Cook was making pastry, while at the other end of the table Lucy was talking to a girl a little younger than herself.

'Oh! I beg your pardon, Miss Bree. This is my sister Penelope. Penny, make your curtsy to Miss Mallory and Miss Thorpe. I hope you don't mind her visiting, Miss Bree, only she's up from the country looking for a position and Mrs Greenstaff at the end of the road is advertising, so I was telling her about the household.'

'That's all right, Lucy.' Bree smiled at the younger girl. She was neatly turned out and her hands were clean and well kept, plump still, with a touch of puppy fat. 'How old are you, Penelope?'

'Seventeen, Miss Mallory.' Something was nagging at Bree's mind, but she could not catch hold of it. *It is hardly a wonder*, she thought, *given what has passed in the last few hours*. She exerted herself to be pleasant.

'I hope you have good luck in securing a suitable position. Lucy, we have an unexpected visitor. La...I mean, Miss Drusilla. She has had a difficult journey and is resting in the spare bedchamber. She has very little luggage and may need to borrow some things— just take whatever seems suitable to you from my room. And, Lucy, she has very bad smallpox scars— do try not to let her see any reaction to her appearance.'

The maid's eyes opened wide. 'Poor lady. I'll be ever so tactful, Miss Bree.'

'I'm afraid that is one more for dinner, Mrs Harris,' Bree apologised.

'No need to fret, Miss Bree. Mr Piers put his head round the door not half an hour since and said he would be eating at the Mermaid, so it all evens out,' the cook said placidly, reaching for the flour.

'I packed him off to the inn,' Rosa explained as they climbed back up to the ground floor. 'I told him you would be more in need of female company and if I wasn't at the inn, he would be most use at the office.'

'Thank you.' Bree sank down in her favourite armchair and let her head fall back onto the cushions. 'Oh, Rosa. I think Max has broken my heart.' And then, at last, the tears came, and with them the merciful release of simply not having to cope, to control herself, to think of anyone else.

Max stalked into the hall and thrust his hat and cane into the butler's hands. 'I am not at home to anyone.'

'Until when, my lord?'

Max paused in the doorway into his study. 'For the foreseeable future, Bignell.'

He shut the door, taking care to do so softly, recognising in that the same instinct for keeping control that he had seen in Bree's eyes as she had politely enquired if anyone had wanted tea.

It would have been easier if she had broken down, had railed at him, wept, accused him of deceiving her. He felt he deserved all of that, but her courage and self-control had imposed the same duty on him to hold back the emotion he was feeling.

About Drusilla he could hardly think at all, beyond anger at her shrinking, her accusations and thinly veiled hints that he meant her harm. He pitied her profoundly, for her disfigurement and also for the fact that she seemed no deeper, no wiser, than she had ten years ago. That kind of tragedy, if one survived, would surely make one stronger, give one the wisdom to cope.

His own feelings could wait. Whatever pain he was feeling, and would feel for the rest of his life, he could lay at the door of his own infatuation and his own reluctance to do anything in the years since Drusilla had left him.

Max splashed brandy into a glass and began to pace to and fro before the cold hearth. What had he done to Bree? To her heart and to her reputation? It was widely known in society that they were intending to wed; now it would appear that she had been jilted, or that she was a jilt. And somehow he did not believe that any story they might put around about her sudden reluctance to marry one of society's most eligible bachelors was going to convince anyone.

The only way he could protect Bree was to reveal the truth about Drusilla. Could he expose her and her pitiful story to the gossip and sniggers and prurient curiosity? He came to a stop in front of a pair of small portraits. On the left was his father, painted on his twentieth birthday, on the right was Max at the same age.

Less than a year after his portrait had been completed he was married. For the first time Max studied his own likeness, glancing between it and his reflection in the mirror over the mantel. Had he ever looked that young? He began to catalogue the changes: laughter lines at the corners of his eyes; a harder, stronger set to his jaw; a sprinkling of grey just touching his temples; the replacement of that look of eager anticipation with one of guarded experience.

Ten years and he was another man, looked another man. And loved, hopelessly, another woman.

Dinner was a bizarre experience. Drusilla said virtually nothing and ate everything that was offered, while the other two women made valiant attempts at conversation.

When the meal finally dragged to a conclusion she took herself off to bed with the announcement that she was very tired after the dreadful day she had had.

'Well!' Rosa exclaimed. 'After the day *she* has had!'

'It must be very difficult for her.' Bree tried valiantly to be fair. The alternative was bitter ranting or to relapse into floods of tears, and that had left her red-eyed and exhausted.

'Nonsense.' Rosa sounded every inch the head-mistress. 'She is reacting just like a spoiled chit of a girl—I have seen enough of them to know. She has no thought for anyone else's feelings and she is totally self-absorbed.'

They sat for half an hour in virtual silence, then Bree said, 'It feels like a bereavement—that awful time when your mind is full of nothing but the fact that someone you love is no longer with you and there is nothing to talk about, nothing you have the energy to do.'

'It is a bereavement,' Rosa said gently. 'Unless...' She hesitated. 'Drusilla will not be living with him. Have you thought of an irregular relationship?' She looked decidedly uncomfortable saying it.

'No.' Bree stared at her. 'No. That never entered my head.' She tried to imagine it, almost seduced by the thought. Drusilla did not love Max, did not want to live with him. She could not be hurt by it. 'No,' she said finally. 'I love him, I want to be with him openly, to have his children. I cannot bear the thought of something clandestine. It would get out, there would be rumours and whispers. There are Piers and James to think about. And what if I became pregnant?'

Rosa nodded. 'That is what I thought you would say. But he might ask you—it is best to be prepared.'

'No.' Bree smiled, thinking about Max. 'He might be prepared to anticipate marriage, but he would not ask me to be his mistress.' Warmed a little by her certainty in him, she got up and stretched. Every muscle ached; it must be from the tension of the day. 'I think I will go to bed too. I don't know if I will sleep, but I must try to.'

She kissed Rosa's cheek and went up, surprising Lucy, who was just turning down the bed. 'Is Miss Drusilla comfortable?'

'Yes, Miss Bree. Dreadful thing that smallpox, she must have been so beautiful. I have lent her one of your nightgowns.'

Bree climbed into bed, blew out the candle and curled up, pulling the feather comforter round her ears, expecting to lie awake for hours. But when she woke abruptly, to complete darkness, she realised she must have fallen asleep almost immediately. It had not been an untroubled slumber. Fragments of dreams, of jumbled memories, of emotions swirled in her brain.

What woke me?

She struggled up against the pillows, disentangling twisted sheets to do so, and forced herself to remember. *Yes!* That was it, the sense of something not being right, of something in the picture being at odds with what it should be.

Then the pieces all slid together and she knew. *She is not Drusilla. She is too young. This is not a woman of almost thirty, this is one who is twenty at most.*

'Then who is she?' Bree threw back the covers and

reached for the tinder box. In the light of the candle she sat on the edge of the bed, bare feet dangling, and put all the inconsistencies together. Those plump, flawless hands. The smooth nape and perfectly black hair, her gauche manner that had so reminded Rosa of the girls she used to teach, that slip of the tongue when she was describing life at Longwater: *It was like being at school, Drusilla said.* That was what she had almost blurted out before she had hastily turned *Drusilla* into *dreadful.*

Fanny, that is who she is. The little sister. No one else could be so like Drusilla. And Max sees what he had last seen, what his memories had preserved, a beautiful woman of twenty, only with the mask of those scars to veil the differences.

Relief swelled through her, so violently that it almost hurt. Max was not married. He was free. He was hers. The clocks in the house chimed three, the sound silvery in the stillness. Was he awake, like her? *Yes,* her instinct told her. He was awake, suffering, believing that his own actions and inactions had led to the end of both their hopes.

Bree slid off the bed and began to drag on clothes, snatching up a gown she could manage without waking Lucy and pushing her feet into the nearest pair of shoes. She found her reticule, checked that there was enough money in it for a hackney carriage fare, then stopped in the act of fastening her pelisse. How on earth was she going to get a hackney at this time of night? And she could hardly walk there, not alone.

Shielding the guttering candle flame with one hand, she crept along the corridor and eased open Piers's door. Goodness knows what time he had come back last night, she thought, guiltily aware that Rosa had probably sat up for him.

'Piers, Piers, wake up.'

'Wha—?' He rolled over, rubbed one had across bleary eyes and stared up at her. 'Bree? What on earth? What time is it?'

'Three in the morning. Piers, get up, please, and get dressed. I need to go to Max.'

'Are you eloping?' He sat up, unfocused, the night's growth of stubble making him look older than he was.

'No, of course not. Piers, listen, he isn't married after all.' Bree sat on the edge of his bed and gave him a shake. 'She isn't Drusilla.'

'But Max recognised her. Bree, I know you're upset, but we've got to face facts.'

'She is what Max remembered of Drusilla.'

'You mean, she's a ghost? I know you need to hope, but, Bree, that isn't possible.'

'No—I mean she's her younger sister. I mean, she is Drusilla's younger sister, Fanny, pretending to be Drusilla. And she is just the age Drusilla was when Max met her.'

'Oh, I see!' Piers looked wide awake now. 'But you cannot go off to see Max at this time of night.'

'Why not? If he is half as miserable as I was until I realised, I cannot bear to leave it until the morning. But I can hardly walk across London by myself.'

'Well, let me get dressed then. But I'll wager you he has sunk his troubles in a brandy bottle.'

Bree had already drawn back the bolts when Piers came downstairs, his hair still tousled and his chin unshaven. 'I've left a note for Peters in case he thinks we've been burgled. Do you think there is any chance of a cab or shall we take the most direct line and walk?'

'We'll try Tottenham Court Road,' Piers decided. 'You never know.'

They were in luck. One weary cabby, obviously returning home, agreed to turn around and head back into the West End for double his fare. Bree could hardly sit still on the battered upholstery as the horse plodded its way down to Oxford Street.

'What are you going to do with her? Fanny, I mean?' Piers asked.

'It's not for me to say. She is pretending to be Max's wife, after all.'

'She nearly ruined your life,' Piers pointed out.

'I know. It has hardly had time to sink in, it was such a shock. I can't imagine doing something that dreadful to another person, but I don't think she understands.'

Piers's snort of derision was comment enough. He peered out of the smeared window. 'Almost there, this is Bruton Street.'

'Here's the money.' Bree thrust it into his hands and tumbled out of the carriage door before it had stopped moving. She was halfway up the steps to the shiny black front door when it opened and a tall, cloaked figure stepped out.

Chapter Twenty-Three

'Bree?' Max's heart seemed to stop, then he saw she was smiling.

'Max! Oh, Max, it is all right! She isn't Drusilla.' She flung herself into his arms and clung. *Hell, I must reek of brandy. She doesn't seem to mind....*

From the pavement he heard the rasp of the hackney driver's voice. 'Blimey! That's a willing tit,' and a snort of laughter. He glanced up. Thank goodness, at least she had Piers with her.

Max bent his head as his arms closed round her. 'Darling, I know, I was coming to tell you.'

'Five minutes either way and we'd have passed each other.' Piers came up the steps to join them. 'You'd be hammering on our door, we'd be upsetting Bignell all over again. Do you think we ought to go inside? I mean, there's a couple of bucks strolling this way, and a carriage has just pulled in three houses along, and I don't know what your neighbours are like...'

'Come on.' Max steered them both inside and into

the study. It seemed impossible to let go of Bree, but somehow he managed to untangle himself and sat her down. 'Pour three glasses of brandy, Piers, I think we need it.'

'You've been drinking it already,' Bree said. 'Piers said you'd be drunk.'

'I've had a few, I'll admit. Bree, what happened? Did Fanny confess? I assume that's who she is.' He wanted to touch her, hold her hands at least, but he knew if he did, then he would not be able to stop himself kissing her and they needed to talk first. Suddenly, opening up in front of him, was a lifetime of being able to kiss Bree.

'I think she must be Fanny. I only realised at three o'clock this morning. I'd been dreaming. All the things I had noticed and yet not realised the significance of, were churning about in my brain and I woke up—and there was the answer.

'She's a woman of twenty, not one of thirty. Her hands, her skin where it isn't pockmarked, her hair, are all those of a very young woman. And to hear her talk, she is so immature—Rosa spotted that and she is used to young girls. If we discount ghosts, then it being her younger sister seems the only solution. But how did you guess?'

Max got to his feet, lifted the small oil painting off the wall and handed it to her.

'Oh, it's you! What a charming study. When was it painted?'

'Shortly before I met Drusilla. I found myself brooding over my brandy glass, staring at it. And then I looked in the mirror and saw how I had changed.'

'You are even better looking now,' Bree said loyally. 'Your face has gained maturity and strength.'

'Thank you.' He smiled affectionately. 'I found myself thinking that I had changed significantly and how little she had, if you discount the effects of the smallpox. And suddenly, about an hour ago, it dawned on me.' How could he ever express to her how it had felt, that relief, that blinding sense that an emotional death sentence had been lifted? Then he saw the love in the blue eyes watching him and he knew that Bree's feelings for him were as deep as his for her. And that her hurt had been as acute.

'I sat for a while, just trying to work it all out, make certain I was not mistaken. Then I knew I had to come to you.'

Piers cleared his throat, jerking them both back to the present. 'Rosa said she knew things.' He blushed. 'Private things about your marriage.'

'I expect Drusilla confided in her.' Max shrugged. 'Not the sort of thing one should talk to girls her age about, of course, but she was angry, bitter, confused and I suppose it all came out.'

'What are we going to do now?' Blinking in the

candlelight, Bree looked as though she had just woken up from a bad dream.

'We send out the wedding invitations. Or at least, I get my secretary to do that.' He couldn't resist it. He got up and went to sit on the arm of her chair, and began to stroke the mass of blonde hair she had bundled roughly into a net.

'Yes.' She leant her head into his caressing hand like a cat being stroked. 'But what about Fanny? Max, what made her do it? I just cannot believe she is intelligent enough to work this out for herself.'

Damnation. He had hoped she would not realise that. Once he had emerged from the shocked joy of realising that Drusilla had not come back to haunt him, Max had wondered that very thing. And then the memory of Ryder's letter fallen to the floor at Latymer's feet in the club had come back to him. This time he was going to call the man out, and this time he had every intention of putting a bullet into him.

And despite the fact that she could not see his face, Bree had sensed his reticence. *Hell*, he thought with the sense of willingly giving up not just his heart but his entire life, *I'm never going to be able to keep anything secret from her.*

She twisted round in the chair to look up at him. '*Max.* You know something.'

'I think it is Latymer again. I suspect he read a letter from Ryder to me. It named no names, but it had enough in it to give him a start if he was wanting to pry into my business.'

'What are you going to do?' Piers demanded, on his feet, fists clenched.

'Call him out. He will not be able to wriggle out of it this time. *I* have no intention of accepting an apology.'

'Max—what if you kill him?' Bree's brow was furrowed with anxiety. 'I don't want to be left standing at the altar while you flee to the continent!'

'You don't worry he might kill me, I notice,' he teased her, amused at himself for the warm glow of pride her assumption of his superior skill gave him.

'Of course not.' She rubbed her cheek against his sleeve. 'But you must be careful. He might be such a bad shot he will hit you by accident.'

'May I be a second?' Piers asked.

Max nodded, ignoring Bree's gasp of denial. 'Yes, you and Ryder. One of you will have to act for Latymer—I can't afford to let anyone else in on this, not even Nevill.'

'Piers is too young!'

'No, he is not. I'll look after him.' Max winked at Piers over Bree's head.

'It is supposed to be the other way round,' she scolded. 'Oh, I suppose it will be all right if Mr Ryder is there—he, at least, seems sensible.'

'That has put us in our place,' Max observed to Piers. 'Now, let's think this through. We will confront

Fanny after breakfast. I want Ryder there. I think it will be useful to have a witness from outside the family.' Bree glanced up and smiled, a fleeting curve of her lips, acknowledging that word. *Family.* 'We will see if our suspicions are confirmed and then deal with it.'

'And Fanny?'

Wring her neck for causing you one moment's pain. Max bit back the words. 'What do you want me to do about her, my love?'

'Give her a modest pension, find her a cottage—a long way away.'

'Reward her for trying to ruin our lives?'

'Show you are as generous as you are loyal and clever and brave.'

'I think I'll, um…go and see if the hackney is still waiting,' Piers announced gruffly.

'We're embarrassing him.' Bree smiled.

'Do him good,' Max rejoined unsympathetically. 'He's learning about affairs of honour, he can start learning about sex.'

'Max!'

'And love, of course. Which reminds me—how long is it since I kissed you?'

'Far too long.' She curled deliciously into his embrace, squeaking with alarm as he slid into the chair with her, bundling her in his arms until she was sitting on his knee.

'You know, you make me feel younger than I did when I met Drusilla.'

'I do? Why?'

'Because you are a grown woman. You don't need treating like a child, you don't sulk, you deal with me as an equal. So I can relax.'

'Oh.' The twinkle in Bree's eyes was decidedly grown up. Max could feel the effect of it solidly in his groin. 'I am not sure I want you *very* relaxed.'

The only answer to that was to kiss her.

'Bree, how many days now until we are married?' Lifting his lips from hers, Max sounded as breathless as she felt.

'Nine?' she hazarded vaguely.

'I don't suppose we can send Piers home in the hackney and—'

'No.' Bree planted one hand firmly on Max's chest and got to her feet.

'*Oof!* I thought you'd say that.' Apparently resigned, he stood up. 'Off you go, then. Ryder and I will be there by seven if I can locate him, then we can decide how best to confront Fanny. Catching her off guard will probably be best.'

He opened the study door for her, then seized her round the waist and bent to kiss her again as he slowly walked her backwards towards the front door. Torn between ecstasy and giggles, Bree let herself be shuffled slowly along, her fingers tight around Max's lapels.

'Do you wish the door opened, my lord?'

With a squeak Bree jumped backwards. Bignell was standing there, immaculate in full livery, a branch of candles in one hand and an expression that she could only call *stuffed* on his face.

'Thank you, Bignell,' Max said with admirable aplomb, rather spoiling the effect by enquiring, 'Do you sleep in your livery?'

'No, my lord. Upon hearing voices, I first came up-stairs in my nightgown, if Miss Mallory will excuse the mention of such a garment. Having identified your voice, my lord, I returned downstairs, restored the blunderbuss to its cabinet and assumed my garments.'

'I see, excellent.' Bree could see that Max was bit-ing his lip, presumably to stop himself laughing. 'Er, carry on.'

Outside he hurried her down the steps and into the hackney, hanging on to the open door and giving in to his amusement with his back safely turned to the butler.

'Oh, dear,' Bree said faintly, 'I really do not think Bignell approves of me.'

'I approve of you, which is rather more to the point,' Max said, struggling to get his face straight before re-turning inside. 'He just has to put up with you. I will see you before breakfast. Sleep well.'

'Goodnight.' Bree reached out and touched his face, the stubble on his unshaven cheek prickling her fingertips. 'Goodnight.'

'Well,' Piers said somewhat breathlessly, as the tired coach horse plodded back northwards. 'Life's not like this at Harrow, you know. It's going to be devilishly dull when I go back.'

'Good,' Bree said with feeling. 'I am certain I am a very bad sister, exposing you to all this.'

'I'm not going to be able to talk about it, am I?' he said, suddenly glum.

'No,' Bree agreed. 'You are not. That's one of the disadvantages of being grown up—lots of exciting secrets you can't brag about.' She reached out and gave his hand a squeeze. 'Never mind, you are going to acquire a very dashing brother-in-law.'

Rosa was already up and arranging her hair when Bree peered sleepily round her door at half past six the next morning. 'Goodness, you look half-awake,' she exclaimed, putting down her brush. 'Poor love, couldn't you sleep?'

'No, but not for the reasons you might expect.' Bree shut the door and came to perch on the end of Rosa's bed. 'Piers and I were at Max's house at half past three this morning.'

'What!' Rosa gasped, then shot a hasty look at the closed door. 'Is it about Drusilla?' she whispered.

'Yes, only she isn't. Rosa, it is all going to be all right.'

Bree's revelations, and the arrival of the gentlemen at the kitchen door, provoked a flurry of activity in the household, for it proved impossible not to tell the staff at least something.

'Well, I never did!' Cook exclaimed, banging sugar snips down with some feeling. 'A confidence trickster in our house, and I was going to make her a nice kedgeree.'

'I think we'd all appreciate it anyway,' Bree said soothingly, although her stomach revolted at the mere thought of anything more than plain bread and butter.

Max and Jack Ryder vanished upstairs, Bree and Piers took themselves off to the breakfast room and Rosa went to roust their houseguest out of her room.

'She must have been fierce when she was a schoolteacher,' Piers observed with a grin.

Fanny drifted in, smiled wanly at them and took the remaining seat with its back to the screen which hid the door to the back stairs.

Bree plied her with tea and toast, sang the praises of Cook's special kedgeree and launched into energetic conversation with Rosa and Piers.

'More kedgeree, Piers? It is very strengthening. Toast, then? Fanny, do be so kind as to pass the butter.'

And quite unconsciously Fanny did just that. It was not until she had the silver dish in her hand, halfway to Rosa's, that the name Bree had used penetrated. 'Oh!' She dropped the dish with a crash and stared round wildly. 'What...what did you call me?'

'She called you Fanny. That is your name, is it not?' Max put the screen to one side and stepped out, leaving Ryder lounging against the serving buffet, one sharp eye on the door. 'You are my sister-in-law, I believe.'

Fanny stared at him, her mouth open, clutched a napkin and burst into tears. 'He said you would never know!' she wailed. 'He said it would be so easy...'

'Brice Latymer told you that, did he?' Ryder enquired casually while Rosa pressed a handkerchief into Fanny's hand and told her briskly to pull herself together.

'Mmm.' She nodded, sniffing miserably. 'He told me what to say, told me to pretend about the letters, so could say I didn't trust you. He said we could split the money.'

'How did he find you?' Bree asked. 'Were you in Portsmouth?'

'No.' Fanny gulped. 'I never left Winchester. I was apprenticed to Mrs Pilgrim the milliner. The girl who cleans the pews came to see me, told me this gentleman was enquiring about the Cornish family. Then Mr Latymer came, enquiring about what the other gentleman had been asking for and the sexton sent him to me.' She looked apprehensively from one face to another. 'What are you going to do with me?'

'Find you a cottage and give you a small annuity,' Max said. Bree saw him wince slightly as the great green eyes fixed on his face. 'And I never want to hear from you again.'

'I'll take her to your attorney,' Ryder offered, 'then put her on the next stage to Winchester.'

'Thank you.' Max looked grateful not to have anything more to do with his errant sister-in-law. 'I'll just write a note for him.'

Bree tried to apply herself to wedding preparations, lists and arrangements, but the constant coming and going of Mr Ryder and Max was distracting, and when they came to collect Piers for their call to Latymer's lodgings she was left too nervous to concentrate. 'Don't forget he has a swordstick,' she called down the stairs after them. 'Don't trust him an inch.'

They came back, hours after she had expected them, all three with the look of small boys who had been deprived of a treat. 'What happened?' Bree demanded, practically dragging them into the drawing room.

'He's done a runner off to Scotland,' Ryder said, running his hand through his hair. 'It's where the family comes from. By all accounts he has been having a watch kept on this house. When the lad saw Fanny being taken off by me, he ran back to Latymer, who must have realised the game was up.'

'He's gone on the stage,' Piers said glumly. 'I thought Max could take his curricle and we could give chase, but he said you'd ring a peal over him if he did that.'

'I am so glad you didn't,' Bree said with feeling. 'That is just what I need, a bridegroom halfway up the Great North Road in pursuit of a duel!'

'But I think we can feel free to tell everyone— in strict confidence, which they will not observe, of course—all about the card-sharping incident. He'll never be able to show his face in London society again,' Max said, stretching long legs out to the fender. 'Do you think, Miss Mallory, that we may now pro- ceed to a trouble-free nuptials?'

'With this family?' Piers snorted. 'I doubt it!'

Chapter Twenty-Four

Bree blinked as they walked out of the bright sunshine of a crisp October morning into the gloom of the church porch. Then the verger threw open the doors and she and Piers stepped into the light streaming down from the clerestory windows, reflecting off the old white stone, catching the glossy leaves and petals of sheaf after sheaf of flowers arranged at the ends of the carved pews.

Beside her Piers looked impossibly grown-up in his new swallow-tailed coat. She tightened her grip on his arm and searched for Max. He looked so far away down the long aisle, between the massed guests.

'Off we go,' Piers whispered and they began to walk, Bree darting quick glances from the shelter of her veil. There was Lady Lucas, her husband beside her, there was James, torn between pride at the match and horror at the choice of location for the wedding. There was Max's redoubtable grandmother, whom she had come to like over the past few days—as she saw Bree her autocratic face was transformed by a wide smile.

Almost there now. Uncle George, well again, beaming at her—and then there was nothing and no one in the world but Max, white-faced as she had never seen him.

Bree gave her flowers to Rosa, turned and placed her hand in Max's. The Vicar stepped forward, lifted the prayer book and began.

'Dearly beloved…'

Bree had expected the service to pass like a dream, yet every moment slowed until it had its own significance and she knew she would never forget a second of it. The moment when Max spoke his vows and she heard his voice break, the moment she said hers and his hand tightened warm and secure around her cold fingers, the feeling as the ring slid on to her finger and the sight of his face as he put back her veil and stood looking down at her.

'You may kiss the bride,' the vicar intoned.

'My wife,' Max said softly. 'My beautiful wife.'

The kiss was long, intense, full of words neither of them had to say. Bree was blushing and laughing when Max finally released her, all the colour was back in his face and the guests were beaming.

Walking back down the aisle, stopping and exchanging words with old friends and new, Bree knew this wedding in the quiet country church, miles from fashionable London, was perfect. Nothing could make the day any better.

'Had you noticed,' Max observed as they emerged from the porch, 'I have not given you a wedding present yet?'

'I rather thought you were it,' Bree said daringly, making him chuckle.

'No. I have something rather larger for you. It will be here in a moment.'

The bells were peeling out overhead, the guests came crowding behind them, spilling out into the churchyard to throw rice, wave and call for Bree to throw her bouquet. They reached the lichgate. 'Where is my present?' Bree teased. 'I can't see anything larger than you.'

Then there was the familiar blast of a coach horn and across the green a stagecoach came at full tilt pulled by four grey horses. 'Max! A stagecoach, what on earth is it doing here?'

It was in *Challenge Coach Company* livery, she realised. Bill Huggins, a vast nosegay in his buttonhole, was on the box, but it was bigger, shinier, infinitely better than anything they had in the yard. Bill brought the team to a snorting halt in front of the gate and Bree saw the lettering on the door. '*The Countess of Penrith*,' she read. 'Max! You've bought me a stagecoach!'

'I wanted to show you that I am proud of my wife,

proud of the company and proud to be part it.' Max staggered back as Bree launched herself at him in an enthusiastic hug. 'Shall I drive you to the wedding breakfast? Will you come up on the box with me?'

Laughing, trying to protect her blue silk skirts as she clambered up, Bree let herself be boosted on to the box. Max climbed up beside her and steadied the team. Looking down, Bree saw Piers assisting the Dowager Countess into the coach, followed by a faintly protesting James.

'Here.' Max offered her the reins. 'It is your coach.'

'No.' Bree shook her head. 'Ours.' And she slid her hand into his, and drove with him, just as they had that night when they had first met.

'I wish we could have driven to Norfolk in my new stagecoach,' Bree said wistfully. 'I don't think any bride has ever had such a wonderful present.'

'It was worth it just for the look on your brother James's face when he realised he was expected to get into it to drive to the breakfast.' Max chuckled. She smiled back, then fell silent, suddenly shy.

She was conscious of his eyes on her face, of the closeness of his long body, the strong, elegant hands, the power in his relaxed frame. He was, finally, her husband. That had implications of intimacy that she had never really considered before. Sexual intimacy, of course. Bree swallowed, realising that she had never seen Max naked, nor he, her. And that was just the start of it.

And then there were all the other intimacies: shared dreams and hopes, things to disagree about and argue over, fears kept private until now, little faults and big failings. How would it feel to share all those things with someone who loved you, someone you were coming to realise you hardly knew?

Except I know the important things. I know he is honest and brave. I know he admits his faults. I know he is loyal to his friends, drives like an angel and kisses like all the temptations of sin. I know I love him, and I believe he loves me.

'You are very serious.' He looked serious too, and a little anxious about her solemn face. 'Regrets?'

'No, never those. I was just thinking about how intimate marriage must be—all those thoughts kept private until now, all our own odd habits, preferences, dislikes. Do you think it will take long to become used to each other?'

'I am not sure I want to become used to you.' Max studied her face, his eyes warm beneath lids that seemed heavy with smouldering desire. 'I want to be constantly surprised.'

She smiled back, reassured, then glanced out of the window. 'Where on earth are we going? The postilions must be lost. This isn't the way to Norfolk—in fact, I think we are going west.'

'We are, and we are nearly there. I couldn't face the journey, not having to stop at some inn on our wedding night. I have borrowed Lansdowne's hunting lodge in the Vale of Aylesbury. He is the only one who knows, the servants have all been firmly instructed to be neither heard, nor seen, and we can stay a week if we like.'

'Oh.' *Nearly there.* Bree ran her tongue over lips that were suddenly dry. She had thought she had hours to prepare herself. It wasn't that she didn't want Max to make love to her, it was just that she didn't feel very ready for it.

He was watching her face. 'Not a good idea?'

'A very good one.' she said firmly. 'How kind of Lord Lansdowne.'

Max merely smiled, leaving Bree with the clear impression he knew just what she was thinking. It was hopeless, one couldn't *keep* blushing, surely?

She did not have long to brood. The carriage swung between a pair of modest brick gateposts, past a lodge and into a small park. The house was a neat Queen Anne, perfect in its miniature detail.

'It is a doll's house,' Bree exclaimed, charmed. Max helped her down and escorted her up the steps to the front door which stood wide open. 'There's no one here.'

'No one visible,' Max corrected, taking her by surprise by sweeping her up into his arms and carrying her over the threshold.

'But...'

He pressed on up the stairs, blithely disregarding her half-hearted struggles. It was quite extraordinarily disconcerting to be carried so easily. Another door stood open on the landing, Max strode through it, set her on her feet and closed it, turning the key in the lock.

Bree looked around. Here was a table set with a cold collation, a bottle in an ice bucket and two chairs. There was a fire crackling in the wide hearth, heavy golden drapes at the windows and around the bed. The very big, very prominent, very *obvious* bed.

'Are you hungry?'

'No.' Where her stomach should be there was a hollow space filled with a mass of butterflies.

'Shall we go to bed, then?'

'At—' she cast a wild glance at the mantel clock '—five in the afternoon?'

'Sounds a reasonable plan to me.' Max reached for her bonnet ribbons and began to untie them slowly. He tossed the bonnet on to a chair and reached for the top button of her pelisse.

Suddenly emboldened, Bree held up her hand. 'No. We take turns. I have no intention of blushing here on the hearthrug while you stay safely clothed.' She reached up and removed his tall hat.

'Hmm. One item at a time?'

'Exactly. Pairs of things count as one,' she conceded. 'And no…no lovemaking until we have finished.'

'Right.' He resumed unbuttoning her pelisse.

'That would be easier if you took your gloves off first,' Bree observed.

'You don't trick me into throwing away an entire garment like that, my lady.' He persevered while Bree struggled with the reality of being *my lady. A countess. Me.*

The thought was so distracting that Max was slipping the pelisse off her shoulders before she could concentrate on the tactics of this new game. It would be amusing to have him struggle with corset strings in gloves. On the other hand, she had to admit that she could not wait to have those long, clever fingers on her skin.

'Gloves next.' Slowly, one finger at a time, she began to ease off the pigskin gloves. She let her fingertips brush against the sensitive skin inside Max's wrists. He drew in a hissing breath. As she pulled off the first glove she let her thumbnail score lightly down his palm, then repeated it with the second.

'Witch.' Max reached for her own hands. The buttons at the wrists were tight and he took his time, teasing the fine skin over the pulse with the pads of his fingers until she closed her eyes in mute supplication.

He changed to start working at each finger, easing back the thin kid. 'I could have dragged Latymer out of his curricle and broken his jaw for him that day in the park,' he remarked, startling her so that she opened her eyes and blinked at him. 'I was trying not to become attached to you. I was trying, with very little success, to tell myself that you did not belong to me.'

'Even then?'

'From the first moment I saw you, that glimpse of your furious face as Nevill took the drag past your stage outside Hounslow. Mine. I knew it.'

Both gloves were crumpled in his hand. They stood, barely a foot apart, swaying together so their breath mingled. She saw his pupils widen.

'My turn.' Bree reached up and pushed Max's coat off his shoulders.

Max growled deep in his throat and dropped to one knee beside her. 'Shoes.'

Removing shoes, it seemed, was just as exciting as gloves. Bree balanced, one hand on his shoulder, looking down at Max's dark, ruffled hair and wondering if he was simply very good at the preliminaries to lovemaking, or whether all men spent this much time reducing their wives to a mass of quivering anticipation.

And not just their wives, she realised, for under her hand she could feel the tension in his shoulder. She could see the pulse thudding in his neck and the warm colour of his nape.

Both shoes off, she stood in her stockinged feet, regarding her husband, making up her mind. 'Your Hessians,' she pronounced. Until those were off, his trousers could not be removed, although she was not at all sure she wished to go that far yet.

Obligingly, Max sat down and offered a foot. 'You'll need to turn round and straddle my leg,' he offered helpfully with a straight face and the air of a man hugely enjoying himself.

Bree narrowed her eyes at him, but did as he said, gripping his knee between her thighs, her skirts tumbling on either side. It felt positively indecent. And exciting. She gritted her teeth, grabbed the heel again and hauled. The boot slid off smoothly. Bree stepped over his other leg and repeated the process.

She expected Max to attack her stockings next, but he walked around her and began to work on the row of tiny pearl buttons down the back of her gown. Was the man capable of doing anything fast? It seemed every button required infinitely detailed attention, and the necessity to caress the exposed line of her upper vertebrae with his thumb before moving on to the next one.

At last, just as Bree was on the point of spinning round, seizing him by the ears and kissing him until he suffocated, Max reached the bottom of the buttons and untied the sash.

'Does this slip down or lift over?' He was easing

it off her as he spoke, his palms caressing down over each shoulder.

'Li…lift off,' Bree managed to whisper.

'Sweetheart,' he murmured in her ear, pulling her back until she was flat against him. 'Aren't you enjoying this?'

'Yes, yes I am. Only I feel so…'

'Tense?'

'Yes.' That was definitely the word. It was like the other times he had made love to her, but all they were doing now was undressing each other. How could it make her feel as if he was running his hands over her naked body, as though his mouth was… 'Yes. Tense.'

'Poor darling.' His mouth was very close to her ear. 'We will have to do something about that.'

'Make me less tense?'

'Oh, no, quite the contrary.' He chuckled and bent to lift the hem of her gown. Enveloped in silk and satin in lush folds, Bree emerged to find Max regarding her wickedly over an overspilling armful of fabric. Somehow it managed to make him look even more outrageously masculine.

Right. 'What of yours would you like me to take off next?' she enquired sweetly.

'Stockings,' Max said instantly. 'There are few things more ridiculous than a naked man in nothing but his stockings.'

'I see.' Bree nodded and reached for his neckcloth.

'You *baggage.*'

'I was only teasing,' she said demurely. 'Put your hand on my shoulder.'

It had never occurred to her that feet could be attractive, or that they might upset her equilibrium. But the sight of Max's lean, bare feet, their long tendons flexing as his toes burrowed into the carpet, made her feel slightly breathless.

'What next?' he asked.

'Garters?'

'So you are counting garters and stockings as two items, are you?' Max leaned forward and ran one finger under the thin strap holding up the petticoat. 'I'll leave those for the present. Just as a man wearing only stockings looks ridiculous, a woman wearing nothing else looks very, very exciting.'

Bree suppressed a squeak of alarm at the purr in his voice. Somehow she had imagined the last garment coming off being followed by a rapid retreat under the bedclothes. It did not sound as though Max had that in mind at all.

The thin lawn slid down to pool around her feet. Bree told herself that she was still very decently clad, although a corset over a shift that reached only to her knees felt precarious covering.

She reached up and untied his neckcloth, standing on tiptoe to unwrap it from around his neck. It brought her close against his chest and Max closed his arms around her. The corset pushed up her breasts and the points of her nipples, covered only in the fine fabric of her chemise, peaked, brushing against the firm fabric of his waistcoat. 'Max!'

'I am just steadying you,' he said earnestly.

'You are not, you are moving against my…against my chest.'

'Heavy breathing.'

She pulled the last turn of muslin free and tossed the cloth to one side. 'Then let me go. You will feel much better.'

'I doubt it. Turn around so I can reach your corset strings.'

Bree turned, resting her hands on her hips and breathing in as she did when Lucy laced or unlaced her. 'However do you breathe?' Max asked. 'I'm going to have to take the scissors to these.'

'Cheating.'

'Well, prepare for a long conversation, then! I have confessed to falling for you at first sight. Are you going to tell me when you first began to feel the same way?'

'In the chaise, after the highwaymen, and you were wounded and we took off your shirt. I found I was becoming very flustered.' She felt herself blush just talking about it. 'That stud—it made me think about what you meant by saying they were considered erotic. And the more I thought about it, the more I wondered.'

Max's fingers tightened on the laces of their own accord, pulling Bree in so the warmth of his breath fanned the flushed skin of her nape. 'I knew all that pain had to be worth it eventually,' he murmured. It had not seemed that his body could be any tighter, the ache in his groin any more acute, but Bree's flustered frankness was having a devastating effect.

'I didn't realise I was falling in love with you until you came with me to see Uncle,' she confessed, hurrying on to slightly safer ground.

'So your concern for my poor, wounded shoulder had nothing to do with you offering me a bed for the night?'

'Yes, of course. It was so kind of you to have come with me.'

'I have a confession to make—' He broke off, muttering under his breath with frustration at the tight knot. 'Ah, that's got it. There was nothing hurting at all. The wound was healed up, I was feeling perfectly fine, but I wanted to go with you, so I did my best to look as though I was bravely suffering in silence.'

Bree spun round, the corset strings pulled out of his hands and the stiffened fabric slid to her hips. 'You *fraud*!' She took a hasty step forwards and it slid further, effectively hobbling her. 'Oh, get this beastly thing off me so I can hit you!'

Max grinned and tugged the corset up over her head. 'I had the best of intentions.'

'You can take your own waistcoat off,' Bree said, trying to look affronted. Max stripped off the moiré silk, its deep blue shimmering as it caught the light, making him think of her eyes.

Bree did a rapid calculation. 'Shirt, pantaloons, drawers. This is very unfair—you have more clothes on than I do.'

'You should have added up first, and made me start,' Max drawled, then yielded a point. 'I'll unpin your hair and count that as one.' It was no concession; he was having trouble controlling his breathing at the thought of that wheaten mass sliding free over her shoulders. Any minute it now it would be slipping over her naked body.

He made a deliberately slow business of it until it slid over his fingers like cool live flame. He caught up the weight of it, then let it go. 'Lady Godiva,' he teased, trying to cover up his own emotion before he lost control.

Bree's eyes were wide on his. This was ceasing to become a game, yet she was not frightened, he could tell. Apprehensive, yes. And aroused. He could see the hard peaks of her nipples, the flushed skin of her throat and bosom.

She took hold his shirt and began to pull it free from the waistband of his trousers, then set to work on the buttons. He wondered just how much more of this he could stand. 'There.' She pushed the linen back off his shoulders. Max put up his hands, caught hers and pulled them down, flattening them against his pectorals, feeling the pressure of her soft palms on the tight, aching knots of his nipples.

'Max.' It was a whisper that fluttered against his skin like the brush of a feather.

He released her and took hold of her chemise, pulling it gently over her head, never taking his eyes off her as he tossed it aside. Then all he could do was look.

Bree's hands fluttered to her sides and she stared back at him, seeming hardly to breathe.

His eyes drank her in. The delicate slope of her shoulders, the firm, uplifted breasts with their puckered, rose-pink aureoles, the sweet curve of waist and hip, the feminine roundness, the mass of curls, darker than her head hair, the shadowed triangle of delights, the provocative pink garters and the shimmer of silk over her calves.

His hands went to the fastenings of his pantaloons, fumbled, freed them and he dragged them off, his thumbs hooked into his drawers so both came together, leaving him naked in front of her. Bree's eyes widened, she touched the tip of her tongue to her upper lip. 'Touch me,' he said softly. 'Put your hands on me.'

But he is beautiful. His shoulders were broad, his chest ribbed with muscle, narrowing down to a slim waist, tight hips. Her gaze froze and she ran her tongue around lips suddenly dry.

She had held him, caressed him, in the drag. But she had not seen. Max, powerful, aroused, naked, was taking her breath away.

'Touch me. Put your hands on me.'

Bree took a step forward, then another. She laid one hand on his chest, over the breastbone, feeling the thud of his heart. She raised her lips for his kiss and curled her other hand around the hard, hot, velvety masculinity that pulsed between them.

'I love you.' They were not playing now. The tone of his voice was as sincere as when he had made his vow in church. His lips on hers were a claiming as much as the placing of the ring on her finger. She slid both her arms around his neck, letting him pull her tight against him, branding the heat of him on her belly.

'I love you too. Show me how to make love to you,' she whispered.

He lifted her, carried her to the bed and settled her on the expanse of golden brocade. 'I should go slowly for you,' he whispered, settling himself beside her, his hand gliding down over the curve of her breasts, the swell of her belly, into the curls that seemed the only protection her modesty and virginity had left.

'Max.' She did not know how to say it, how to tell him that she ached for him, that she was wet for him, that tiny quivering darts of pleasure were shaking her.

'Max, I need you *now*.' Daring, desperate, she touched him again, taking him firmly as he had shown her, caressing up the length to the crown, then down again.

'Sweetheart…stop, or I will lose what very little control I have left.' His finger moved into the hot, wet, aching folds and she pressed against him, knowing the pleasure that would give. But he avoided the aching bud and instead slipped inside. Bree felt her muscles closing around him, trying to hold on to him, then a second finger joined the first and she arched up, pressing against his palm, whimpering with delight.

Max shifted over her, nudging her legs apart, and she moved to cradle him, feeling the tip of his erection at the very spot she so yearned for him. 'I love you,' he said again, and surged into her.

Bree gasped, shocked by the stab of soreness, then shaken to her core by the sensation of his body within hers, of the movement that was driving the pain away, building that tension that was racking her to the point where she arched hard against him, desperate for it to sweep her away.

'Open your eyes. Look at me.' Barely able to focus now, as his body drove hers into a tighter and tighter spiral of sensation, Bree dragged open her eyes and looked up into his face. His eyes were wide, dark, intent. His jaw was locked hard, the tendons in his throat taut with effort as he took them both higher, harder, further.

'Max—' His name was dragged from her lips as the dam burst, the tension splintered into pleasure that racked her from head to toe. She was conscious of his body surging against hers, of his shout, of his body driving impossibly deep into hers, and then the world went dark.

She came to herself to find Max's weight still on her, his forehead resting on hers, their panting breath mingling.

'Max?' He rolled off her with a sigh, but gathered her against him as though fearful of letting her go. 'Max, is it always like that?'

He pushed himself up on one elbow. There was sweat on his forehead, his hair was in his eyes, his mouth looked bruised. *I did that?*

'Not in my experience,' he admitted. 'Never before.'

'Will it always be like that?'

'Slower,' he said. 'Sometimes slower.'

'Oh. Slower would be good. Sometimes. We'll try that next, shall we?'

'Shall we have a glass of wine first?' Max slid off the bed, clutched the bedpost for support and grinned at her. 'You have unmanned me.'

Bree sat up against the pillows. Her muscles seemed to have been turned into jelly. 'Then pour the wine and come back to bed,' she said softly. 'And teach me how to show you just how much I love you.'

'If it is as much as I love you,' Max said, pressing

a cool glass into her hand, 'we may need to stay here for ever.'

The glasses clinked together, they sipped, then he put them both down beside the bed and took her in his arms again.

Outside, the autumn dusk fell like dark velvet. Inside the fire crackled, flared up, catching sparks of light off the crystal on the table, and two voices, merging and blending, whispered, 'I love you.'

* * * * *

Mills & Boon® Online

Discover more romance at
www.millsandboon.co.uk

- 🌹 **FREE** online reads
- 🌹 **Books** up to one month before shops
- 🌹 **Browse our books** before you buy

...and much more!

For exclusive competitions and instant updates:

 Like us on **facebook.com/millsandboon**

 Follow us on **twitter.com/millsandboon**

 Join us on **community.millsandboon.co.uk**

Visit us Online   Sign up for our FREE eNewsletter at
www.millsandboon.co.uk